THE HUNGER REBELLION

A DYSTOPIAN TALE

G. F. CUSACK

The Hunger Rebellion

A Dystopian Tale

By

G. F. Cusack

First published in the US 2019

ISBN: 978-0-473-49969-3

Cover Design by Sarah Oliver
www.saraoliverdesign.com

CONTENTS

ESCAPE FROM THE REBEL REFUGE

10 August 2202

Pepper was in the bathroom when he heard the first rattles of gunfire. Pausing from drying his hands, his first thoughts were that there was an internal skirmish underway. The rebels in this refuge weren't a family, more of a collection of smaller individual gangs. The Company was the real enemy but the rebel groups weren't a peaceful alliance. It wasn't unheard of for petty squabbles to escalate into violence.

Although the rebels had a selection of guns, Pepper knew immediately that he was listening to sustained gunfire. The volumes of the bullets could only mean one thing: they were under attack from the forces of the Company.

Standing over two metres tall with a muscly frame and battle scars over most of his dark skin, he projected an imposing figure. Ripping the door open, he was outside of the bathroom in no time. The sound of the bullets was getting closer and a quick assessment of the situation told him that although his whole life he had stood up to bullies, today was not the day to fight and survive.

The Company was not here to take prisoners and its heavy firepower was rapidly cutting down the few resistance fighters left alive. Directly in front of him stood a young woman with long dark hair. She was rigid against the wall and Pepper was overcome with an urge to help her. Without a second thought, he grabbed her and swept her along with him as he ran down the narrow corridor, past the bathroom towards an escape tunnel.

Noticing that her hands were tied, he quickly drew a knife from his pocket and cut the ropes.

As he exposed the hidden hatch, he paused for only a second to address her. "What's your name?"

"Flo," she murmured weakly.

"Okay Flo, if you want to live, you are going to go through this tunnel as quickly and quietly as possible. Don't stop once you are in there as I'll be right behind you and I don't want to hurt you with my big heavy boots!"

It was a tight squeeze for someone of his build but the incentive to stay alive was enough to make him compress his broad shoulders to fit. He sneaked a quick look over his shoulder to see if anyone else was going to escape but the only people in view were Company men and he just managed to secure the hatch before they reached it.

Pepper emerged from the shaft into the dark, cloudy night. Flo was there, standing stiff against the wall, just as she had been inside. Luckily, because the cloud was covering the moon, the two sentries hadn't noticed her.

Her initial lack of movement had been an advantage but time was against them – he needed to get her to move quickly. The two sentries with their grey coveralls and assault rifles meandered along a lax route. Pepper mused that if they'd worked for him, he'd have stern words with them after the assault. As it was, their limited movements did allow Pepper to easily track them.

After the troops turned away, without waiting for a response from Flo he hastily shepherded her into the woods. Once they were safe within the dark cover of the forest canopy, Pepper placed his hand over Flo's mouth and shook her to get some response. It was not safe to remain where they were and, if they were to have a conversation, it needed to be further away from the ears of the Company forces.

Pepper said quietly to Flo, "Come with me and say nothing, our lives depend on this." Taking her by the hand, he guided her further into the woods and she reluctantly followed. Only after they had walked silently through the woods for around twenty minutes did Pepper believe that they were far enough away to attempt a conversation.

2

WILL'S VIEW OF THE RAID

10 August 2202

The Company's assault team had been waiting outside the warehouse for over an hour in the dark. With no moonlight, it was difficult for Will to make out the outline of the main doors.

Will had been dispatched from the Sanctuary to disrupt any pockets of rebels in this area. Other members of the Company council perceived Will as just a ruthless thug but supreme leader Brand valued his particular set of skills.

Brand's patronage had marked Will as his right-hand man. No one had the authority or inclination to mess with the supreme leader's man, allowing him to amass power and privilege well above his station.

The resistance member that he had bribed was to give the signal when at least fifty percent of the rebels were present in the building. In the past, Will had used threats against families as a way of leveraging his victims. But now that the value of human life was so low, he found offering food was a much more successful incentive.

The rebel went to the vehicle and turned the lights on and off three times in succession – the signal.

Will pressed the button on his radio. "Go, go, go," he shouted. An explosion lit up the night as the charges on the main doors exploded.

Even though they were taken by surprise and were outmatched by the superior firepower, the rebels put up a valiant fight. The flashes of automatics fire lit up the dark of the night.

Following in behind his advance troops, Will was surprised to find that some fighting continued. The rebel leader had barricaded himself in the reinforced part of the building and was resisting till the end.

"Hello in there," Will shouted during a lull in the gunfire.

The smell of smoke remained in the air and a ring from the previous shots echoed but no reply was forthcoming.

He tried again. "If you come out now, I promise you'll not be harmed. We have done what we came here to do. This place is done but you have no reason to sacrifice yourself for a few broken buildings."

"I've never met a Company man I could trust," came a voice from the other side of the barricade.

"Who am I talking to?" Will asked. He wasn't really interested but if he could build a dialogue, he could resolve this matter faster. It was getting late and he was sick of dealing with these low lives.

"My name is Paris. Make sure that you spell it right when you write in your report how many of your troops I have killed," he replied defiantly.

"If you are not concerned for yourself, think of your people. We have captured ten of your fighters alive and if you want them to stay that way, I suggest you come out."

Paris was unsure of his next move. There was every chance that the Company man was lying. "Give me their names, if you have them."

Will kicked one of the wounded rebels. "What's your name?"

"Graeme," came the faint reply.

"And you three?" he said to the others.

"Donna." "Gil." "Pat."

"Okay, I've got a Graeme, a Gil, a Pat and even a Donna. The other six are too injured to speak. If you don't want all of their blood on your hands, you need to come out in the next five minutes." After a pause, Will finished, "Some of these are women – can you live with their deaths?"

Paris relented. However slim a chance, he had to try to save his people. He had seven fighters left fighting with him and he gave them the signal to remove the barricades.

As the rebels came out with their hands in the air, Will waited. When they were all in view, he asked, "Which one of you is Paris?"

A Latin-looking man stepped forward and raised a hand. Before he could say a word, Will raised his rifle and shot him in the head. "Take the rest of these outside and dispose of them," he ordered his troops.

With no exact figures on the number of rebels he had started fighting, Will was unsure of how many might have slipped through his net. The final body count was at least fifty-three dead rebels, plus two dead and ten seriously injured among his own troops. He would report the action as a success to Brand and hope that the supreme leader thought so too.

Still, even though they had removed another rebel cell from the landscape, the girl's escape made Will doubt that Brand would class this mission as a success.

Slaughtering the remnants of the cell after they had surrendered removed the chance that these scum would cause the Company any further trouble. Will thought it ironic that the bodies of the people fighting against the liquidation process would all contribute to a batch of gel packs.

3

DISCUSSION IN THE WOODS

10 August 2202

Pepper was unsure why he had experienced an overwhelming feeling to help this young woman, both when he first encountered her inside the building and when he had emerged from the tunnel to find her again standing rigid. Initially he'd put it down to sympathy – the fact that he towered over her by over a foot and outweighed her by five stone made him think that she was scared of him. Now he was unsure if any of that was true.

Even though he thought that they were safe from listening ears now, he spoke quietly. "Who are you really? Is Flo even your full name?"

Receiving no response, he asked again, "Who are you?"

After his fourth attempt at the question, Flo murmured under her breath, "Flo, Flo".

Although he felt some unexplained empathy with her, with his limited time he thought they weren't making enough progress. His instincts made him believe that she wasn't a threat but he hadn't survived this long on the run from the Company without having some kind of strategy.

"Okay so your name is Flo. Is that short for something? "

She was becoming a little more animated, as though she was coming out of a trance. Her voice wasn't much more than a whisper. "My name is just Flo."

"I need to know what you were doing in that place. I need to know what a young woman like you was doing with the rebels. What were you doing there?"

"I was a prisoner."

"A prisoner of who? Why were you a prisoner?"

"The Murdochs had brought me to the refuge to trade me with another group, I don't know its name."

Pepper was aware that many groups made up the resistance. They were a disorganised, ragtag bunch of a coalition and not all of them were savoury.

He was unsure what value this young woman could have to them but she was clearly suffering from shock. Rather than digging into the reasons for trading, he focused on his immediate goal: to decide whether to trust her.

"Where are you originally from?" he asked.

"My home is Pandora," she murmured.

"What or where is Pandora?" Pepper asked quizzically.

"It's a farm, far to the north."

Because the woman was young and her answers were laboured, Pepper decided to wrap things up quickly. "How do you know the farm's in the far north?" he asked.

"I spent most of my life on a farm in the countryside. I understand the movement of the sun and the location of the stars enough to know that I have been travelling south for a long time. Will you take me home?"

Pepper was taken aback. Without thinking, he blurted out, "I've saved you from whatever was going to happen to you, but I don't need a travelling companion."

He was torn between a feeling of responsibility now that he had saved her and an unwillingness to retain that responsibility for too long. Pepper's main criterion for survival was his "what's in it for me?" attitude. Some people might see that as selfish but, as a large African-American male, he stood out from the crowd and this was the only way he knew to stay alive as a long-term deserter from the Company forces.

Pepper thought fast. "Here's what I can do. I have a friend who lives not far away. Rogan has a cabin and it is safe there. I'm willing to take you there and you can stay with him for a while."

He needed to replenish his supplies anyway, having lost his backpack full of resources in the refuge. The last time he'd seen it, it was in the hands of the rebel leader Paris. He could have beaten himself up for leaving the pack behind when he went to relieve himself, but it wouldn't have been so useful right now, as it mainly contained the medicines he had brought to trade.

Figuring that self-deprecation was not going to help him, he decided to go back to the cabin and collect some supplies he had stashed there. Rogan was a bit more hospitable and older than Pepper, and Pepper believed that Rogan might find a use for the girl –

cleaning, cooking, who knew? Perhaps, coming from a farm, she could prepare food or even grow some kind of plants.

"Is that okay?" he asked her. "I can take you to a cabin where a man I know lives. He's a nice guy and then we can discuss what you want to do. I think for the time being we need to get as far away from the place that was just attacked as possible."

Flo nodded.

"This is only going to work if you do what I say, when I say. Do you understand that?"

Flo again nodded feebly.

"I mean it! I haven't survived this long without trusting my instincts. If you are not going to do as I say, tell me now and I will leave you here."

Flo murmured under her breath, "I will do what you say."

Although she seemed in a fragile state, Pepper reiterated, "Then it is agreed: I will take you to the cabin and you will do exactly as I say, when I say it?"

With that, he headed north and she followed him closely behind.

4

WILL TRAVELS BACK TO THE SANCTUARY

11 August 2202

As Will was driven away from the rebel stronghold, he could see flames billowing out of the ruins behind him. This was the sixth cell that he'd wrapped up in as many days and that should have made him happy. Yet it gave him little comfort to know that soon the buildings would be just a large pile of ashes.

He wasn't looking forward to explaining to Brand that the girl had escaped. He had taken out a large percentage of the rebels in this area, including this last compound, but he knew that Brand did not reward failure.

Heading to the landing site, he heard the rotor blades speeding up. One bonus of the helicopter ride was that it would take him home faster than his troops. They would spend the next couple of days on the rough roads and tracks heading to the border.

Of course, the flight was not direct. It would have to

stop off at a couple of places to pick up warriors for the pits. Yet, even with these detours, his travels would be faster and more comfortable. The reinforced suspensions on the purpose-built armoured trucks would help but, without well-maintained roads, there was no such thing as a smooth ride.

As Will flew in to Newtown, it seemed unusually chaotic. Below him was a large group of people, although that was to be expected as he had arrived on gel distribution day.

This wasn't the first gel distribution point he had seen and distribution points were never orderly as there never seemed to be enough gel packs. It was not supposed to be a case of survival of the fittest but, as the strongest always pushed to the front of the queue, they got fed first.

Scheduling the same distribution day at the same time throughout the kingdom stopped people from travelling between locations to try to get extra gel packs. Even though barcodes needed to be scanned to get gel, there was always a black market in food when life was so cheap.

When he landed, he could hear the radio message blaring over the speakers. It was the same message that would be going out on a loop at all the gel points across the kingdom.

It was supposed to be a message of hope. "The gel rations have been increased by ten percent today." Will knew that this wasn't true as they had actually decreased the rations by thirty percent. "In order to continue to increase gel supplies for all our valuable citizens, we will be reducing the compulsory age at the next aging ceremony from forty-five to forty-four. We are grateful for our elderly citizens' sacrifice to keep the rest of us alive. We are stronger together." The same message repeated over and over.

Will was aware that there was no need to reduce the gel distribution or to reduce the compulsory age. The increase of supply was not to benefit the masses but to provide more wealth for the elites. This dark economy provided kickbacks on the black market that even Will benefited from. What they stood to gain was always on the mind of the elites.

Brand chose not to get involved directly but he still benefited financially from these dealings and, like everything else the elites did, his spies kept him updated on any developments.

Will's helicopter had a short stopover in Newtown to pick up future warriors – prisoners – from the local sheriff, who seemed very happy to see two large men bundled into the helicopter. Will was told that these two miscreants had killed several people in a fight over a small amount of food. The current shortage of gel packs made food expensive even though the value of life itself was becoming cheaper, almost worthless.

The prisoners were bound, gagged and then, rather than being allowed to walk into the helicopter, stacked like luggage. Their comfort was of little concern to Will; they were just excess baggage burning valuable fuel and making the journey riskier.

Transporting prisoners in this manner saved on the number of troops required to guard them. This was a logistics matter to be considered against the impact of the prisoners' extra weight on the fuel reserves.

Will was relieved when they eventually reached the border staging point and unloaded their cargo. A sergeant who met the helicopter instructed his troops to bundle the prisoners into the back of a couple of trucks. On the outside the sergeant seemed unusually happy to see the prisoners but that was only because it reminded him that this was the end of his three-month tour at the staging point.

Soon the replacement shift would arrive and his troops would return home, taking the prisoners back to the Sanctuary with them. Transporting a bit of extra cargo was a minor inconvenience when it came with the chance of returning to the Sanctuary. At least home offered some kind of entertainment – unlike here, where the only activities were servicing vehicles, manning guard towers and patrolling the border.

Will stayed in the vehicle while the helicopter powered down and took on its valuable fuel, which Will had ordered the pilots to do even though the stop was supposed to be a drop and go. The emergency fuel at the staging point wasn't meant to be used without higher authority. Possibly Will would upset both the logistics teams in charge of the fuel and the scheduling personnel in charge of the flights. But he didn't care. As long as he had Brand's backing, no one could argue with him.

In what seemed to Will like no time at all, he heard the "wop, wop, wop" of the rotors as they began to rotate. After a slight shudder, once again Will felt his stomach drop with the rapid ascent into the sky. The next time they landed, he would be reporting to Brand – and that made him more worried than the thought of the helicopter crashing.

5

PEPPER AND FLO REACH THE CABIN

13 August 2202

While they were still some distance from the cabin, Pepper noticed the smoke. The nights were already getting colder so this could have been a little smoke from the cabin's stone fireplace. But Pepper doubted this was chimney smoke.

He cautioned Flo to be wary. His gut was telling him that something bad had happened.

"Stay here and I will be back for you. Do not move until I return. But if I don't return in the next hour, do not come into the cabin to find me – head north."

With no response from Flo, Pepper asked, "Do you understand me?"

"Yes, I understand," she said meekly.

With that acknowledgement, he circled around so he could approach the cabin from the back; he had spent so much time around here that he could have walked this area blindfolded. When he got closer to the cabin, he crouched down and stayed perfectly still for ten minutes, listening for any out-of-place sounds until he was sure that he was alone.

When he emerged into the clearing, his first view was of the smouldering remnants of the cabin.

He judged that, in its current state, the cabin had been burning for some time – over twelve hours, by his estimation. So he was fairly sure that whoever had started the fire was now gone.

With empty shell cases scattered all over the site, Pepper assumed that his old friend must have put up a strong resistance. Unfortunately, though, the Company forces would have had more firepower and must have worn him down.

Stapled to the trees were the regular Company posters. The Company's standard method of operations was to burn down any habitable buildings and then display warning posters. Destroying buildings removed any potential shelter for rebel forces. The posters were meant to instil fear – and by and large they were effective. The posters had the standard words:

•These resources and the surrounding buildings were destroyed by the forces of the true governing body.

•The inhabitants were traitors to the rule of law. Their sole goal is to shatter our fair and civil society.

•Anyone sheltering or harbouring survivors from this punishment will be liable to summary execution and their bodies will be transported to the gel plants.

Pepper always smiled bitterly when he read the last line of the posters. Once you were summarily executed, why would you care what they did with your body?

But then he also realised that he would not find a body here as, if the Company forces had killed Rogan, they would have taken the corpse to the gel plants. After scouring the area thoroughly and deciding it was safe, he went back into the woods to retrieve Flo.

He found her exactly where he had left her, cowering behind a tree.

"It's okay, the bad people have gone," he said quietly and calmly.

"Are you sure?" she asked timidly.

He took her by the hand and shepherded her into the clearing. "Trust me, it's okay."

The cabin and the smaller buildings had been ransacked. Their contents would have been either destroyed in the fire or plundered by the soldiers.

Luckily Pepper knew of a stash of supplies within walking distance of the ruins and he motioned for Flo to accompany him. A hundred yards from the clearing at the base of an old maple tree was a shovel hidden in the undergrowth.

With the shovel, he dug down to uncover a moulded plastic strongbox.

Opening the lid, he was glad to see that the monthly checks had ensured that the cache was in good condition. Knowing that the cabin was always at risk, Rogan had insisted on this lifeline and, right now, Pepper was very grateful for it.

After extracting the two backpacks, he began to fill them with the other contents of the box. Although he divided the dry foods evenly between the two packs, he gave himself the weighty stuff such as the canned food and blankets.

He took both of the Glock pistols and the bullets, placing one pistol and the two silencers in his bag and the other pistol in his waistband. The silenced pistol had long been the preferred weapon of the rebels as they needed to depend on stealth to give them an advantage over the Company's superior resources.

Pepper tossed Flo a winter jacket, a hat and gloves. They were a bit large for her small frame, but they were heading into winter and her survival could depend on them.

As it was still light, Pepper was conscious that the smoke remained visible from some distance. Worried that it would attract more attention, he decided to vacate the area as quickly as possible. He did not want to take Flo with him but he was also aware his previous plan of leaving her with Rogan was now literally up in smoke.

"We need to get away from here right now. Come with me and once we are far enough away to be safe, we can discuss what to do next, okay?"

Flo was clearly tired and confused but her instincts seemed to tell her that Pepper was her best option. "You won't leave me, will you?"

"I know you're tired but as long as you keep moving, I won't leave you. Can you keep putting one foot in front of the other?"

"I think so."

"Put both of those straps over your shoulders. It will spread the load and you'll not tire as fast."

They headed off, bearing north. Pepper knew that they would be walking for some time, until he felt safe enough for them to rest up.

6

WILL REPORTS HIS SUCCESSES

11 August 2202

The wind was whipping up clouds of dust as the helicopter touched down. To the side of the landing pad, two large armoured vehicles waited to take Will to Brand.

As he exited the metal bird, Will took a few minutes to stretch his legs and reach his arms up towards the sky. After the circulation had returned to his limbs, he rolled his head from side to side until his neck seemed looser. He had been sitting in the helicopter for hours and, although the armoured vehicle would have more comfortable seats, he needed to gather his thoughts before he began the journey to the council buildings.

Climbing into the passenger seat of the lead vehicle, he motioned for them to head off. When the powerful engines gunned into life, they headed away from the airfield and towards the impending briefing.

It took less than thirty minutes for the vehicles to pull up in front of the council buildings. Will realised

Brand would be aware of their arrival as Brand seemed to know everything. He bounded out of the vehicle and up the steps. As he hadn't been restrained by his escorts, he assumed that they hadn't been sent to apprehend him.

He could have taken the elevator but Will decided on the steps to give himself a bit more time. Whether that was time to think or just a little longer to live, he was unsure as yet. As he ascended the six hundred steps, he knew this was a balancing act. He couldn't climb too slowly as this might inadvertently anger Brand; he didn't want to arrive out of breath or Brand might see this as weakness. He cursed himself for not taking the elevator.

The six security guards at the door nodded to their boss as he approached them. Will knew that only Brand and he could get through this door without having their documents checked. The guards had orders to shoot first and ask questions later, as one previous council member had found to his detriment.

Councillor Hurst had been lucky that his wounds weren't fatal but that incident had impressed on all of the council that, no matter how important they perceived themselves to be, there was only one supreme leader and it was Brand.

When Will entered the room, he was struck as always by the contrasts in its design. The room was large and almost empty. The floors were dark polished wood and the walls were deep red up to a wooden border. The bright white on the top half of the walls extended up to a high ceiling of the same colour.

The browns and red made the room feel warm yet the whites made it feel stark and cold. It was said that the lack of furniture was to reduce the number of potential weapons but it also gave visitors nowhere to sit.

The one purpose for which this room existed was for Brand's enjoyment. It was his domain and he controlled it.

Brand was sitting behind a large ornate wooden desk in a huge carved wooden chair. The only chair in the room, its leather upholstery and brass buttons made it look like a throne from centuries gone by.

Clad in a pin-striped three-piece suit with a crisp white shirt, Brand gave the impression that he wasn't the type of boss to get his hands dirty. That notion couldn't be further from the truth. On more than one occasion, Will had seen Brand beat a man to death with his bare hands. Will had been the only observer of these killings, which placed him in danger as he was all too aware. He was seen by most as Brand's loyal right-hand man but Brand would despatch him quickly if he felt this witness was any kind of threat.

"So what have you got to report?" Brand got straight to the point.

"It was a successful mission. We destroyed six rebel dwellings and killed over a hundred rebels. As well as the six larger groups, we picked off some individual trouble-causers."

"You think it was a successful trip?" Brand said sarcastically. "So you got the girl?"

"No, we didn't capture the girl but I thought that was only the secondary part of the mission. Our primary mission was to destroy the rebels and we did that."

"I set the mission parameters." Brand's voice was getting louder now. "I say what your priorities are and I wanted the girl captured. Do you seriously expect me to believe that with all of the resources I have provided you, you couldn't capture a teenage girl?"

"My source at the final compound we routed said that a teenage girl was inside. I got my people to check all of the bodies closely but there was no sign of one. If she had been present, I would have brought her back with me, dead or alive."

"Dead or alive." Brand spat at him. "My express instructions were that she was to be brought back unharmed. Am I speaking to myself when I give these orders?"

Knowing this was a rhetorical question, Will did not say a word in response. He could feel the rage in Brand's words and he couldn't chance angering him any further.

"You may think that this mission was a success but I see it as a failure."

Will reflected that his assessment on the journey home had been correct. No matter how many rebels Will had killed, Brand would be disappointed that he hadn't captured the girl that he seemed obsessed with.

The reason why the girl was important was immaterial to Will as Brand always had his own agenda. Will only knew that capturing her was important to his survival. Making Brand happy was the best way to stay alive.

After a short pause, it seemed to Will that, rather than calming down, Brand was growing increasingly angry. "I give you responsibility but with that comes a great deal of rewards. Never forget that you can be replaced in seconds. I have given you my patronage over the years and that has allowed you to lead a privileged life. I gave you that life and I can just as easily take it away."

Will realised that he was in a dangerous situation. He chose to say nothing and that was just as well because Brand had a lot more to say.

"Today you are able to eat the best foods and drink expensive beverages but tomorrow you could be part of the next gel pack consignment. Remember that the next time you fail me."

After a few more seconds, Brand seemed to regain control. "You will be glad to know that I have decided to be merciful. Today is not a day to send you to the gel plants."

Because he hadn't been dragged here by the team escorting him from the helicopter, Will had been cautiously confident that he might survive the day. Unfortunately, when dealing with a paranoid narcissist like Brand, there were no guarantees.

"There are more rebel enclaves in the regions further north than the ones you destroyed this week. As you seem to have a talent for neutralising these enclaves, that is where you shall focus your energies. I have other resources that I will employ to pursue the girl. Don't think that you are being rewarded for your failure though – you should feel fortunate that you can still provide some value to me. Have you anything else to report?"

Will just shook his head. He felt like he was getting the chance to leave and he would happily seize the opportunity. He decided continued silence was the best option as his words were unlikely to improve the situation or, worse, if they were wrong they could result in his death.

As it turned out, Brand's patience wasn't helped by Will's lack of verbal response. "Get out my sight and ensure that, the next time you present a report to me, it is a real success and not just half a job. Do you understand that?"

Again, Will nodded silently.

"Go on then, what are you waiting for? Get out of my sight."

Will didn't hesitate any further; he turned and headed to the door. As he exited the room, he pondered that he could have offered some elaborate excuses but with Brand, less was more. The less time you spent in his presence when he was angry, the better your chances of survival.

Again he opted for the stairs after leaving the office as the thought of being in an elevator box made him visualise being caged in, but this time he walked at a more leisurely pace. The reprimand he had just suffered was still stinging him and he would ensure that the next time he'd have the right information, whatever the cost.

Walking down the steps, he reflected that Brand wasn't happy with the results of the raids. From his own perspective, one teenage girl escaping seemed insignificant when it was compared with the killing of over a hundred rebels.

One never knew what Brand's plans were. That was one reason why he'd survived so long. Another was that he was so brutal that few people would have the courage or resources to challenge him and survive.

When Will eventually reached the bottom of the stairs, he flung open the external doors and took in the fresh, cold air, thankful that he had survived another day.

7

PEPPER AND FLO NORTH OF THE CABIN

13 August 2202

During the two-hour trek from the cabin, Flo was developing a plan. It was clear to her that Pepper was primarily a mercenary as, unbeknown to him, she had been reading his mind.

He had been thinking of ways to leave her that wouldn't prey on his conscience.

Although the Farm had plentiful resources, she didn't know if it provided enough of an enticement to guarantee he would take her all the way there.

She did sense some empathy in him though so she decided to take a chance. Then she began to mentally prepare for the time that they would rest.

Pepper had deliberately taken an erratic route and had not identified anyone following them. As soon as he felt they were clear of the cabin, he motioned for her to stop.

Seizing the moment, Flo surprised him by beginning

to talk. "Before we go any further, I want to ask if you will escort me to the farm."

Pepper didn't reply straight away. He remembered his old adage of 'what's in it for me' and was reticent to actually agree to accompany her even though he doubted if she could survive on her own.

Sensing his resistance, she continued with her pitch. "The Farm has lots of resources – not just produce; we also trade with nearby strongholds of rebel fighters. If you escort me, I guarantee you will be rewarded handsomely."

"How handsomely?" Pepper asked. He was slowly warming to the idea of a payday at the end of a relatively simple trip.

"More than you can carry on your back," she replied.

"You'd be surprised how much I can actually carry on my back!"

Pepper had lost his trade goods at the rebel stronghold and his remaining supplies had literally gone up in smoke with the cabin. Realising that his immediate options were limited, he was tempted by this opportunity to quickly replenish his losses.

Trying to put on an air of indifference, Pepper laid out his terms. "I will accompany you north as far as your so-called Farm, but only if you do exactly what I say, when I say. If you don't, I'll leave you where you stand, do you understand?"

Although she could read Pepper's emotions as well as his mind, she sensed some kind of edge in his demeanour and felt he wasn't joking about the chance of abandoning her if she failed to meet his demands. "Okay, if you keep me safe, I will do as you ask."

With that, Pepper extended his hand. "I always shake on a deal." She took the hand and the bargain was struck.

"If we are heading on a long journey, I need to be sure that you can make it. Is your pack comfortable? Is anything rubbing?"

"My shoulders are a little sore."

Pepper pulled back her jacket to check her shoulders. She might have been a farm girl when she was abducted but she had become soft during her captivity. He noticed her shoulders were already red after only this short distance.

"Take off your jacket and your top. I've got some ointment in my pack." As she was disrobing, he wrapped a spare pair of socks around the shoulder straps of her pack for extra padding. Pepper also took more of the stores out of her pack and stuffed them in his. "This should help but if it gets too sore, let me know."

"Thank you," Flo said as he rubbed the ointment into her shoulders. For such a powerful man, he seemed to have a gentle side.

"I'm used to travelling alone so I tend to travel fast. Don't try to be a hero. If you feel that you can't keep up, let me know. I will give you regular breaks and supply food and water. But no whining."

She nodded to show she both understood and accepted his words.

As they headed north, Pepper cautiously viewed their surroundings. He was still unsure why he had taken on board this young woman. Why had he deviated from his normal self-centred survival instincts? The fact was that he now felt responsible for someone and it was not a feeling that he liked.

8

INTRODUCING ZAP IN THE SANCTUARY

01 August 2202

Ethan had been a computer programmer since he'd been a young teen. Everyone called him Zap but his stepfather had named him Ethan.

As a Company data analyst, he had access to lots of information, including details about all of the Sanctuary's food supplies. He knew that plenty of food was being produced. Even though some of the crops were being used for biofuels, plenty of food was left over to feed everyone, if it was properly distributed.

Like most people among the masses, growing up he had been taught that the Water Wars had happened because of a worldwide shortage of water and other resources. Whether it was greed or necessity that had led the companies to fight for control over these resources, the fact that they had fought was in no doubt. The people had been told that the fighting had not just reduced the planet's population but had damaged the food chain to levels where humanity was struggling to survive.

The Water Wars had been over for a hundred years now. Maybe the shortages at that time would have justified some of the Company's draconian measures but Zap was unsure why it was still using them.

Maybe it was because he was too young to have become set in his ways or maybe it was because of his logical way of thinking. He couldn't fathom why the needs of the few were leading to a shortage for the many – the huge inequalities just made no sense to him.

So many people were starving, being forced to fight for the entertainment of others and finishing up in the gel plants once they reached forty-five years of age. At the same time, a small minority was allowed to lead a life of excess and greed. It was for these reasons that, at an early age, Zap had decided to join the resistance.

Because of his technical skills and intelligence, people saw him as a lot older than he was. Still, with the standard life expectancy set at forty-five years, at seventeen he was fast approaching middle age.

Zap was conscious that the fear-mongering propaganda of the Company played on the anxieties of the masses. The Company pushed the narrative that the resistance was causing more damage to the fragile environment – an environment that the Company pretended to protect.

Working on the main computer systems, he had identified that the technical setup was designed for misinformation. As he was uniquely positioned to access this data for the resistance, he had chosen to investigate this discovery further.

It was a dangerous pursuit because the Company

was brutal in stamping out any dissension. Being caught (or even accused of) breaking the Company rules could spark an early trip to the gel plants. Yet very few people, not even his friend Dick, were as skilled on the computer as he was. Zap had spent most of his life working on machines and was well practised at hiding his tracks on the technical highway.

Zap had been very young when his stepfather had noted his proclivity for technology and machinery. Their privileged position also gave him access to machines that were out of reach of many others.

It was this access and encouragement to learn more, tinged with his natural curiosity, which had made Zap a formidable computer hacker. The Company's dedication to developing his skills had only heightened his curiosity. Little did the Company know that the resource that it had created had become a weapon against it.

Initially he had only supplied the rebels with small amounts of information – locations of supply depots, access codes to storage vessels and security timetables. These acts could put him in danger but he was confident that he'd covered his tracks so none of it could be traced back to him.

Recently he had noticed an increased pressure from the resistance for more information. His communications with his contact were becoming more frequent and Angus was asking him to provide ever more detailed information.

He felt that he was heading towards a tipping point: soon he would be seen as a full member of the resistance. For some time, he had been wondering how far he would go.

In an ongoing self-talk, he had been considering the balance between salving his conscience and looking after his own safety. In reality, though, he knew that he had long passed the point of no return. If he was caught now or caught doing something more serious in the future, the punishment would be the same.

He would be tortured until they got as much information as they felt possible and then sent to the gel plants. There he would become just another ingredient in the diet of the masses.

9

THROUGH ANOTHER'S EYES

10 August 2202

Zap was hoping for a good night's sleep as the last few nights had been restless with weird dreams. He assumed that everyone dreamt of somebody they recognised at some stage. He often saw people in the streets, the poor, the starving and even beautiful young women. He dreamt of all of these people on occasion, especially the young women.

For the last few weeks his dreams had been different. He wasn't dreaming about somebody, he was dreaming of being somebody. It was as though he was in that person's body, feeling their breath rise in their chest, feeling the softness of the pillow under their head. It was all very strange.

The person he was in his dreams lived somewhere different. He could tell this because the pictures in their head were unlike any he'd ever seen.

Zap had lived his whole life in the Sanctuary and the locations in his visions didn't seem like anywhere he knew. Some of the people in the visions, though, seemed similar to the commoners he encountered travelling around the Sanctuary and in the fighting pits.

He was aware of the disparities between his life and others' – not everyone was as fortunate as him. He had his own apartment with fresh running water, as well as a good job that supplied plentiful food and other luxuries. Some people might even call Zap one of the elites, but he knew that he wasn't on their level of greed and gluttony.

The person in his dreams had a very different life. At times it felt as though their wrists were sore from being bound. He assumed that they were a prisoner although his gut feeling was that this wasn't the kind of bad person who would commit a crime. They also seemed to have a feminine side, although dreaming of being a woman seemed strange to him. To be honest, the whole thing felt strange but for now he assumed that he was in a female head.

There was something else about this person – the way they felt about men. He got an overwhelming sense of fear of men as predators and he assumed that the female wasn't very old, perhaps around his age. Yet a male even of his age wouldn't feel so timid so this convinced him of her gender.

Zap had been fortunate that he had never had to survive off gel packs. The thought of eating another human being, however much they had been processed, was repulsive to him. The person of his dreams had been forced to survive on whatever scraps she was given. Sometimes she was given parts of gel packs, and the memories of eating them were burnt into her psyche for him to experience. The revulsion that she felt, knowing that someone else had needed to die for her to survive, was almost too much for her. She had great empathy with her fellow humans.

Zap didn't see himself as a bad person but he was clearly dreaming with someone a lot nicer than him. Someone with a strong moral compass. While Zap hated to see others bullied and he felt angry about some of the Sanctuary's elite inhabitants, this person seemed to see the good in everyone and wanted everyone to survive.

Zap had been brought up with the view that for him to survive, others needed to suffer. He had recently started questioning this upbringing, especially after his discussions with his trainer in the pits, Angus.

As he'd had two restless nights, he decided to go to bed early. Most nights Zap caught up with Dick, his work colleague and neighbour. Zap was better with machines than people so finding someone who he could chat to was a bonus. Dick was an easy listener – never judgemental and seeming really interested in everything Zap said. Tonight Zap just wanted a rest.

That also cut out going to work out at the fighting pits, which he did some nights without Dick, who did not share his enjoyment of it. Zap relished the primal nature of being sweaty among all the warriors and pushing yourself in that environment.

On more than one occasion, Zap had asked Dick to accompany him. But after the last rejection, he had stopped asking. Dick was not a skinny person – in fact, he was a bit overweight – but he was a good friend to Zap so he didn't push it.

The dreams had been getting more vivid and it was becoming harder to relax. Angus had taught him some mind-clearing techniques. After years of training warriors, Angus knew what worked. He said that some people suggested letting your mind go blank but for a warrior with an active mind, you needed movement to relax. A blank space could be filled with the nightmares of previous battles and bloody opponents.

Zap focused his mind on clear running water, filling the space in his mind with images of a torrent of water flowing steadily through rocks and boulders. He was becoming one with the water and felt his body flowing through the space between the rocks, without a care in the world.

Very quickly Zap found himself sinking into a blissful sleep. Yet he had not been sleeping long when he felt a mental jolt. It was hard to tell if he was still asleep, was dreaming or had woken up. Suddenly he was inside her head. He felt as though his body was frozen against a wall, as though his limbs were too heavy to move. He could only sense the dark as his eyes seemed frozen shut.

At first, Zap felt like he was lying in bed but frozen with fear. He couldn't move any of his muscles; his arms and his legs were all stuck rigid to the bed. She was also rigid – he could feel her fear. She was unsure of what was happening, but she knew that moving would draw attention to her.

He could hear loud noises, bangs. It sounded like gunfire. He had heard gunfire before from his apartment. But that had been at a distance: apparently a night patrol had opened up on some trouble causers and the sound of the gunshots had travelled easily through the still, silent night. After curfew, not much moved in the capital.

These shots were closer and there were lots of them.

He could hear people screaming – although he wasn't sure if he was hearing or feeling them screaming. The sensations were alien to him, like feeling somebody else's sensations but muffled. He could feel that her hands were tied behind her back. In previous dreams they had felt sore after she had been unbound; this time, they were still tied.

A feeling of desperation was overwhelming him. She felt as though she could do nothing so Zap felt it too. He could do nothing. He was just an observer of his own life, or more like someone else's life.

He felt the eyes closing tighter as though not seeing the danger would make it go away. He knew this was irrational and so did the woman he was inhabiting. Fear sometimes overcomes rationality and it was clear she was terrified. He was unsure how long she had been frozen stiff with fear.

Slowly he felt something grab their arm, like he was now one with this woman. Her eyes shot open and, even though he was still asleep, he could see through her eyes. Staring back at him was a tall, dark man, with several visible scars on his arms. The sight of a large man made the woman even more scared and her breathing almost stopped.

The man was trying to pull her away from the wall and, although she was resisting, the man seemed genuinely concerned. Using his superior size, he swept her down a hallway with him.

When they paused, he quickly drew a knife from his pocket and cut the ropes.

The man was opening up some kind of passageway when he suddenly spoke. "What's your name?"

Zap felt himself murmur, "Flo."

He heard the man say, "Okay Flo, if you want to live, you are going to go through this tunnel as quickly and quietly as possible. Don't stop once you are in there as I'll be right behind you and I don't want to hurt you with my big heavy boots!" Suddenly the spell was broken and Zap was back in his own head.

What had just happened? Where had he just been, whose head was he in? This was getting stranger and stranger and the link was growing stronger. He knew she was in danger and, even though he didn't know who she was or where she was, he felt an unexpected bond forming. He wondered if he could do anything to help her.

He would have to discuss this with Dick and even Angus the next day. Two heads are better than one and three are better than two – but only if they are trusted heads.

Anything out of the ordinary could get a person an early trip to the gel plants. He had already told Dick that he had been dreaming of someone, but this was taking it to another level.

On second thoughts, perhaps it was too early to share this information with anyone at all.

10

THE WARRIORS ARRIVE AT THE PITS

15 August 2202

The convoy had been on the road for three days and the prisoners had been bound for the whole journey. They had been fed a small amount from gel packs, but they hadn't been allowed toilet breaks so most of them were covered in excrement and urine.

Karla had seen this all before, having run the pits for some time. She instructed her lieutenants to hose them down.

The lieutenants cut the prisoners' clothes off and quickly set to work with high-pressure hoses. Karla thought that it was good to see people happy in their work and her trainers did seem to take pleasure in degrading the new recruits.

It was hard to tell what kind of warriors these rookies would be. Height was not always a sign of prowess. The fact that they had received little food on the journey and it was unknown when they'd last trained could also disguise any potential they might have.

After the prisoners had been stripped and hosed down, they were forced to stand naked in a line.

Karla walked in front of them, stopping at each one and casting her eye over the new meat.

Karla was feared and respected among the warriors in the pits. She kept the new recruits' hands tied behind their backs until she knew that they had learnt to respect her.

She began her usual welcome speech. "Listen up, you have been spared the gel plants, although that might only be temporarily. Here at the pits, you have one choice: fight or die! If you fight well and don't die, you may end up with your freedom. So despite your previous crimes, however bad or minor you may think they were, this is your life from now on."

Although Karla was a woman of large stature, most of the warriors were taller than her. "Make no mistake that your lives, for now, are in my hands. It is my decision when you eat, it is my decision when you sleep and it may be my decision when you die. If you put on a good show, you may be rewarded; if you choose not to fight, you will die quickly; if you choose to try to escape, you will die painfully. Am I making myself clear?"

Karla eyed the largest of the prisoners. Even if size wasn't a measure of a man's ferocity, usually if you singled out the largest prisoner, it made the others pay attention.

She motioned to Miyamoto, her personal bodyguard. Casually strolling over to the largest prisoner, Miyamoto kicked him squarely between the legs. The prisoner collapsed in a heap. Miyamoto followed up by spinning around and kicking the prisoner in the head, knocking him out cold.

"Have I got your attention now?" Karla said. "I will not tolerate disobedience. Do you understand that?"

She noticed that one of the prisoners was smiling. He was smaller than some of the others, but her strong judgement of character told her there was something about him. Although she was never told what crimes the prisoners had committed, this one seemed dangerous. Perhaps he would be a good warrior or even a dirty fighter but first he had to be controlled.

Karla again looked to Miyamoto. Raising her eyebrow, she motioned to the smiling prisoner. Miyamoto needed no further instructions. Receiving a sharp kick to the back of his knee, the prisoner quickly fell to the floor. Miyamoto inflicted several more punches to his head and torso while he was going down.

The next target was the scrawniest prisoner among them. Miyamoto walked down the line of men and unleashed a barrage of kicks and punches, breaking the wretch's nose and busting both his lips. After ensuring he had left plenty of visible bruises, he resumed his place by Karla's side.

This demonstration was usually an effective way of instilling in the prisoners that she held all of the power in her hands. Singling out both the largest and the smallest warriors tended to make all of them consider their situation. They would realise that not only did the larger warriors have no power, the smaller ones could not act like grey men and blend into the fringes of the group. The third warrior was usually picked at random and it just so happened that today the smiling warrior had been singled out because Karla felt he would need it in the future anyway.

"I don't want you to get the wrong impression," Karla said. "If you do as I ask, if you fight and you put on a good show and you survive, you will be treated well. The food that you receive will be more than you got in your past life. But make no mistake, your survival relies on you doing what I tell you. The sooner you realise that, the easier your life will be – however long it may last."

With that, she signalled for her guards, who were also her fighting instructors, to take these raw recruits away and start their training.

11

____

THE ATTACK ON PEPPER AND FLO

18 August 2202

Having decided where to camp, Pepper had set a small fire but it needed more fuel if it was going to keep them warm through the night. Although they had the blankets and warm jackets from the cabin, the damp fog that they'd been walking through all day had sunk into their bones.

The light of a fire would make them stand out in the dark, perhaps attracting unwanted visitors. Pepper decided that the benefits of the fire outweighed any risks. Added to that, they were deep in the woods. The trees weren't particularly thick here but they would provide some cover for the fire from anyone looking from a distance.

"I've put some food in the pots. Just keep an eye on that and make sure it doesn't boil over," he told Flo. "Remember, this is gonna be hot so if the water starts to boil over, use your gloves and lift off the pot with a big stick."

Although she seemed to be a young adult (he hadn't asked her age), she seemed fragile. Not wanting to waste food, he was treating her more like a child than he would normally when giving someone instructions for cooking. "Do you understand?"

Flo nodded. "I have cooked before, you know."

Her response was a little reassuring to Pepper. Not so much the information that she could cook but that this was the first time she had spoken more than a couple of words to him. Apparently cooking was important to her.

"I'll be back in about five or ten minutes. I might leave your line of sight but I will not be far away. If anything happens, if anything or anyone comes towards the fire, scream my name as loud as you can and I'll come running. Do you understand?"

"If anyone comes, I'm to scream, 'Pepper' as loud as I can."

Pepper had to venture further away from the clearing than he would have liked but all the wood in the open was slightly damp. If they were going to have a fire that would last through the night, he needed to find wood that had been sheltered under a thicker canopy of trees.

Finding some older, drier branches, Pepper started to stack them in his arms for the walk back to the clearing. He still had a bad feeling, a tingling in his senses, like they had been observed as they had travelled through the fog today. He had just started walking back to the clearing when he heard her screams.

"Pepper, Pepper – help"

Dropping the wood, he sprinted towards the clearing, at the same time drawing his pistol from his waistband. Entering the clearing, he could see three figures by the firelight. They were dishevelled, wearing almost nothing more than rags. Hair and skin were covered in dirt but he could just make them out to be two males and a female.

The larger of the males had a knife in his hand and was approaching Flo, while the other two were rifling through the packs. Wasting no time, Pepper took aim at the man with the knife and fired two shots into his head.

He was just taking aim at the second man when he saw movement to his right. He sensed rather saw a man charging towards him. More by instinct than by anything else, Pepper side-stepped and avoided the full impact of the man. All the same, he was caught with a glancing blow, and they both crashed to the ground in a heap.

Pepper managed to keep hold of the pistol but his assailant's flailing arms engulfed him and made it difficult to aim the barrel for an accurate shot.

In the distance he caught an occasional glimpse of the other two who, no longer rifling through the bags, were looking at him and Flo. The woman headed towards him, while her male companion went for Flo.

He could see that Flo still had her knife in her waistband. He had told her to keep it handy but she was again frozen with fear. If they survived this confrontation, Pepper vowed that he would teach her some survival skills.

His first priority was the fight at hand. Although the man he had been struggling with was smaller than Pepper, he was like a wild animal, clawing at his face while perched on top of him. Pepper growled loudly in the hope that the extra adrenalin would give him some added strength. It seemed to work as he pivoted to his left and managed to dislodge the man.

Before he could take a shot, the approaching woman pounced onto his arm holding the gun.

Even though Pepper was a big man, he wanted the struggle to be over as fast as possible. He had been in many fights over the years and he knew that anyone could score a lucky hit, no matter their size. He had the scars to back up this theory and even though he currently had a pistol, that advantage could soon change.

He didn't know what part of his assailants the gun was aimed at but, as he could feel the muzzle was against someone's flesh, he figured his only option was to fire. With two rapid shots, the bullets ripped through the thigh of the man. Although this stopped his struggling, it seemed to embolden the woman, who started scraping and scratching, hitting him with her head and using anything she could as a weapon.

The man was still alive but was screaming in pain, clearly no longer part of the fight. Pepper took this opportunity to drive his advantage against the woman. Manoeuvring her frame, he hurled her to the ground. As soon as his gun was clear, he fired two rounds into her head and another into the squirming man on the ground.

With three assailants down, he hoped that he could quickly deal with the last one. Looking around cautiously to check no others were ready to pounce, he levelled his gun in the direction of the man next to Flo.

Although the last man was shorter than Pepper, he was larger than Flo and had a knife held against her throat. When he opened his mouth to speak, he exposed a few broken yellow teeth framed by his grimy face.

"I kill her, I kill her," he grunted.

With some memory of how to speak, it seemed that he wasn't totally feral yet.

"Drop your weapon," the man continued.

Pepper quickly ran through the scenarios in his head. This was not the first time he had been in this type of situation. What was unusual was that the person in danger was someone he cared for. At the moment, he had the advantage: he had a gun trained on someone armed with a knife. If he put down the gun, there was every chance that the man would kill Flo anyway and Pepper would have lost his advantage.

"Give me the gun," the man said.

Pepper made his decision. Feigning to lower the pistol, he kept a tight grip on its butt. As the man temporarily lowered his guard and seemed to loosen his grip on the knife, Pepper swiftly raised his hand and fired two shots into the man's head.

He had been worried that he might hit Flo, but the only option was to think and act fast. The longer situations like this dragged on, the greater the threat became.

Flo had a lot of blood on her face but it all belonged to the dead man. His head had exploded as soon as the rounds impacted. His hand still had a deadlock on the knife but it was no longer held against Flo's throat.

As Pepper got closer, he saw that she was still sat rigid and the dead body was slumped over her. Pepper manoeuvred him away and wrapped his arms around her.

"Are you okay? Are you hurt?"

She slowly seemed to come round and the colour returned to her face. "I was so scared. But I think I'm okay."

After checking the attackers' pockets for anything useful, Pepper dragged the bodies into one pile. The pockets had been empty as he had suspected. All the same, he was determined that the attackers could still provide some benefit.

Conscious that he couldn't leave Flo again to collect enough dry firewood, he realised too that she might see his next actions as barbaric. Giving all of the blankets to Flo, he waited until she drifted off to sleep before he began the process of dismembering and burning the bodies.

The sickening smell of burning flesh was not pleasant but the fuel kept the fire burning as he remained on an alert vigil through the night.

12

THE ATTACK THROUGH ZAP'S EYES

18 August 2202

Zap had finished work for the night and was back in his apartment. Having prepared a pot of food for dinner, he was just placing it on the stove top.

Suddenly he felt an overwhelming rush of fear that froze him to the spot. In his head, blaring like a klaxon, all he could hear were the words "Pepper, Pepper – help!"

It was fortunate that he hadn't started to heat up the pot yet, as he was unable to move and couldn't put it down. His eyes closed involuntarily and it seemed as though he was somewhere else.

In his head, Zap found himself in a clearing in the woods and it was getting dark. A fire was burning and he wasn't alone – he could make out three other figures in the clearing. He knew he was in danger, he knew these people meant to do him harm but he couldn't move. His helplessness was fuelled by the fear that these three people were going to hurt or kill him.

Two of them seemed more interested in a pile of clothes and other items. But the biggest figure was staring straight at him. The man was ragged and dirtier than any man he had ever seen before. He had dirt in his hair and his face looked thick with mud. What clothes he had on were more like rags. He had gnarly fingers with long, black fingernails. He wasn't a large-framed man but he seemed taller than the other people in Zap's vision.

The tall man had a knife in his hand and he was getting closer. As he approached, the feelings of dread and fear grew. Suddenly, out of the woods, a large dark-skinned man appeared, bounding into the open. Even from a distance, this man seemed cleaner than the other three. For some reason, the sight of him made Zap feel more comfortable. He seemed familiar but Zap hadn't had a chance to see him fully yet.

This new arrival had a gun in his hand and, within seconds of his appearance, he'd fired two bullets into the man with the knife. Although it wasn't totally dark, the shadows from the fire obscured Zap's view. His vision was also limited because his head was frozen in place. This made it difficult to work out all that was happening around him.

The man with the gun was looking round frantically. His gun was still outstretched and it came to rest in the direction of the two people who were rifling through the contents of the backpacks.

Before he had a chance to fire another round, another figure rushed out of the woods and tackled him. This latest arrival looked dishevelled and more like the first three people Zap had sensed, dirty and in rags.

At the last minute, the man with the gun seemed to sense that he was under attack. Although he didn't move fast enough to fully avoid the charge, he pivoted at the minute of impact. With this last-minute move, he avoided the full brunt of his assailant's attack.

The two people rifling through the bags, a man and a woman apparently, suddenly stopped what they were doing and glanced between him and the two men. As the woman headed to join the fight, Zap could feel the last man staring into his eyes. The man drew a ragged knife and headed towards him.

It was all happening so fast. He heard two large bangs in the direction of the two fighting men. The smaller man rolled off the man with the gun and, even at this distance, it was obvious he was covered in blood. Just as quickly as this scuffle ended, the woman saw an opening and pounced on the victor.

Zap was suddenly distracted as the final man approached with his knife. He could feel the blood in his veins pounding. He wanted to get up and run but all he could do was sit there frozen, watching this horrible beast approaching with his knife.

Zap's sole focus was now on this man. He knew a struggle was still going on at the other side of the fire but that was not his concern. He needed to do something, he needed to get away from this man who clearly intended him harm. He wanted to stand up and run; he willed his legs to move but nothing was happening.

The man seemed momentarily startled at the sound of another two bangs. Zap was becoming more orientated to his surroundings and he was pretty sure it was gunfire.

Although hearing the shots had slowed him down at first, the man now increased his pace. By the time a third shot rang out, Zap's assailant had arrived.

Zap could feel an arm around his throat and the knife blade flashed in the firelight. Even though the attacker was not giving Zap his full attention, it felt hard to breathe.

He was terrified; the threat that he had perceived was now here and he could feel his breath labouring as the man's arm cut off his oxygen supply. The knife was above this arm, which seemed to be the only thing stopping his throat being cut.

At any time, he expected the man to slit his throat but for some reason the man had slowed his assault.

He heard the man speak but it didn't seem like the man was speaking to him.

"I kill her, I kill her. Drop your weapon."

Across the fire, Zap could make out only one figure left standing and this figure was pointing a gun in their direction. He hoped that the weapon was aimed at his assailant but his eyes were bleary from the lack of oxygen.

"Give me the gun," the man next to him growled in a voice that hardly seemed human.

The other man looked to be lowering his gun, filling Zap with a sense of dread. This man seemed to be the only one keeping him alive and, if he gave up his gun, it could be the end for Zap. The pressure around his throat seemed to relax slightly and he could actually breathe a little. But he was now worried that the arm was being moved to give the knife better access to his neck. Either way, the outlook did not seem good.

As the other man lowered his gun, Zap started to panic. He felt sure he was going to die. His attacker was going to slit his throat and there was nothing he could do about it.

The arm with the gun was getting lower when, without any warning, it darted upwards, gun hand raised. Two bright flashes in front of Zap were followed by two loud bangs. He felt a whistling past his ear and then a shower of warm fluid over his face and neck.

He experienced so many feelings all at once in the deafening noise and time had seemed to slow down once the bullets started rushing towards him. He felt fear, exhilaration and then suddenly he felt like he was being crushed. The full weight of the man behind him slumped on to him and he felt the last of his breath being forced out under the man's dead weight.

Out of the corner of his eye, he could see part of the man's face – he could actually see inside the man's face. It was a horrible bloody mess and his flesh seemed to have exploded at the impact of the bullets. He realised that the warm liquid had been not just blood but flesh, bone and even brain matter. He suddenly felt sick.

The tall man approached him quickly. Zap felt safer, even though he was still frozen with fear. The tall man pulled the body off him and he felt friendly arms wrap around him.

"Are you okay? Are you hurt?"

Zap heard himself say, "I was so scared," and then after a pause, "but I think I'm okay."

As quickly as all this had happened, it was over.

Zap's eyes shot open. He realised he was still holding the pot and, although he hadn't noticed the weight during his vision, he now felt its full burden.

He just managed to bang it down on the stove top before it had the chance to fall to the floor.

Once again Zap found himself questioning himself: "What happened? What have I just seen? What have I just felt?"

He lowered himself into an armchair and tried to figure it out. It seemed like he was himself yet he was someone else – he had been perceiving things through someone else's senses.

This whole experience was new to him. It felt similar to his previous dreams of the girl, he'd felt her emotions before but never this vividly.

It was a strange feeling to be in somebody else's body, someone he recognised as the person in his dreams.

In this waking dream, everything had been more intense; clearly this was something new and deeper. He had to figure out why he'd been inside someone else's head – or had she been in his?

It was one thing to dream this stuff when sleeping but he didn't like losing control in this way while he was awake. He noticed that he was shaking in the chair; this whole event had drained him. As soon as the shaking subsided, he poured himself a tall glass of water and drank it.

As he calmed down, he felt a surge of euphoria. Whoever's eyes he had been looking through had been in grave danger and Zap now had a great sense of relief. For now it seemed that the person he shared this bond with was safe and that made Zap feel better.

Abandoning any idea of food for the night, he left the cold pot on the stove and climbed into bed, hardly stopping to undress.

As soon as his head touched the pillow, he fell into a deep sleep. His sleep this night was to be the best he had experienced in a long time. This was a sleep void of any dreams; the kind of sleep that any insomniac would give anything to experience.

13

SMIT'S LAST CHANCE

18 August 2202

Captain Smit, head of the Sanctuary defence forces, was never a fan of being the bearer of bad news.

Delivering bad news to someone like Brand was certainly risky for his career but, worse still, it put his life in danger.

"I'm starting to think that you are becoming a liability," Brand said. "This is not the first time that you have stood in front of me to confess failure."

While he didn't like answering back to Brand, Smit also knew that the supreme leader despised weakness. He had to provide some kind of defence. "I appreciate that we lost some troops, but we did actually capture some traitors."

"Was I misinformed? I was under the impression that you actually killed the resistance before they could be interrogated."

It was true that the traitors had been killed. In fact, it

was all one big accident that the confrontation happened at all. The resistance had been smuggling contraband and had by chance been stopped at a checkpoint.

In a place the size of the Sanctuary, and with the disparity between rich and poor, a black market resourced by some smuggling was inevitable. Usually the resistance kept their noses clean but lately, with the shortages of food and the reduction in the distribution of gel packs, the rebels were becoming more emboldened.

"It is rare that these confrontations happen," Smit said. "The resistance tends to stay under the radar."

The comment only seemed to stoke Brand's rage. " So what you are saying is that normally your forces are even more incompetent. You're standing here admitting that you do not usually capture them and they get away with their crimes? On this one occasion when you accidentally stumble upon them, instead of capturing them for valuable intelligence, your incompetent soldiers kill them all."

Seeing this was a no-win situation, Smit decided to argue it no further.

"How many soldiers did we lose?" Brand demanded.

"Four of our troops were manning a checkpoint. A vehicle that they stopped for a regular check contained six armed rebels. They had the element of surprise and, when confronted, they killed the four guards. As soon as the alarm was raised, a quick reaction force was dispatched. The QRF force pursued and in the battle that ensued we lost one more man. All six of the traitors were killed."

"Have you managed to identify any of the bodies or

are your intelligence forces as incompetent as your soldiers?"

Smit was happy to at least have some good news for Brand. "Although a lot of these scum look the same, we did verify that one of them bore the 'W' mark of the warriors from the fighting pits."

This revelation seemed to pique Brands interest. "So Karla was involved?"

"We have no evidence to identify if he was a current warrior or one of her victors who had been granted his freedom for his fighting prowess," Smit said reluctantly.

Karla provided a service for the state by running an operation that gave an outlet for the violent tendencies of the Sanctuary's lower classes. Although through his wide network of spies Brand knew that she had some dealings with the black market, he had previously turned a blind eye to her activities. The benefits of the service that she provided made it worth overlooking a few minor transgressions.

Knowing unofficially that Karla traded in contraband was one thing, but this kind of disrespect could not go unanswered.

"Bring me the head of the warrior," Brand ordered.

"Just his head?" Smit was bemused. With Brand in a bad mood, it was not a great time to question an order but equally he needed to get it correct.

Brand's eyes widened. "Yes, that's what I said – the head. Is there something wrong with your hearing today? Put it in a bag or a box, I don't care as long as it's not dripping blood everywhere. Get it brought to me here by morning and ensure that the W brand is still visible."

"Of course, sir." Smit took this opportunity to leave the office.

Brand had the kernel of a plan forming in his head. He had decided it was time to reiterate who held the real power in the Sanctuary. The head might seem a little theatrical but it would help drive home his point.

14

IN THE WOODS THE DAY AFTER THE
ATTACK

19 August 2202

Pepper had survived the night and keeping the fire burning had helped to dry out his clothing.

After their confrontation with the attackers, he had no intention of sleeping and hoped that giving Flo all of the bedding would allow her to rest.

He was hoping to move faster today and, as she was holding them back, he wanted her to be at her best.

From time to time, as he worked through the daily camp routine, he tried to wake Flo up but was having trouble doing so. Gently rocking her shoulder had brought no reaction, so he was increasing the ferocity of his shaking. "Wake up, wake up, it's time to wake up."

He had some soup waiting for her to combat any residual effects of her shock from the night before. Apart from the breakfast supplies, he'd packed up most of the kit before attempting to wake her.

Suddenly Pepper realised that Flo was actually awake, but staring off into space. It was like she was dreaming while conscious, in some kind of trance. Her lips were moving as if in conversation but no sound was coming out of her mouth.

Although he wanted to break her out of this state, he was unsure how healthy it would be to continue to shake her. He was worried what the shock would do to her.

He decided it best to wait a few more minutes, until the food was ready. Going over to the pot of soup, he got it boiling before trying to rouse her again.

This time he touched her gently on the hand. After a momentary delay, her facial expression changed and she looked straight at him. She moved strangely, as though her consciousness had just arrived in someone else's body.

"Are you okay?" he said. "Are you awake?"

Still somewhat drowsy, she managed to murmur, "Yes."

"Are you with me?"

"Orm, urrr … yes."

"You looked like you were talking to somebody. Who was it?" he asked quizzically.

She was unsure about how much of her abilities to reveal. Previously she had told him that she could read people but her skills were now growing exponentially.

She decided that if she didn't answer, he would just keep asking questions. Plus Pepper had risked his life to save her and she felt he deserved some kind of explanation.

"I have been dreaming of someone for some time now. No, it's more than just dreaming – it is like I am inside his head looking through his eyes and he is in mine seeing through my eyes. At least, it has been like that but then, since last night, something has changed."

"What is this person saying? What information is he after?" To Pepper, it sounded like a risk that he couldn't guard against.

"Since I woke this morning, it is like I am having a conversation. Our communication is now like chatting. As if he was standing in front of me, where you are now. He doesn't seem like a threat – he feels like a friend, like someone I have always known. He was concerned about what happened last night and felt the fear in me."

"Has he asked you where you are?"

"No, it's not like that, he was concerned about me. He said he felt all of my pain. He explained that he too was unable to move when we were attacked. He was frozen with my fear. I can't explain it any other way."

"Do you know where he is? Have you recognised anything when you looked through his eyes?"

"He is in a strange place that he calls the Sanctuary. When I see through his eyes, it seems different to anywhere I have ever been, but faintly familiar."

Although he was keen to pursue the topic further, Pepper thought she should eat something first. "Here, I've prepared some soup. You need to get something warm inside you before we leave." Once they got moving, he would question her more.

15

BRAND ARRIVES AT THE PITS

20 August 2202

Smit had supplied the head of the warrior on schedule the next day but Brand liked to plan for contingencies. He had waited until now to deliver his message.

Brand arrived at the pits with twenty of his elite bodyguard, all well-armed. To a man, they held the pistol grips of their automatic rifles and they were ready to pull the triggers at the first signal from Brand.

It was late morning and the warriors were doing some light sparring in the amphitheatre.

Karla was sitting at her desk when one of her lieutenants, King, barged into her office.

"Supreme leader Brand has just arrived. He has a large force of soldiers with him and has made his way to the premier's box."

"What? He's here now? Why wasn't I informed earlier?" Karla was rarely flustered but Brand usually liked them to make a fuss over him on his visits. If he'd turned up in force without notice, it was not a good omen.

She rushed down the stairs flanked by Miyamoto and found Brand standing in the premier's box.

"I'm sorry, I didn't realise that we were expecting you."

"You weren't expecting me, which is the point!" Brand replied. "That is the point."

Before Karla had a chance to reply, Brand continued. "Assemble all of your warriors in a line in the arena."

It was clear that Brand had an agenda and the sight of his troops in the arena gave her few options. "Miyamoto, go round up the warriors and line them up in the arena," Karla instructed before turning to Brand. "Can I get you anything to eat or drink?"

Rather than speaking, he replied by sweeping his hand in a dismissive manner.

Brand looked out at the warriors forming up in the arena. The premier's box was designed to provide an optimum view of the arena so Brand could watch the warriors while his troops observed him.

When all of the warriors had assembled, Miyamoto waved to Karla from the arena.

"That's all of them," Karla said.

As Brand motioned to his troops, they surrounded the warriors and raised their guns. "Who is your best warrior, who is your star?" he asked.

"Obviously," Karla said, "it is David. He has never lost any of the last twenty fights and they have all involved in a quick kill."

"Tell him to step forward."

"David, take two steps forward," she shouted down

to the warriors. Without any hesitation, he did as he was told.

"Okay, who is your worst warrior?"

"Fred has the least experience."

"Tell him to step forward and instruct another three random warriors to do the same."

Thinking that this was going to be some kind of fight display, Karla chose two more of her best warriors and threw in an average warrior so that this would be a good performance.

She hoped that they wouldn't be expected to fight to the death. It was not unheard of for Brand to request warriors to be brought to his residence or to the council buildings to fight. This could happen at his whim or for a special occasion, although it was unusual. This was the first time he had appeared at the pits outside of a scheduled fight.

"Fred, Rook, Bass and Trip. Take two steps forward also," she shouted to the group below, wondering what kind of fight Brand expected to see.

But no further instructions followed. Instead, Brand raised his arm and the troops instantly fired two rounds into each of the five chosen warriors. Karla watched on transfixed.

Before she could react, Brand addressed Karla and the remaining warriors. "I have been informed that rebels are among your people. It is important that you realise you live by my whim. If you fight well, you have a chance for freedom and forgiveness of your previous crimes. This is not true if you fight against the state! You notice today that I have killed one of your best warriors and one of your worst. This is to show you that no matter how well you fight, if you choose to rebel against the state, your life will be forfeit. I take it that I have made myself clear?"

Karla had no idea what it all meant but, before she could question Brand, he gathered his troops and left the pits.

Miyamoto bounded up the stairs to check on Karla. When he reached her, she was looking slightly confused but quickly regained her composure. "Go check they have gone before we try to work out what just happened."

Then she shouted to the group below, "King, get those bodies out of arena. Angus, I want an intensive training session for the rest of the day. Make the men sweat." From her vantage point, she saw Angus and King nod.

When Miyamoto stepped outside, he was confronted by a severed head impaled on a spike. The spike had been driven into the ground in a prominent position for passers-by to see.

He recognised the head as Zeus but before he could remove it, one of the stadium guards shouted, "Leave that head where it is. No one is to move that head for twenty-four hours. If you try, we'll have to shoot you."

The guards were supposed to be there to protect the warriors but they were Company troops and their prime purpose was to follow orders. Brand's message was clear: the general public would see the head and the word would get out that he was serious.

Karla was still trying to work out what had happened when Miyamoto returned.

"They've stuck a head on a spike outside and the guards have been ordered to stop anyone from removing it. The head is Zeus's." His voice was tense with anger as he clearly struggled to stay emotionless in the aftermath of Brand's visit.

Karla had provided Zeus to Hubert to help out on a gel pack run for the black market. These ventures always held some risk but she had to maintain her alliances with the other black market leaders.

For the immediate future, she could not remove the head but she would need to schedule a meeting with Hubert and the other resistance leaders. It was unclear how much Brand knew and today's demonstration could be the start of a crackdown.

Even though she showed very little emotion on the outside, inside she too was seething with anger.

As a businesswoman, she realised that her livelihood was no longer guaranteed. Yet, although Brand's actions may have been designed to quell any rebellion, they had the opposite effect.

As one of the supposedly criminal leaders in the Sanctuary, she had shied away from open acts of rebellion. It had made no business sense to draw attention to her activities but things had just changed.

The other leaders had been rumbling about resistance for some time, while she had felt safe so had seen no reason to take on extra risk.

It was now obvious to her that the only way to increase her odds of survival was to wholeheartedly join the rebellion.

16

WEATHERING THE DOWNPOUR

30 August 2202

Pepper decided that they needed to head for the woods to seek some kind of shelter from the constant rain.

He was wary of the dangers that can lurk in the dark but his main concern was the health of his young charge. Flo could hardly walk, had developed a fever and was becoming delirious.

Although he was soaked to the bone, he was in a much better shape than her. She needed to be supported so much that he was almost carrying her. As they reached the edge of the trees, he noticed movement and drew the pistol from his waistband.

His soaked gloves offered little comfort. His hand was shaking a bit in the freezing rain but he made a conscious effort to keep it steady as he scanned the area. Years of practice and training meant that his gun hand mirrored the movement of his head.

Out of the woods emerged two figures, one holding a shotgun and the other a rifle.

"Stop where you are, drop the gun and put your hands in the air," the taller one shouted.

In a more controlled environment, Pepper might have attempted to shoot both of the men at the same time. Here, weighed down by Flo and with the rain in his eyes, he couldn't guarantee taking out either of them.

That they had not fired immediately was a good sign that he might be able to reason with these people. In the back of his mind was the hope that neither Flo nor he would be injured or killed.

Placing his gun slowly back into his waistband, Pepper raised his right hand while keeping his left arm around Flo for support.

"Where are you going? What do you want around here?" the taller man asked.

"I am escorting this young woman home. She comes from around here." He had decided that his best option was to present Flo in the hope that somebody around here would recognise her and avoid further confrontations. "Who are you guys?"

"I'm Neville and this is Ryan. Where is she from?" The smaller man spoke now, keeping his shotgun aimed firmly at Pepper's head. Ryan didn't seem impressed about his name being given to a total stranger.

"She is from a place called Pandora. Do you know it?" Pepper asked.

This information seemed to stir Ryan's interest. "What do you know of Pandora?"

"She said it's a farm and that she's lived there for several years."

"Show me her face," commanded Ryan. "Take off her hood so I can see her face."

Clumsily Pepper took down Flo's hood while attempting to keep her body supported against him.

When Ryan examined her pale face, Pepper noticed his eyes light up in apparent recognition. "Where did you find this girl?"

"It's a long story but basically, I rescued her from somewhere during an attack by Company soldiers."

"Did they follow you?" Ryan had concern in his voice.

"This happened well over a week ago. We've come a long way since then and she needs medical attention!" Pepper shouted.

Ryan hesitated, like he didn't really trust Pepper, but he seemed to understand the urgency of the situation.

"The Farm is on the other side of these woods. We'll take you there – if you hand over your weapons first."

Pepper slowly removed the pistol from his waistband. Holding it by the barrel, he extended his right arm towards the men. Both men kept their guns trained on Pepper, while Neville took the pistol and stashed it in his own waistband.

"Okay, walk in front of us, no funny stuff," Ryan said and then turned to Neville. "You keep your eyes on this guy, don't take your gun off of him." He then took the smaller backpack off Flo's shoulders to make it easier for her to move.

Pepper didn't know much about this guy but it was clear that Ryan was in charge. Although his first impressions were positive, his main concern was not to make Flo's situation any worse.

Once they were under the cover of the trees, Ryan

took a small radio from his pocket and spoke into it. "Hello Eagle's nest, hello Eagle's nest, this is Patrol one, over."

A crackled voice came over the radio. "Hello Patrol one, this is Eagle's nest, over."

"Eagle's nest, this is Patrol one. We have encountered a male subject accompanied by what seems to be the young female Florence, over."

"Say again, you have encountered a male subject and he is accompanied by Florence, over?" The voice on the radio seemed surprised.

"That is correct. I am referring to Florence the Farm's daughter. She is suffering from what seems to be hypothermia and we need to get her medical assistance as fast as possible, over. "

"Hello Patrol one, this is Eagle's nest. Get her to the edge of the woods and a vehicle will meet you there, over."

"Patrol one, message received and understood, out to you."

"Hello, Patrol five and Patrol two. Please confirm you will cover Patrol one's arc until told otherwise over."

"Patrol five, will do, over."

"Patrol two, will do, over."

After ten minutes of almost dragging Flo through the woods, they emerged into a clearing. Pepper could see fields of crops and a group of buildings in the distance. Speeding towards them was a flatbed truck.

Pepper was surprised that the Farm actually existed and even more surprised at the size of the operation. Perhaps he was indeed going to get a large reward for returning the girl home.

Almost as soon as the vehicle stopped, a young bald

man jumped out of the vehicle and rushed towards the group. Initially Pepper thought this guy was going to attack him. Although he wasn't as tall as Pepper, he was definitely agile and muscly. Yet he needn't have worried as the new arrival's sole focus was on Flo.

Reaching Flo, he unceremoniously nudged Pepper out of the way and encompassed her in a bear hug. "Are you okay, are you okay? It's me, Eric."

"Yes," she murmured feebly.

Pepper noted that he'd been correct about the strength of this Eric. He lifted up Flo like a baby and carried her effortlessly to the truck.

As Eric was positioning Flo softly in the back seat of the truck, Ryan relieved Pepper of his backpack and tied his hands behind his back. Ryan then motioned for him to get into the back of the truck, assisting him in his newly restrained state.

Ryan and Neville then mounted the truck while keeping their weapons trained on Pepper and the vehicle sped off towards the buildings.

It was around 6pm and, as they reached the main building, a group of people were already waiting outside on a deck. Over the deck was a pitched roof, which was providing cover from the still heavy rain.

As soon as they stopped, Eric exited the vehicle, cradling Flo, and carried her into the building.

Pepper could see smoke coming out of the chimney and hoped that, whatever came next, he would at least be able to dry off and get warm.

One woman stood out from the group – an elderly woman with a check shirt, long grey hair, and creased skin that Pepper assumed she'd accrued from years of working outside.

The woman motioned for Pepper to be brought to her. Ryan and Neville helped him out the truck and took him over, his hands still tied behind his back. Neville emptied the two backpacks onto the deck alongside the pistol.

"So who do we have here? Who do we have to thank for bringing our Florence home?" the woman said.

Pepper was unsure how they were viewing him but, as far as he was concerned, he was a hero returning the prodigal daughter. He decided that was the role he'd play.

"My name's Pepper and I rescued this girl from certain death. I escorted her here because she said I would receive a reward if I did so. Who are you?"

"My name's Kath and I'm Florence's mother," she said as she looked Pepper up and down, as if assessing whether what he said seemed true.

Florence wasn't well enough to question yet and so Kath had to use her intuition. Surveying the contents of the upturned packs on the dry deck, she noted the main pack had contained two pistols and silencers – the preferred weapons of the rebels – a knife and several other survival stores. The second pack had also contained a knife.

"When we encountered them, Florence was carrying the smaller pack and this guy had the larger bag," Ryan said.

Kath immediately noted that Florence had also been allowed to carry a knife. Although she doubted that even in full health Florence would have been able to overpower someone of Pepper's size, allowing her a knife did show some element of trust existed between the two.

"Okay, instead of us all staying out in the rain, let's take this inside," Kath said. "Untie his hands, put his things back in the packs and take them to the store room. Mr Pepper, you can have your guns and equipment back once we have corroborated your story."

Looking at Pepper's sodden figure, she added, "For now, let's get you out of those wet clothes before you catch pneumonia. If you are truly the hero bringing home our Florence, the least we can do is offer you some hospitality."

Pepper didn't hesitate to walk into the building. He was presented with the sight of a blazing open fire. Flo was lying on a cot in front of the fire, her wet clothes now removed and dry, warm blankets swaddling her.

Kath had called for some towels and a set of large, warm clothes for Pepper. Never one for embarrassment, as soon as the pile of clothing and towels arrived he began to strip off his garments.

At the sight of the triangle branded on Pepper's left shoulder, Eric's facial expression changed. He was no longer the caring nurse, tending to Florence. It was like someone had flicked a switch that turned him into a wild animal. Eric started to advance on Pepper.

Seeing this, Kath quickly put a hand up and shouted, "Stop!" Eric faltered momentarily. Quickly Kath said to Pepper, "I see you bear the brand of the Company. It's not very clever coming here under cover with a brand on your shoulder."

Eric looked ready to pounce at any moment so Pepper chose his words carefully. "Yes, once upon a time I worked for the Company as a soldier in its army, but we parted ways. We had a difference of opinion."

Kath noted that, as well as the triangle brand on his

shoulder, he had a badly scarred back. The roughly healed strips of skin showed the kind of injury inflicted by the public floggings that she had seen the Company inflict over the years. "So you are a deserter?"

"As I said, we parted ways through a difference of opinion. That was several years ago and I get the feeling that they have not forgiven and forgotten."

Kath decided that this was not the time to delve too deeply into this in front of the gathering crowd. He seemed genuine and apparently felt he had little to hide given that he had brought Florence here and immediately revealed the brand by taking off his shirt.

She did, however, have one important question "If you are no longer with the Company, why do you keep their mark? Surely it would make sense to remove their brand, for your own safety?"

Pepper contemplated a moment before his next words. "The brand could never be removed fully and having a partially removed brand would be even more suspicious than keeping the full mark." After pausing again for that point to sink in, he added, "There have been times when the brand has come in handy, when it has been useful to play the part of a Company man."

Once Pepper had changed into dry clothes, he was guided to a long table where he was given a bowl of thick vegetable soup. He devoured it quickly.

Taking into account his size, Kath motioned for a second bowl, which he devoured almost as quickly.

"So this is what we are going to do," Kath stated. "Until Florence is better and can fully substantiate your story, you will remain secure in one of the rooms. You are not a prisoner. However, you will not be given any weapons and your movements will be restricted until we are more confident about who you are."

Pepper reflected on his current situation. He had been given dry, warm clothes and food. It seemed that these people were just taking normal precautions and, if he had been in danger, he doubted he would still be alive.

Kath said, "I am sure you have had a weary journey, so I would ask that you take this opportunity to rest. Your room will be locked and a guard will be posted outside your room."

Considering the way that Eric was still looking at him, Pepper wondered if the guard was for the Farm's safety or his own.

"We will keep your possessions safe and talk more tomorrow."

When she raised a hand, two armed men escorted him to a room on the same level as the common room. The window was barred – although it seemed more like a storage room than a cell – and it was furnished with a freshly made bed.

After nights of broken sleep while protecting Flo on the road, he was due a good night's sleep. He was grateful for the bed and, even though it was still early, he fell asleep, almost as soon as he rested his head on the pillow.

Although Kath had been desperate to hold Florence in her arms, her first duty had been to assess the new visitor. Now she could give her daughter her full attention. Eric had already spoon-fed Florence some warm soup and she was covered by dry, warm bedding. But she was still shivering and had a fever. Kath applied wet cloths to her forehead, in an effort to bring down the temperature.

Unsure how sick Florence was, Kath had a roster drawn up so that somebody would be watching her during the night. In reality, though, Kath knew that Eric wouldn't leave her side all night.

17

THE AGING CEREMONY

31 August 2202

This was not the first aging ceremony that Zap had attended. His stepfather had not been classed as an elite but, for some reason, he and Zap had always sat in exclusive seats. Since his stepfather's death, Zap had inherited this privilege but rarely used it as he preferred to mix with the warriors.

The wall of the stadium has been designed with a dual purpose. As well as being part of the stadium's external structure, it formed part of the stands and seating that gave a view of activities staged outside of the stadium. The elite and the Company officials overseeing the ceremony sat up there. They were both physically above the proceedings and immune to the compulsory age limit for liquidation.

Huge crowds had congregated in front of the stadium to witness the roll call of the chosen. They stretched far into the distance.

Standing at the lectern, the announcer read out

today's long list of the condemned for this month. For as long as Zap could remember, these ceremonies had preceded a fighting event.

At the end of the aging ceremony, people who had reached forty-five years of age were euthanised and fed to the gel plants. The Company deemed it merciful to allow their loved ones to attend and say one last goodbye.

Although this public ceremony was presented as part of the survival process, it was starting to stoke resentment in the masses. They saw the privileged overindulging in luxuries, while they were forced to sacrifice their own families to be processed for food.

It was an emotional time for those saying farewell. The barcode tattoos that all Sanctuary inhabitants were given at birth contained their personal information, including the day of that birth. This ensured that the Company never forgot anyone's forty-fifth birthday.

The barcodes were compulsory for anyone wishing to receive their gel rations as they were scanned at the distribution points. The Company had used this branding for so long that no one could remember being without a barcode; most people were identified by their surname and the last three digits of their barcode.

Some people would always try to avoid the ceremony but the Company took precautions.

Tattoo removal wasn't recommended because if a Company patrol caught anyone without a code, it meant an instant journey to the gel plants.

If you failed to show up for your ceremony, the Company retribution was swift. Two of your family members were chosen at random and immediately processed at the gel plants.

After killing your family members, the Company still pursued you. If you managed to continue to evade pursuit, each year for the next five years it took another member of your family to the plants. Family units weren't very big among the masses so removing five people left a huge hole in most families.

The result was that, although very few people relished ending their lives at forty-five years of age, most showed up for their ceremony to spare the rest of their family.

The age of forty-five had initially been set to allow Company soldiers to retire at thirty-eight with seven years of freedom left to enjoy. Lowering the age to forty-four, supposedly due to food shortages, was not popular as the masses believed that there was enough food for everyone, if the privileged weren't so damn greedy and wasteful.

Today's graduates for the ceremony stood near the front of the large crowd. They could move forward easily as no one else wanted to be inadvertently swept up into the waiting trucks.

Lots of people were crying. Before each block of names was announced over the speakers, the announcer proclaimed, "We would like to thank all of you for your contribution to our society. You are giving the ultimate sacrifice so that we may live."

The message offered little comfort to children losing their parents or to others losing siblings.

As always on these occasions, the elites were dressed in their finery. It was late in the year so their wardrobes consisted of large coats, beautifully woven gloves for the ladies and fur hats for the particularly privileged.

From an early age, everyone was taught about the

origins of the gel plants. After the Water Wars, the plants had emerged as a sustainable way for people to survive in a planet starved of resources.

Zap couldn't understand why resources were abundant in the Sanctuary, yet the poor had such a shortage of food. The average member of the elite consumed over one hundred times more resources than any of the workers or servants within the Sanctuary. This made no sense. Why was there such disparity between the two classes?

The history they had been taught was that the elite had saved the planet. The three companies that had started the Water Wars were radicals fuelled by socialist ideals. It was only the foresight of the elites that had managed to stop the total obliteration of the human race.

The stories of how the elites had saved the planet were vague but Zap accepted that anyone saving humankind deserved some respect. What he didn't agree with was that all elites had a birth right to maintain their status until the end of time.

Zap didn't know who his real father was but he must have been somebody powerful for his stepfather to take charge of him. His stepfather had been fair and never cruel to him. Whenever he asked about his real father, his stepfather had said that he had been a soldier who'd died fighting for the Sanctuary.

As a child, Zap had accepted this story but, as he got older and gained access to more information, his belief had weakened. After all, in the hierarchy of this society, even those in the officer class were never accepted into the ranks of the elites. Given his stepfather was a law official who lived on the fringes of the elites, he would never choose to endanger his own status by bringing up the child of a member of a lower class.

When the next name was called – "Byron 623" – a man walked forward to the waiting trucks. Two small, crying children were holding his hands tightly, trying to hold him back but to no avail. He turned, kissed them slowly on their foreheads and pulled away to walk through the line of Company soldiers. The barrier closed behind him and the children were left standing there alone.

No one came to collect the children. As more and more sacrifices advanced towards processing, the two small figures disappeared into the crowd.

Zap thought it a smart idea for the Company to follow the ceremonies with a fighting event. The atmosphere inside the stadium and the fights to the death tended to take over most people. Yet the blood lust didn't work for everyone. Children who had lost their parents were particularly scarred.

The ceremony continued until the last name was called and the woman chosen slowly walked towards the trucks.

The Company had tried to make the ceremonies an enjoyable spectacle but it was a solemn occasion for many. Even those in the crowd who were not losing somebody this time were well aware that next list could include a family member – or themselves.

One feeling that tended to overcome grief was hunger, a link the Company capitalised on.

As soon as the gates opened, the crowd surged into the stadium. A limited supply of gel packs was available inside. If you were lucky enough to be at the front of the queue, you received one of these free gel packs.

The pack didn't come as part of your normal gel rations – instead of having to scan your barcode, you were just handed one as you walk in. With the recent shortages of gel packs, some might have been surprised that the Company continued to give the free ones away at the stadium.

Although Zap was suspicious, hungry people tended not to question free food. There were rumours that at the next ceremony, the big ceremony that preceded the festival, the age limit was going to be dropped to forty-three. This was just a rumour but there were lots of murmurs of discontent around the Sanctuary, especially in the capital.

Not everyone could travel with their family to the capital for the ceremony: the Company provided free trains only for the chosen. Perhaps the Company bureaucrats saw the provision of free transport as merciful but, for people who would never see their loved ones again, the farewells at the train stations were filled with emotion.

Zap wondered if the time would ever come when they would not need the gel plants, when people could live longer and survive just from the planet's resources.

He understood the stories that the Water Wars had decimated resources but his data analysis indicated not all of the stories made sense. The story that the qualifying age for liquidation might have to keep being reduced because the planet had been even more damaged than they were taught in history felt like pure propaganda.

A group of Company soldiers called the eco-warriors were supposedly working tirelessly to protect the planet. Their existence put more pressure on the average person to sacrifice for the planet too.

Zap thought it strange that the eco-warriors expected the sacrifice from the masses, but not from the elites. Officially the elites were always sacrificing themselves for the good of the people but that didn't seem true to him.

For today he would soon be distracted from such questions. The elite seating was revolving so that, whereas they had previously looked out onto the ceremony, the elite now were viewing the arena. This was a prime viewing position for the fights that were about to begin.

18

KATH'S REQUEST TO PEPPER

03 September 2202

Pepper had been at the Farm for three days now.

The routine was the same each day. His door was unlocked and he was escorted down for breakfast. He was not allowed away from the main building and he had not had his weapons returned.

The Farm inhabitants were amiable enough to him and it helped that Flo was now up and talking. She had corroborated his story, which had earned him a certain amount of trust.

Over the last few days he'd had many conversations with Kath, informing her about the state of the kingdom further south. They had also discussed the attacks by the Company forces.

He'd told her how he came across Flo in the rebel compound during the assault by the Company forces. Kath explained that this Farm was supplied by rebel guards. Although it was run (if not owned) by her and her husband Mitch, it was seen more as a coalition. The

Farm provided valuable resources for the rebels and, in exchange, the resistance kept them safe. It worked in a time when food was life.

This Farm was clearly an important resource, which is why rebel guards – more than thirty by Pepper's reckoning – were stationed there. Some farm workers also carried weapons, but they lacked the bearing of the rebel fighters.

Kath had been keen to know about Flo's journey north. Pepper was nonchalant about the attacks he fought off on the journey but Flo's recollections were that she owed him her life. Even though a reward was supposed to be the reason for his help, Kath had heard from Flo that she had felt his empathy towards her.

Most of the people at the Farm remained wary of Pepper, yet they seemed to be staring less and less by the day. As time went on, they were viewing him as less of a threat even if not enough to see him as one of them.

The one exception was that, whenever he was around Eric, he could feel the hate coming through the young man's eyes. Even when Pepper was facing away from him, he could feel Eric's eyes burning into his back.

A bit of mistrust was understandable but he'd done nothing to this boy. Seeing how Eric reacted to the return of Flo, you would think he would've been suitably grateful for her return.

Eric's issue with Pepper had been there for all to see, ever since the night Pepper arrived, ever since he had taken his shirt off. On the third of his daily talks with Kath, he decided to broach the subject.

"So what's the boy Eric's story?" Pepper asked. "Why do I get the feeling he would like to plunge a knife between my shoulder blades?"

"Eric has been here for several years," Kath began, apparently deciding that Pepper was owed some kind of explanation. "About seven years ago we discovered a young boy in one of the barns. The few clothes he was wearing were nothing but rags, he didn't talk and he was more like a feral animal than a person."

When Kath paused, Pepper held his silence, waiting for her to continue.

"Initially he stayed in the barn. Although we left him provisions, including food and water, he didn't even try to wear the clothes but snuggled in the blankets like a dog in its bed. Around that time, Florence started to pay attention to him and ended up adopting him as a pet project. There wasn't much for a young girl to do on a farm like this and, besides her chores, she had a natural way with sick animals."

"So she is like his master and he's her pet?" Pepper perked up.

"No, it has become much more than that. After many months of patience, she managed to coax him out of the barn and helped him communicate, eventually teaching him to read and write. Although he talks more now, back then he only talked to Florence and the bond between them is closer than brother and sister."

"Did you ever find out where he came from or how he ended up alone and feral?"

"Florence called him Eric because he couldn't remember his real name. It took a long time but eventually she got him to open up to her. It turned out that his parents had been miners and he'd been in the mine with them on the day it collapsed, which left him in the dark alone. At the time he was only seven or eight years old – it's hard to tell exactly as his memory is still fuzzy on some things."

Kath took a sip from a glass of water and before continuing. "His parents had been killed in the rock fall and, because life was cheap, the Company hadn't even tried to rescue them. It was cheaper for the Company to just sink a new shaft nearby and leave any survivors to rot."

She took a bigger gulp of water. Even though she knew this story by heart, it still made her sick thinking of the cruelty of the Company. "Eric is a survivor and managed to dig himself out of the rubble on his own. Who knows how long it took him to tunnel out by hand – days, weeks, maybe even months? He survived by eating rats and whatever other creatures he managed to scavenge. You may not have noticed, but his hands are badly scarred from their use as human shovels. He wears dark glasses during the day because his eyes have adapted to the dark, like some kind of nocturnal animal. The scars on his forehead are from his fights with animals in the mine. It's hard to imagine what a child of that age went through, and what primal survival urges he would have needed to drive him to escape the tomb he found himself in. Whatever he endured, somehow he managed to escape."

"That doesn't explain why he hates me," Pepper said, a little more subdued this time.

"One thing that is burnt into his memory is the Company troops who abandoned him and his parents. Apparently in the heat of the mines they used to strip to the waist, even though they weren't workers. The Company brand on their shoulders is ingrained in Eric's mind too. Whenever he sees a triangle brand, it is like fire touching dry tinder, the rage just erupts in him. Seeing your brand did just this."

"How often does this happen?"

"We have tried to keep Eric on the Farm as much as possible but he's a strong young man and is sometimes needed on supply runs. On a couple of supply runs, he's been involved in skirmishes with the Company forces. From what his companions have said, these incidents have not ended well. He has spiralled into a rage and in his ferocity has killed several soldiers. Keeping him here is for the safety of others but also to avoid retaliation from the Company.

"When Florence initially disappeared, he wanted to go looking for her. Knowing the way he might behave and the chance that he would lose control, we decided to keep him here."

"How did he react to the enforced confinement? He doesn't seem the kind to listen."

"He was not happy with my decision and for a time I felt some of his anger directed at me. Since you've arrived, you seem to have become the sole focus of that attention," Kath said with a wry smile.

"Great, so I've got a young psycho who hates me for being part of the Company, which has actually been hunting me for most of my adult life?" Pepper said indignantly. "Well, the young girl is healthy and safe, so I think it's time to discuss my reward. The reward I was promised."

Kath, who had been expecting this conversation for some time, was actually surprised it had taken so long. "What kind of reward are you expecting?"

"I was offered as much as I could carry and although it's very nice to have crops to eat, I need things that I can trade – weapons, tools and medicines if you've got them."

"We can supply you with some medicines that we make from the plants we grow here. We trade them for other resources and they are highly sought after. We have limited weaponry to spare. However, we trade regularly with the rebel compound and they have a lot more resources. If you are willing to go on our next supply run, I can promise you enough weapons and tools to fill that pack of yours."

Pepper felt that he was being played. "Excuse me, the bargain was that I get the girl here and I get my reward. I have kept up my end of the deal. Now you need me to go somewhere else to get the reward? This is not what I agreed to!"

"Perhaps the bargain you struck with a young girl wasn't as precise as it should have been? I am willing to provide the reward you require. All I am asking is that you go on the supply run to collect them. The next supply run is in a week's time and, if you are willing to go, I would ask that you take Florence with you."

"Why would I take the girl with me when she's just arrived? I thought you wanted to protect her?"

"She has some important information and I need her to give it to the rebel leader in person. In the interim, you have the freedom of the Farm. I will have your pack and weapons returned too. If you choose to leave without all of your reward, you can be on your way. If you want the tools and weapons, you will have to go on the supply run. We will continue to feed you and provide you a room while you're here for the next week. I will check on your decision in three days' time."

"Okay, we'll talk about it again in three days," Pepper agreed.

He wasn't happy with this arrangement but at least he could now get his weapons back. He'd felt naked without a weapon. Even though most of these people seem friendly enough, you never knew. He had not survived this long through blind trust.

19

———

THE NIGHT PATROL

05 September 2202

The wedding was a typical one for any of the poorer class in the Sanctuary. As most of the guests had jobs servicing the elite, the wedding was scheduled for later in the day.

Food wasn't abundant but one of the groomsmen was related to the butcher, who had done them a good deal on some grade B meat. The farm workers among the wedding guests had also managed to collect some meagre food rations. Some of this food had even been turned into a local alcoholic hooch.

It was almost nine thirty and, with the ten o'clock curfew approaching, most of the guests had already gone home. As the few people remaining had drunk a little too much of the hooch, the groom's family suggested that they spend the night. Although there wasn't much room, they had the option of sleeping on the floor.

Simon, a friend of the groom, had a counter-offer:

they could sleep at his place. Simon and his parents lived in a larger house than most and it was only twenty minutes' walk away. He was loudly confident that they'd reach it well before curfew. They could travel between most houses in this area within twenty minutes.

The threat of the night patrols was serious but they were safe until the curfew claxon sounded. People could achieve a lot in twenty minutes – and that could be the difference between life and death at this time of night.

Simon decided to chance it. He and six other young men left the house at nine thirty. Even if they didn't complete the journey in the next twenty minutes, they had a ten-minute buffer. Simon doubted that the patrols waited for the curfew ready to pounce – surely they had some safety margin? Perhaps the drink was clouding his judgement.

Carl was the leader of the patrol this evening. They had been out since eight thirty, driving round and preparing for action. Although curfew wasn't officially until ten o'clock, he liked to patrol in advance and look for potential captives early on so that they could move in as soon as the curfew claxon sounded.

The initial purpose of the patrols was to provide security in the Sanctuary but, as the elite had their own security, the role of the patrols soon became to find victims to supplement the gel plants. They only patrolled the poor areas and some patrols had been known to turn a blind eye for a price.

Previously, if they came across any black market activities, they had usually impounded the goods and let the criminals go. But now, with their increased quotas for the plants, they might still impound the goods but take the criminals to the gel plants instead of accepting a bribe.

Anyone caught out after ten was immediately transported to the gel plants. Some of his previous captives had pleaded that they worked for a member of the elite but that wasn't Carl's concern. He had quotas to reach and Carl always met his quotas. There was no reprieve for anyone supposedly protected by the elite. By morning they would be gel packs, beyond rescue.

Earlier that day, Carl had heard rumours of a wedding in this quarter, which gave him a good place to start. Carl's troops had instructions to keep their eyes peeled any time after nine. This close to ten, not everyone made it home.

Carl had four vehicles under his command that night. They were spread out around the sector looking for anybody on the streets. At nine thirty, a message came over the radio. "Hello Bravo one, this is Bravo Two, over."

Carl keyed the mike. "Bravo one, send, over."

"I am observing a group of seven young males. I am on the corner of Stanton Street and Mill Road. They are staggering down the road, over."

"We are five minutes away from your location. Do not let them get inside," Carl shouted into the handset.

"Message understood."

"Put your foot down," Carl snapped at the driver, who immediately sped up.

Within a few minutes, they turned the corner to see a group of young men hobbling and staggering towards the vehicle. "Bravo two, this is Bravo one. Cut them off at the rear. We have them at the front, over."

"Understood," came the quick reply.

With that, the two vehicles blocked both ends of the road and immediately became noticeable to the seven men.

Although slightly under the influence of the hooch, Simon checked his watch and noted that they still had twenty minutes to curfew.

"Keep calm," he said to the group. "We've done nothing wrong and, if we don't cause any trouble, we'll get through this."

There was nowhere for them to go. The vehicles blocked their advance and retreat but at the moment they hadn't broken the curfew. Five Company soldiers stood in front of each vehicle, most of them with clubs drawn.

James, at the back of the group, was not as sober as Simon and he panicked. He assumed it was after curfew and decided he wasn't going down without a fight. Apparently becoming more focused, James began to run towards the rear vehicle. The troops from this vehicle were ready with their clubs. James had a muscular frame and Carl initially thought that his momentum might allow him to break through the group. He watched as James picked up speed, getting faster and faster, as he approached the vehicle. When he reached them, the crewmen were ready.

The fact was that the troops were sober and James wasn't. As he headed for a perceived gap between two of them, they both swung their clubs at the same time. Mid-flight, James crashed to the ground and crumpled into a heap. Almost immediately, the two soldiers continued to club him until he no longer moved.

Simon realised that James was either dead or pretty close to it. Was there anything he could do to save the rest of them? One of the other young men was still carrying a half-full bottle of hooch and attempted to throw it at Carl's vehicle, but by this time the soldier's weapons were drawn and one of them shot him twice before he even let go of the bottle.

The remaining five men from the wedding raised their hands, resigned to their fate.

"It's not ten o'clock yet, you can't do this, the curfew time is set, you can't just change the rules." In desperation Simon tried one last gambit. "I've got connections, my uncle is Hubert the butcher."

"It is by my watch," Carl said jovially, "and yes I can, even if you're connected." He had his troops restrain the five conscious men before putting them in the back of his vehicle. Then he waved for the other vehicle to collect the two dead bodies.

At the gel plants gates, the security guards acknowledged Carl with a wave. It was hard for Simon to move with his hands tied behind his back but he manoeuvred himself to look through the back windows of the vehicle. If this was to be his last view of the outside world, he wanted it on his terms.

The gates were opened quickly as Carl regularly contributed a full load. After depositing his haul at the plants, Carl headed back to the scene of the wedding. The night was young and he hoped to encounter more unlucky victims.

20

KATH AND FLORENCE DISCUSS HER ADVENTURES

01 September 2202

A day or so after her arrival with Pepper, Florence's fever broke and she was able to tell Kath of her journey.

"What happened to you? You were off on a supply run about twelve months ago and then you just disappeared. I knew I shouldn't have let you go, but you were so insistent!" Kath said in desperation.

"We were attacked by members of the Macadam Clan. They were after anything they could steal and then, as quickly as they'd attacked, they melted into the bushes so no one would pursue them. I don't know why they took me at first but when they discovered my skills they decided I'd be useful for negotiations. I told them I could read people, hoping it would keep me alive, and it worked."

"That was very risky for you but I'm so glad it worked."

"I didn't have many options. As time went on, word

of my skills was spreading and, once I was outed, I became less useful to the Macadams. That was when they decided to trade me to another rebel band. Since then, I've been traded between various clans. The last one to hold me was the Murdoch Clan but not for long – as they waited for the trade to be completed, the Company attacked the building." After some hesitation, Florence said slowly, "Mum, I need to tell you that my powers have changed!"

"What you mean, 'they've changed'?"

"Not only can I read people's emotions, I have started to hear people's thoughts. And more than just hearing the thoughts of the people around me, I have seen through someone else's eyes. There is a boy who seems to be of a similar age to me and I sometimes feel as if I'm actually inside him. I can see through his eyes and he's in a strange place."

"What makes you think it's strange?"

"It's very bright and has lots of power, food and strange machines and lots of things that I just don't recognise. It seems like a dream, but we're communicating: he has been saying words in my head and I have been saying words in his head. He says he lives somewhere called the Sanctuary. Have you ever heard of that?"

Kath had heard of the Sanctuary. Many years ago a sick woman calling herself Mary had come to the Farm with her daughter. Mary had told how she had escaped from a bad man in a place called the Sanctuary. During the escape, she had been fortunate enough keep her daughter and her life but she hadn't managed to bring her son with her.

Mary was very ill when she arrived and Kath had

promised to raise the girl as her own, while her mother lay dying. She had explained to Kath that the Sanctuary was a very dangerous place. It was a place north of here, and she had also made Kath promise not to tell Florence about the existence of her brother.

Mary knew that if Florence tried to find her brother, she would be in great danger. Kath tried to push Mary to get more information on the Sanctuary but all she managed to find out for certain was that Florence's father was a bad man.

She only mentioned that Florence had a brother, Mary said, because they were twins – gifted twins – and she thought that as time went on Kath might have to deal with issues that sometimes occurred between twins like this.

"Gifted?" Kath had exclaimed. "What does gifted mean?"

Unfortunately from that time Mary had very little to say that was lucid. All these years later, Kath was starting to understand the meaning of gifted.

21

THE RESISTANCE COUNCIL MEETING

09 September 2202

This was not the first time that Karla had dealt with Hubert and the other resistance leaders. All the same, the term 'resistance' made it sound like they were an organised force when in reality they were just a group of self-serving survivors.

Each of the leaders had their own speciality. She controlled the fighting pits and thus had ready access to muscle.

Hubert was a tall, well-built man with a slight paunch. He was called the butcher for two reasons. First, he controlled all the meat distribution in the capital and, second, anyone that crossed him was known to disappear. Perhaps he had started the rumours that some meat cuts contained human body parts but, whoever was responsible for the stories, they helped to solidify his reputation.

Next was Spider, an ordinary-looking man who seemed to blend into the background. Nobody knew his real name but he was revered for his intelligence network. It was said that his web of informants was rivalled only by Brand's own band of spies and this inevitably led to some crossovers between the two. This detail was not lost on the others, who eyed Spider with a healthy dose of mistrust. A spy was by definition duplicitous and he could easily be sharing information with them and the Company, playing both sides for his own ends.

While their survival strategies differed, all of those strategies were built around self-preservation. If at times Spider traded information with the Company, it didn't make him any worse than the rest of them. They all did what was needed to survive and although they were wary of Spider, he seemed open about what information he shared. Sacrifices were necessary for survival but he did what he could to limit the impact on the rest of them.

Hook was well named. As a recruit in the Company naval forces, he had lost his hand in a training exercise. Hook had a part in everything that went through the ports of the island Sanctuary. His naval background had set him up well for this position so he was a powerful member of the group.

The final member of the group was Clarence Thomas. Known as CT, he supplied the alcohol to all of the elites around the Sanctuary. Although the elites might rule the Sanctuary, they relied on people like the individuals around this table to do the dirty work. CT not only supplied regulated, clean liquor to the elites, but was also responsible for the trade in illicit hooch to the masses.

They all had deals to provide kickbacks to certain

Company bureaucrats, but together they had more power than anyone else outside of the Company.

Hubert started to talk. "I have called this meeting because we are being squeezed more and more every day. Since the last aging ceremony, it has been broadcast that the compulsory age for the gel plants is to be reduced to forty-four. The other evening my nephew left a wedding thirty minutes before curfew. It was only a twenty-minute walk home and he never made it. Through various means, I found out that he and his companions were picked up by a night patrol and delivered to the gel plants. Although a society survives by rules, the elite have for too long treat us like cattle and they are becoming more and more emboldened.

"You people in this room may be under the illusion that we have power but we all know that we survive at the whim of the elite. Once we reach the age of forty-five, or forty-four as the Company has just announced, or whatever other age the Company determines, it will cull us like cattle – we will end up in the plants just like any other member of the masses."

"What do you propose that we do?" Spider asked. He was a man to look at the big picture. He was trying to figure out if anything said at this meeting was going to benefit him more than it would hurt him.

"We need to rise up," Hubert said. "We need to overthrow the elites!"

Hook was not the kind of person to react first. This occasion was no different. He was studying the others in the room and waited for the others to respond.

CT was normally seen as a jovial person but when he spoke he seemed more reflective. "Why do we have to worry about other people? We have all got comfortable lives. We are all going to die some time so why not make the most of the time we have left?"

Karla stood up from the table. "You all know that I am not one prone to theatrics. We all think we control our own areas but we don't. On occasions I have lent muscle to most of you for your illegal activities."

"And you've been compensated for that," CT interjected.

"That's not the point I'm making. I'm here to tell you that I do not control my own house. Recently Brand came to the pits and killed three of my warriors. His excuse was that one of my warriors had been caught in a firefight with the Company during an illegal gel run. The gel run was one of your operations, CT, which failed due to your lack of planning." She paused to let that sink in.

"This is not about just you, CT, but I want you to understand that our fates are all linked. Brand was not punishing me because one of my warriors had broken some rules – he was merely proving who had the power. He killed one of my best warriors a few months before the festival, just to emphasise that he has the power to do whatever he wants. We are all on borrowed time. Although Brand is the most savage of the elites, it is pointless trying to assassinate him. Aside from the difficulty of getting to him, even if we succeeded it would only lead to another dictator being installed and city-wide retribution for our actions. I am open to hearing more from Hubert."

With that, Hubert continued, "I realise this is not a five-minute plan. This will take planning, secrecy and coordination. We are currently planning this year's festival. I believe that if we work together, the festival will give us our best opportunity for success. It is the one time of the year that the elites are vulnerable. Most of them retreat to their winter homes and the troops are preoccupied with internal security for the capital. All the same, it will take all of us working together to make this happen."

Looking around his companions, he decided that they needed more convincing. "If we do this, we are risking our lives – but we risk our lives every day for the pleasure of the elites. Wouldn't it be fantastic to take control? To get rid of the illusion that we have the power and make it the truth? We can give the people back the power."

Hook eventually spoke up. "Are you suggesting that we ditch the elites and take their place? We have some manpower under our control but even our combined numbers aren't enough for anything like that."

Hubert replied straight away, "I am not suggesting that we would control the Sanctuary or even lead the capital. But there will definitely be opportunities for us once the elite are overthrown."

Hook paused for a minute before he replied, "I've spent a lot of time on the water and I spend a lot of time around the water, so I know the wildness of nature. If we unleash the masses, we might not be able to control them. I realise that our current situation is tenuous and that we live at the whim of the elites. But as CT said, at the moment we all have pretty comfortable lifestyles. We have food in our bellies, roofs above our heads and even CT seems to always have a warm body in his bed. I need more convincing that this venture is worth the risk."

Hubert was next to speak. "Am I right in believing

that when you lost your hand, Hook, they sealed it by sticking the stump in hot pitch?"

"Yes, it was very hot!" Hook replied. The memory of the pain never went away, so he was unsure why Hubert was asking this stupid question.

"Did you recoil from the pain?" Hubert asked.

"I would have if I hadn't been held down by two men. They placed a piece of plastic in my mouth, which I bit through with the pain."

"You reacted to intense pain as anyone would – but if someone had put your hand in a pot of cold water and slowly heated it, you wouldn't have noticed the pain right away. We are somewhat insulated from the discomfort of the masses because of our creature comforts but, make no mistake, the elites are constantly turning up the heat. At any time we may be in the Company's crosshairs and, if we don't take action now, it may soon be too late."

Hook pondered before saying, "I have had three of my crew arrested for speaking Spanish this month." This crime would normally mean the gel plants for the offender but Hook had managed to bribe an official to get them released. He looked towards CT and Spider. "Perhaps we should listen to Hubert and Karla."

Karla seized the chance to build on her argument. "The combined forces of the five of us are still not capable of overthrowing the elites' Company forces. Even with my warriors from the pits, we just don't have the numbers. We have to work smart. The masses have already started rioting in the capital. If we can increase the pressure and stoke the fire of unrest among the people, we can gain an army. The people outnumber the Company, which rules by fear. If we can let the people know that they are being played and that enough resources are available for everyone, their hunger can power our revolution.

"We need to build on this dissension. The riots in the streets are increasing. The people are starving, and hungry people make motivated recruits."

"Even if they are unwitting recruits," Spider added with a smile.

"A remark I would expect from a master manipulator," Hook said.

"If this is to work, we need the masses to see rebellion as the only option – not just as one of their choices," Spider pointed out.

They all nodded their heads in agreement.

"How are we going to make this happen?" asked Hook.

"I think we all have some tough decisions to make. I suggest we meet again in two weeks. Everyone is to bring their suggestions then and we can strategise. Has anyone got anything else to say before we close this meeting for the day?" Hubert asked.

Everyone shook their head and with that the meeting ended.

Karla left the meeting with a seed of a plan germinating in her head. She wasn't prepared to share her full plan with the rest of the leaders yet, although maybe she would at the next meeting.

The young man named Zap who hung around the fighting pits was a computer hacker that she had used previously. He had access to technology and information; perhaps she could use his skills to stoke up anger among the masses.

He was young and understood technology better

than she did. She excelled in blood and bone rather than electronics and mechanical things. Perhaps their combined skills could be put to good use. She would get word to him immediately and set up a meeting.

He had carried out illegal activities for her before so she knew that he wasn't averse to breaking some rules. She had come across people like this before, who lived a good life compared to everybody else. Because he was not starving and had no need to fight the system, she had to tread carefully.

The minor tasks he had previously performed could have got him into trouble but she didn't know if he was willing to risk everything. Was he willing to bond his survival with the rest of them? Zap might not see himself as one of the Norm class but surely he realised he wasn't an elite?

She did not know if his previous activities had been distractions for some spoilt rich kid or if they were stepping stones to him becoming a full-blown resistance member. Her own survival could depend on his commitment so she needed to be sure.

22

PEPPER AND KATH PLAN HIS JOURNEY TO THE REBELS

06 September 2202

It had been three days since Pepper and Kath had last spoken. When he walked out onto the porch for their arranged midday meeting, she was already sitting behind the steering wheel of a truck. She beckoned for him to climb in. As soon as he sat down and closed the door, she drove off around the Farm.

Even though the Farm had lots of wide-open spaces, when they weren't out working most of the people tended to congregate around the buildings. It was clear that Kath had wanted some privacy to discuss his decision, so had chosen to chauffeur him around the grounds.

"How are you enjoying your time in our settlement?" Kath asked, in an attempt to break the tension.

"I suppose it's not the worst prison I've been in," Pepper said abruptly.

"I'm sorry you feel like that. We've tried to make you

as comfortable as possible. Has the food and accommodation not been to your liking?"

Pepper did not answer. If he was trying to get a rise out of Kath, it worked.

"I told you last time we spoke that you aren't a prisoner – you can leave any time!"

"Yes and you also told me that I would have to go on a supply run, to get a reward that I have already earned."

"As you brought up the matter, have you considered my request yet?"

"Apart from telling me that you want me to escort Flo on another journey, to deliver some secret message, you haven't made clear the full extent of my latest contract. You said that I wasn't precise enough in the terms last time, so I won't make the same mistake again. I want to know what exactly the deal is."

"The deal is this: you will escort Florence to the rebel stronghold. You will be travelling by vehicle – not on foot this time. Once she has delivered the message, you will escort her back here and we will supply you with as many rations as you can carry, along with weapons and your choice of any other resources that you can carry in your pack."

"What's this message all about? If I am to risk myself yet again for your aims, I would like to know what kind of information I am carrying and how much danger this information is placing me in."

"That's a fair request," Kath replied. "I would say it's important information because the rebel stronghold, and by association our Farm and all of the nearby settlements, are in danger from the Company. I know that you are aware of Florence's abilities."

"Yes, she told me about her communications with somebody in another place when we were on the road. It didn't make a lot of sense but lots of things today don't make much sense. What has this to do with the message?"

"The boy that she is communicating with is the source of the message. He lives in a place that the Company uses as a central base and he has access to important information. He's aware of the Company's preparations for large-scale assaults in this area and during his communication he has warned Florence of this."

"How do you know if any of this is true? Perhaps these visions are just dreams. Even if she is communicating with somebody, how do you know that you can trust them? This could be some ruse to find out your strengths and weaknesses and make any attacks easier." Pepper was deadly serious now – being cautious was what had kept him alive.

Kath gave him the outline of the story. "Although Florence isn't my biological daughter, I have raised her as my daughter ever since the death of her mother. I believe that the person she is communicating with is her twin brother. She's never known about this twin but when her mother brought her here, she told me of the boy. She begged me to keep the secret about her twin from Florence as it could put her in danger."

"If it's such a secret, why tell me?"

"When her mother arrived with Florence, she was dying but she also had abilities. She warned me that the twins might have inherited the same abilities and I believe that they have. I'm not sure of the extent of their powers but it seems to allow them to read minds and to communicate with each other over a distance. We've all heard stories of people affected by contaminated food or water – leaving some sick or dying and others with special abilities. The information that Florence has received is very detailed and, if it is true, we are in grave danger. I know that you are only concerned with your own survival but surely if the Company is successful in destroying another rebel stronghold, it will be one less safe haven where you can ply your trade?"

Pepper stayed silent while considering his options.

"Before you make your decision, I have one final request," she said. "I want you to take Eric with you on this journey."

"Are you crazy?" Pepper blurted out. "That boy wants to kill me. Why would I take him on the road with me?"

"Believe it or not, Eric does not hate you as much as you think. Since Florence's return, he has rarely left her side and I think he would be reluctant to see her go again without him. She has convinced him that you are responsible for getting her here safely. He would be useful as an extra pair of strong hands to help you unload the supplies. If the Company is planning an attack, it may already have scouts in this area and he is an accomplished fighter."

Despite his initial instincts to turn down the deal, Pepper now hesitated. He considered the usefulness of the boy, who was as strong as anyone else on the Farm. As Eric was so devoted to Flo, he was also likely to put himself in harm's way to protect the girl during any attack. She would therefore be less of a burden and make his own task easier.

"Let's be very clear and precise here," he said. "I

want no confusion this time. I take the girl to the rebel stronghold and deliver the message and the supplies, then return her here. Nothing else! I don't want to get back here and find another mammoth task waiting for me. This is the deal, I take her there, I bring her back and then I leave with my reward. Do we have a deal?"

"Yes, that is exactly what I am suggesting." Kath offered her hand to seal the deal.

As it seemed the best option, Pepper wasted no time in taking her hand and shaking it. "Then it is agreed. When do I leave?"

"Tomorrow afternoon. We need tonight and tomorrow morning to load the stores and prepare the vehicles."

Pepper nodded. "I'll need armed escorts. How many fighters can you spare?"

"We time the supply runs to coincide with the rotation of the sentries. You will have eight armed fighters as your escort for both legs of the journey. Is that acceptable?"

After a moment's consideration, Pepper nodded.

23

ZAP RECEIVES AN INVITATION FROM KARLA

10 September 2202

Zap's previous work for the resistance could be classed as low-level crime. He'd first been approached by a member of the resistance while he was hanging around the fighting pits. He was there because the pits reminded him of his childhood visits to fights plus he wanted to stay fit and the training facilities there were second to none.

Angus was a one-eyed veteran of the pits who now trained warriors. He had taken Zap under his wing and ensured that no one else at the pits messed with him. As Zap's training progressed, a strong bond had developed between the two. When Angus asked for his help, Zap had seen no reason to say no.

When Zap found Angus outside the door to his balcony tonight, he was surprised. Although the security at Zap's apartment complex was not as strong as the security for the elites, it was still formidable – yet somehow Angus had circumvented it.

Angus had only visited once before to drop off some steel bars for training. On that occasion, Zap had to escort Angus through the security barrier.

"Hi Angus, what brings you here?" he asked as he opened the door. Angus just smiled. Realising that it was not safe for him to stand out on the balcony, Zap ushered him in.

"Would you like a drink of water?" Zap offered. He knew he was more fortunate than most to have fresh drinking water and he was always willing to share.

"A glass of water would be nice," Angus replied. The drinking water piped around this apartment building was pristine compared to the water, filled with lead and other poisons, supplied to the poorer quarters of the city. Angus took the glass of drinking water and sat down. "Do you remember when I asked you to get some information for me?"

"I was just thinking about that the other day at work. Do you want more information? What kind of information do you need?"

"I don't need more information. I've been asked to bring you to a meeting. That last favour wasn't for me – it was actually for my boss Karla and she wants to meet you. You may have seen her around the fighting pits."

"Of course," Zap said. "Everyone knows about Karla. She's a very scary woman."

"True," Angus said. "She's a scary and powerful woman but fair. She's asked me to come and arrange a meeting with you."

"It's only a couple of hours until curfew. Will we be back in time?" Zap asked hesitantly.

"It's okay. You don't have to come with me right now.

I've just been asked to set up the meeting. When you come to the pits for training on Sunday, come half an hour earlier than normal. I will meet you in the training area and take you to Karla. You must not tell anybody else of your meeting with Karla. Do you understand?"

Zap was confused. "Why does that matter if I'm only going there to talk to her?"

"Because she has many enemies and if anyone knew that you were meeting with her in person, it would put you in danger," Angus said quietly.

"Okay, I promise, I'll tell no one." Zap was now curious to know what the meeting would be about. The only person he might have told would've been his workmate Dick. He pondered about telling him anyway because, if someone knew where he was, it might give him some insurance. On reflection though, he assumed that, as Angus had breached his security, he could have killed him here if he'd really wanted. For now, Zap would stick to his agreement of secrecy.

He trusted the old fighter, who'd lost an eye in his last fight but still managed to win. His determination made him a great trainer although he no longer fought in the pits due to his disability.

When Zap first went to the pits, he had been seen as easy meat for the savage warriors. When a couple of the warriors started hassling Zap, Angus had stepped in. Once word got around that Zap was under Angus's protection, no one bothered him again. Ever since that first time Angus had intervened, Zap had felt an obligation to him, which is why he'd got the information for him, without question.

It was Friday evening, only two days before the

meeting, but Zap was impatient. "Can't we meet tomorrow? I am on call but I can meet her then."

"No," Angus answered immediately. "Karla has other commitments. You need to take precautions. Make sure that you are not followed!"

"Why would anybody follow me?" he wondered to himself. He had never thought to check if he'd been followed anywhere. He knew dangerous people were in the Sanctuary because the Company had spies everywhere, and his position gave him access to privileged information.

He'd heard of people disappearing but had always assumed that these were just random people off the street and, as his work was important to the Company, the spies would keep him safe. Now it struck him: for the spies to keep him safe, they would need to follow and monitor him. It was dawning on Zap that, for someone that others classed as intelligent, he'd been pretty stupid about this matter.

Among the thoughts that buzzed in his mind was that he might be asked to do something at the meeting that would put the Company at risk. Although this raised some dilemmas for him, he decided he would listen to Karla and then assess his options.

After finishing his water, Angus headed to the front door but then paused. "One last time, I must impress on you: do not tell anyone about this meeting."

"Okay, okay, I've got the message, I understand," Zap said although he didn't really understand. He just knew that Angus was very serious about this and, if it was important to Angus, it was important to him. Nobody would know of this meeting.

Five minutes after Angus left, there was a knock at

Zap's front door. Perhaps Angus had forgotten something? Opening the door, he found Dick standing there and could not hide his surprise.

"Were you expecting someone else?" Dick asked.

Zap deflected. "What are you doing here at this time of night?

"I've run out of sugar. Could you please share some from your rations?" Dick asked.

"Yes of course, come in."

"Have you been alone all night?" Dick asked. "I thought I heard voices through the wall."

Zap wondered how much he'd heard from the next apartment.

"Did you have a woman in here? Have you got a girlfriend?" Dick continued to probe.

Clearly Dick was just fishing. "No, you must be mistaken, I've been alone all night. Have you had a woman in your place then? Is that what the sugar is for?"

Dick eyed Zap with some suspicion. He knew that he'd heard some voices. They had sounded mumbled through the walls. But perhaps it was a girl and Zap was just embarrassed. Either way, Dick was determined to keep a closer eye on him.

"See you in the morning," Dick said as he left the apartment with the sugar.

Although Dick was an accomplished programmer, that wasn't why he had been given the position, with the apartment and the other benefits that came with it. He had been chosen for this role in order to make friends with Zap and spy on him.

Dick didn't know who needed the information. He just knew that he had a contact in the Company who visited him weekly to collect it. He also had a phone number to call, if anything out of order happened between the weekly meetings.

When he closed the door to his own apartment, he considered calling the number tonight but then he realised that all he'd heard was voices. He couldn't even be certain if it wasn't just Zap singing.

If he missed something important, he might lose his position but then again if he rang the number without sufficient evidence, it might get him in trouble too.

For tonight, he would leave the phone alone and try to gather some more information tomorrow.

24

FOOD RIOTS

14 September 2202

Smit's troops were controlling the gel distribution point as the speakers blared out the pre-recorded message.

"The gel rations have been increased by ten percent today to continue to provide enough gel supplies for all our valuable citizens, we will be reducing the compulsory age at the next aging ceremony to forty-four. We're grateful for our elderly citizens' sacrifices to keep the rest of us alive. We are stronger together."

The message over the speakers was meant to be one of hope. In reality, Smit was aware that the amount of gel being distributed was not enough to feed everybody gathered here. Despite the promise of an increase in supply, the gel supplies would run out and he knew the masses wouldn't be happy.

It was easy to control a crowd of scared people in the same way that you would deal with a stampede of wild animals. Firing a few rounds into the air was usually enough to make the Norms disperse.

As they grew hungrier, the people became harder to control and regressed to their primal instincts. The fact that the gel packs were made from human beings was not lost on the population and rumours were that people had been abducted and cannibalised in some areas.

Smit had doubled the size of his patrols so that they now deployed in groups of four vehicles, rather than the previous two. This initiative was supposed to project strength but actually his intention was to reduce the chances of his troops being overwhelmed and suffering the fate of the abductees.

Over ten thousand people were waiting at this one distribution point. Although his soldiers were well armed, they still numbered only three hundred troops and a hundred civilian distribution workers. The thirty soldiers standing in front of the screens to the gel vehicles kept their fingers on the triggers of their assault rifles.

Their survival was their first concern. They'd been briefed that, if the need arose and they couldn't see Smit or his lieutenants, they had authority to shoot without further orders. If a mob was to overrun this site, it would create a precedent that could embolden others and encourage mass riots in the future.

It was Tom's first time guarding a distribution point. Having only recently graduated from his company training, he was more expendable than most. He'd followed his elder brother Ben into the service and was fortunate to have him watching over him today. Even the thought of Ben's sniper rifle providing cover, however, gave Tom only a marginal amount of comfort today.

The screens in front of the vehicles hid the amount of gel inventory that was available as a way of keeping the crowd calm.

From Tom's vantage point, he observed some of the larger, stronger people pushing to the front and they were being fed first. The lucky ones ate the gel packs as soon as they were handed them. Whether they were adults or children, no one dared to take food away, in case they were assaulted for it.

The crowd was densely packed, shoulder to shoulder. Looking down from the second floor of a building on the outskirts of the crowd, Smit imagined it would be hard to breathe. Even from this distance, it was hard to see any gaps between the people.

He knew that, as usual, they would discover casualties once the crowd had dispersed. Today was cold but even the light drizzle in the air would do little to diminish the heat in the crowd. Heat exhaustion and people being trampled had become increasingly common whatever the time of year.

As the distribution session proceeded, the stocks became dangerously low. The stocks were almost gone when a few thousand people were still waiting to be fed.

Particularly on edge, Tom was one of the first to see Smit's signal, waving from above. It was time for them to retreat. The plan was to try to limit the disturbance by getting themselves out of sight from the crowd.

The troops pulled further back to the screens, creating a small buffer zone between them and the distribution tables. This would only give them a few extra seconds if the crowd rioted but it was at least something.

Ben was the first among the soldiers on the outskirts of the crowd to put the butts of their rifles in their shoulders. He had already taken up his position at his chosen firing point and, like most of the snipers, he was on a raised area. The troops were far enough away that they weren't observed in their actions but there was a sense in the air that the situation was about to change.

The crowd was focused on the tables, which had boxes of gel packs stacked at the side. Individuals were handed packs as their bar codes were scanned and, because they were eating them straight away, it created a bottleneck, delaying the next in line from going over to the food.

This was annoying for those waiting, but they accepted it as part of the process. The bottleneck also meant that it was some time before the crowd started to notice that the piles of boxes were not being replenished.

Tom had been briefed that the people being fed last were usually the children and other weaker ones so had less energy to fight. Today, however, because of the shortage of gel supplies, some of those still in line were not so weak. The noise from the crowd was growing. People who had been standing there for hours, and hadn't eaten since who knew when, were becoming more desperate. The usual pushing in the crowd was starting to escalate.

He could see that the people at the front noticed that the troops had retreated to the screens and they were starting to point and shout at them. They had attended enough of these sessions to recognise that the troop movement was a sign that stocks were getting low. Today it actually meant that stocks had almost run out.

With building unease, Tom saw people trying to grab the last gel packs before they were scanned. In an effort to prevent them, the civilian distributors at the tables were constantly using their clubs.

This is how it began: not from a rifle shot but from six or seven people being clubbed to the ground. The prone bodies created a visible gap and allowed more people to see for the first time how little food was left.

Tom became transfixed as he observed one of the crowd clubbed to the ground was still holding a gel pack and two others pounced on him to wrestle for the food. Very few gel packs remained in the boxes. Smit must have seen that things were about to devolve. Tom saw him lift his left arm, giving the prearranged signal for his troops to fire a volley

Without any hesitation, Tom and the other troops with him simultaneously fired one round each into the air.

From his high perch, Smit could hear the thirty rounds echo across the open space, but the noise of the crowd was growing louder and the sound of the bullets seemed to spark more panic.

The large open space had the effect of dispersing the rifle shots. The sound of them echoed, making it hard for the crowd to work out where the bullets had come from. Although the plan was for these initial warning shots to disperse the crowd, they had the opposite effect.

With no obvious source of the danger, the crowd

was always going to head towards the food. Armed soldiers may have dissuaded rational people but these people were desperate for food, not as a casual snack but for their very survival.

With a crowd this big and so few soldiers, control was always going to be a challenge. Tom watched as the civilians with the clubs succumbed first. They were closest to the last few gel packs and were quickly overwhelmed. Seeing them trampled and fearing for their own safety, Tom and his fellow troops opened fire. But the relatively few bullets had little effect on the rolling mass of bodies.

Still looking through his rifle scope, Ben had started shooting at the people in the crowd closest to Tom. He watched as the tables and distributors became encompassed by the mass of bodies. Next Tom and his unit ran out of bullets. They tried to use their rifle butts as clubs but it was futile for so few to try and hold back so many. They were standing in front of the screens that, in the minds of the crowd, hid more gel packs.

Ben and the other snipers were trying to cover their comrades but while Ben was being selective in his targets, the others were firing to the edge of the crowd instead of the front of it, which was the threat to their comrades. The crowd's anticipation of food beyond the screens increased their momentum.

Despite his several years of experience as a soldier, seeing his younger brother in danger made it impossible for Ben to stay detached. Tom had clearly run out of rounds as he was now using his rifle as a club. Very few of the troops around Tom were still firing their weapons and, as Ben was fast running out of bullets too, he was becoming more anxious for their safety.

He watched as the masses steadily overwhelmed the troops in front of the screens. Some of the troops had been disarmed and were being beaten with hands, fists and even their own empty weapons. Ben was down to only three bullets and Tom was one of the last troops standing.

A large group was approaching Tom. Ben emptied the last of his magazine into them. "Tom," he shouted as he watched him disappear into a mass of bodies. Then the screens fell down.

This was when the hysteria really took hold.

Behind the screens was nothing. The delivery trucks had left. There were no more gel packs, just an empty space. The discovery enraged the desperate horde. They had developed a bloodlust. As they swarmed over the tables that had held the remaining gel packs, they had become wild beasts. Anyone who had grabbed a gel pack was set upon by at least five others and not only lost the pack but also suffered injuries including bite marks on any exposed flesh.

Ben was still looking through his scope at the area that Tom had disappeared when suddenly one of the crowd stood up holding a human arm. The arm was covered in blood but it looked to be clad in the grey of the Company uniform.

He wasn't sure if the arm belonged to Tom or one of the other dead soldiers but either way he knew his brother was lost. Thinking of his kid brother, he felt a lump in his throat and the pit of his stomach started to feel hollow.

Along with the stinging loss of his brother, he had other concerns. A group of well-trained soldiers had been no match for the number of unharmed masses they'd faced. After spending most of his military career feeling invincible, he was beginning to get a sense of his mortality.

Then people in the crowd began to turn on each other, tearing off limbs to satiate a primal hunger. In a very short time, about a tenth of the crowd had been cannibalised.

Ben wasn't the only one monitoring the situation. Smit realised that he could do nothing to save his fallen troops. His first priority was to save himself so he rallied his remaining troops to fortify his stronghold.

"Hello Ariel command, this is Captain Smit at distribution point Alpha. We need gunships and we need them now, I say again we need gunships now," Smit shouted into his radio.

"Captain Smit, this is Ariel command. They are in the air and will be with you in fifteen minutes, over."

"Thank you, message received. Captain Smit out." He was thankful that he had prepared for this support in advance.

Within ten minutes the sound of rotors could be heard above as two gunships hovered and began firing randomly into the crowd. It was a pointless act as the rioting had slowed now the rioters had full bellies. Most of the people who remained were squatting on the ground, eating the less fortunate.

The gunships became more tactical, spraying the centre of the crowd with machine gun fire in bursts designed to disperse it. Eventually the people began to move, some carrying the limbs of the fallen over their shoulders.

Today was not the day to pursue them. Today was a

day for Smit to prevent any further casualties on his side. He was not looking forward to reporting this event to Brand.

25

PEPPER AND FLO WARN FRANK

10 September 2202

When Frank's right-hand woman approached, he was surprised to see her. Debs was supposed to be meeting the supply run from the Farm and supervising the unloading and security of the goods.

"Is there a problem?" Frank asked.

"I'm not sure. We've got unexpected visitors from the supply run," she said cryptically.

"What kind of visitors?"

"Florence the girl from the Farm, remember she went missing last year? She's here with a man I don't know. He's called Pepper."

"What do they want?"

"Pepper says they have an important message and they will only give it to you."

As always, Frank was suspicious of unexpected visitors. However, he was intrigued that the man was accompanied by Flo. After being missing for a year, here she was suddenly appearing on a supply run.

"Where's this Pepper now?" Frank asked.

"He's waiting outside with the girl. I thought that you might want to talk to them. They've been searched and relieved of their weapons so they should be harmless."

"Bring them in." Frank cautiously pulled his pistol from its holster and placed it on his lap, under the table.

In walked Flo with a tall, dark-skinned male. The man's noticeable scars gave him a rugged look, telling a story of an interesting life lived.

For his part, Pepper was surprised that this was the leader of the stronghold. He looked quite handsome, almost pretty – clean-shaven, with greased-back hair and Latin features.

Frank sized up the new arrivals. Not being one for small talk, he began, "I understand that you have a message for me."

"It's really the girl that's got the message, I'm just the muscle," Pepper said with a dry smile.

"Okay," Frank said, turning to Flo. "What's this secret message you have for me?"

Flo seemed subdued. She had wanted Eric to come with her too but the rebel guards had only allowed Pepper as her companion. They weren't prepared to present another threat to their leader.

Slowly and quietly Florence composed herself and said, "You are all in danger."

"I'm sorry," Frank said. "You better have a stronger message than that. We are always in danger. It's the nature of our lifestyle and career choice."

Clearly frustrated, she replied, "No, I mean you're in

danger right now. The Company is preparing for a large assault on this compound and the surrounding area. It is going to attack with aircraft to obliterate this place. This is going to happen soon."

"Well, that's a very interesting story," Frank said. "Can you explain how you came across this snippet of information?"

Flo looked at Pepper, prompting him to intervene. "This might sound crazy – to be honest, it sounded a little crazy to me when I first heard it. This young woman has certain skills or abilities."

Frank was losing patience. "What type of abilities are we talking about? Can she cook, can she fight? I have a lot of skilled fighters around here and the kitchen is well staffed."

"The best way for me to explain it, is that she has a mental connection with somebody else, between her mind and theirs and she can also read other people's minds."

Frank was almost ready to kick them out of the room. He wasn't sure what he'd expected but this messenger and this message were definitely not it.

"I must admit, I hear strange things every day. I'm a busy man but I'll indulge you for a short distraction." Figuring she might have some kind of trick up her sleeve, he asked Flo, "What am I thinking of right now?"

Flo quickly responded, "Right now you're thinking that you'll play along with us so that you can make a fool out of me."

Frank was not convinced. "Well, that's hardly news, is it? Someone turns up with a strange story that they can read minds. When they supposedly read my mind, they say that I don't believe them. That seems very convenient."

Flo hesitated before she spoke again. "What about Paris?"

This gained Frank's attention. "What did you say?"

"Before we came into the room, I could hear your thoughts. From the other side of the door, I heard you thinking about your brother Paris, who was recently killed in a Company attack." She paused. "Your brother Paris was the leader of the rebel compound further south. He and the rest of his people were killed in a Company attack there, a few weeks ago."

Frank looked hard at the girl, unsure if he was being played. He didn't know how she knew this information but it was definitely a surprise. Although people knew he communicated with other rebel strongholds, few knew that his brother was the leader of a rebel base. He and his brother Paris had similar features but for their own security they never openly disclosed that they were related. They presented themselves as comrades and, like a lot of rebels, they worked well together. All messages between the two were coded so this girl's knowledge of their relationship made him consider her words more carefully.

"So you heard rumours of a Company attack. That doesn't really prove much," Frank said.

Flo thought for a moment and then spoke again. "I'm not sure but from the images in your head of where your brother was, I think we were there too."

Frank had only ever been down to visit his brother's compound once. It was some distance away and he couldn't leave his own compound unattended for too long. He had gone for a meeting with other leaders as it was central to several rebel strongholds, reducing the amount of time they would all have to travel.

"What do you mean, you were there?" Frank asked. He was focused solely on Flo when Pepper spoke up.

"Hold on," Pepper said. "This base your brother controlled, was it near New Ohio?"

Frank's attention turned to Pepper. "Why do you ask?"

"Because that is where I met this young girl. She was a captive of some members of the Murdoch Clan, who had taken her there to trade her. When the Company attacked, I was there to trade with the rebels. I met their leader and now I look at you, I can see some resemblance in your features."

This was all starting to sound a bit too convenient for Frank. "What other proof do you have? Apart from this young girl supposedly locking minds with someone, who is supposedly feeding her information?"

Pepper answered, "To be honest I don't really know much more but if what she says is true, you should probably listen if you want to live. I saw what they did to your brother's place. As far as I know, we were the only two that escaped alive and that was only by pure luck. I assume that, if they are going to attack with aircraft, they will have spotters in the area. Have you come across more Company patrols than normal recently?"

Frank thought for a moment. Only the other day, one of his patrols outside the base had caught someone lurking. Although he didn't have the mark of a Company soldier, he had some strange electrical equipment with him. Frank's people hadn't figured out what the apparatus was but it seemed to transmit some kind of signal.

Not wanting to add two and two together and get five, Frank decided he needed to investigate this matter further. If the warning was accurate, he didn't have any time to waste.

"It's mid-afternoon now. Debs will take you to the mess hall and then I'll meet you in the tavern at seven o'clock – Debs will show you where that is too."

With that, Frank motioned for Debs to escort his visitors out of the room.

Frank had things to do and people to talk to. First, he was going to interrogate the recent captive. The prisoner had been kept locked up for a couple of days now and Frank needed to find out more about the technology that he was carrying when he was captured. If it was linked to a potential attack, Frank needed to know today – or, preferably, yesterday.

26

THE BAR MEETING

10 September 2202

Frank was waiting at the bar when Pepper arrived. After watching the stores getting unloaded from the Farm delivery, Pepper had spent over an hour walking around and inspecting the layout of the settlement.

The fortifications here were pretty good although the place was a bit compact for his liking. Being compact would help against a ground attack but a few well-placed bombs from an aircraft could certainly do a lot of damage to this stronghold.

Frank was sitting at a table in the far corner. Planted on the table in front of him was a bottle of cloudy liquor with two glasses. Frank cradled a third glass, already half-empty.

Flo had not come to the bar. She'd insisted on going somewhere quiet so that she could continue to communicate with Zap and Eric had stayed by her side.

Pepper had been concerned that they were running out of time and had tasked her with gathering as much information as possible, as quickly as possible. She had grown to trust him, so was doing as he'd asked.

Frank motioned for Pepper to sit down. "Would you like a glass?"

"What's in it?" Pepper enquired as he sat.

"It's brewed locally. Not the best-tasting drink in the world but it does what it needs to do. It sometimes makes life a little easier around here," Frank replied, filling Pepper's glass.

"It's been a while since I've had something decent to drink, so anything's better than nothing. Have you had enough time to consider our information?" Pepper asked before taking a gulp from the glass.

After taking a sip from his own glass, Frank said, "Yes, I have had a little chat with a recent captive. It took a while but he was eventually forthcoming with some information."

"It was nice of him to cooperate."

"I didn't give him much of a choice."

As the conversation went on, Pepper was taking the measure of Frank. Although he looked a bit of a pretty boy, Frank was well built and he must have a dark side if he could control a place like this.

"So what did you learn?"

"I learnt some more about the equipment that he had with him. It is designed to mark a target for an aerial bomb. My captive was not able to give all the technical details of the equipment. But the basics are that it marks a target, so that when an aircraft drops a bomb the equipment guides it to the target," Frank explained. "He and some others have been sent to mark these buildings for an attack."

"It looks like you caught him just in time," Frank said.

"One of the last things he said was that if he didn't report back to the Company, others would be sent to mark the targets."

"One of the last things he said?" Pepper repeated accusingly. "Are you convinced of the threat now?"

"I'm not totally convinced but I'm willing to accept we need to take some precautions."

Pepper took another gulp and grimaced as it burned the back of his throat, making him cough a little. He had hidden the effects of the first taste but this stuff was lethal.

Frank smiled and seemed to even laugh a little. "Careful, this stuff is a bit of an acquired taste. Luckily we make it on site and it helps that we get the raw materials from the Farm, so it's plentiful."

Once he'd cleared his throat, Pepper became more business-like. "So you want to wait until you've got more information. That's fine in principle but in reality it sounds like you haven't got the time to wait. Currently the girl is communicating with the boy in her head. He says we have one, maybe two days at most before the assault. Unless you've got some magic plan that I don't know about, the only way I see you surviving an aerial assault is to evacuate this place. Do you have an evacuation plan? And if you do, how fast can you deploy it?"

Frank hesitated, cautious not to give too much information away. Although Pepper was supposedly on the same side, he didn't know him well enough yet to trust him unconditionally.

"I took a bit of a walk around today," Pepper carried on. "If my estimates are correct, with the number of people, vehicles and equipment you have, it would take at least a day to pack this place up. The next question is, where would you go?"

Pepper gave Frank time to consider his questions before adding more food for thought. "If the Company have recced this place, there is every chance that it knows about your relationship with the Farm. The Farm has too much open space for an aerial assault to have much effect but a reasonably sized ground force could cut off your supply lines."

Frank was in uncharted waters; he had built a stronghold, expecting to defend it against a large ground assault. Someone dropping large quantities of explosives from the sky was not something he could protect against. Even though a large part of the compound was hardened underground, the prospect of being down there and buried under tonnes of rubble didn't appeal to him.

His initial escape plan had been to head for the Farm. If it was also at risk, they needed to take action fast. Assuming Pepper's information was correct, the attack would occur in the next day or two. It would take at least a day to get to the Farm, leaving very little time to build defences that could repel a large-scale assault.

Taking into account the information that he had gleaned from the Company scout, which was verified by the equipment he carried, they were definitely in some kind of danger. The arrival of this girl with abilities and Pepper with his experience at the rebel base with his brother, along with the info from the scout, was fuelling his sense of urgency.

"Did you spend much time with my brother?" Frank asked.

"I traded with his people a couple of times but didn't spend much time with him. He was more a 'hello, goodbye' and a short period of negotiation type of guy. It was only on my last visit to him, when I was trading essential medicines, liberated from the Company, that we spoke for a little longer."

"Paris was never one for small talk," Frank said with a smile. "How was he when you last saw him?"

"He seemed okay. He wasn't injured or sick or anything before the assault. That's about all I can tell you."

"Is there any chance that he escaped?" Frank knew the answer as soon as he asked. He knew that if Paris had escaped, he would have made it here by now.

"I'm sorry to say that I don't think anyone else survived the attack. I was lucky that on a previous visit somebody had pointed out an escape hatch. I was also fortunate that I was in the bathroom when the attack happened so I was close to the hatch. If I'd been anywhere else, I doubt I'd have escaped either. As fate would have it, when I left the bathroom I came across the girl. I'm not sure if it was something to do with her abilities but I felt sorry for her. Without thinking, I managed to manhandle her through the hatch. If I'd hesitated and hadn't acted on instinct, I don't think either of us would be here."

"You had a gun, didn't you?" Frank asked accusingly. "Why didn't you fight?"

"I'm sure that as a survivor like me, you've had times

when you've had to decide when to fight and when to run? This doesn't make us cowards, it makes us survivors. In that situation, we were outnumbered and outgunned – it would have been suicide to stay and fight. I am not the kind of person to commit suicide."

Frank found Pepper's openness refreshing. He could have lied or told any story as one of the only survivors. Yet the tales he told seemed plausible and, in the same situation, if his brother hadn't been there, Frank would have taken the same path. Pepper was right: choosing self-preservation over heroism is what made them survivors.

Pepper was suddenly aware that Debs was approaching the table – the woman who had shown him to the mess hall earlier. Even though they hadn't talked much, Pepper realised by the way she carried herself that she was not someone to be messed with.

It would have been unusual to find a woman as second in command in any group of rebel fighters, let alone in a stronghold like this. Pepper could see women fighters had the advantage of being less noticeable than men. Aside from her undercover abilities, she needed to be strong and resolute to survive, even more so to maintain her current position.

Debs took a seat without asking and poured herself a glass of liquor. It was clear to Pepper that her arrival had been prearranged. Frank had probably suggested she gave them ten minutes to talk before she joined them. It was also telling that Pepper hadn't noticed her when she entered the bar.

Frank said, "I realise that time is not on our side. Although I'm not one hundred percent sure that this attack will happen, I'm not prepared to wait until it's too late to act. I'm going to split my forces in half. Debs will take half of the fighters with you in the morning and head to the Farm. As soon as they arrive, they'll start to reinforce the defences. The rest of us will stay here to create a few surprises, so that if we do come under attack, we can choose the narrative and not become just a by-line in a Company report.

"Debs will be in charge of the fighters – make no mistake, you are only there as a passenger. She knows these roads, she has my full authority and trust. She also has the trust of the fighters, which is just as important. They would never listen to a stranger like you, but they will listen to her."

Frank poured another round of drinks and then continued his briefing. "You can take the boy with you but Flo will stay with me."

Pepper immediately objected. He had a deal: to bring the girl here and escort her home safely, and then he'd receive his reward. "You might not believe this but I don't do this kind of thing for a pat on the back, a round of applause or cheering from other people. I do this because this is how I survive: I trade wherever I can. In this case, I have traded my services to escort this girl here and then back to the Farm. If I don't take her back, I don't get the reward that I've been promised. Make no mistake about this – I am doing this for the reward!"

"Don't worry," Frank said. "The girl will come to no harm. If the attack doesn't happen, in a few days she will be returned to the Farm, when I come to collect my fighters. If this imminent attack is truly happening, I need her by my side to provide advance intelligence."

Pepper couldn't fault this logic. It gave Frank a lot of

wins: he had a hostage in case they were trying to play him, the fear of losing his reward gave Pepper a reason to behave and Flo's presence also gave Frank a means of advance warning of the attack.

Having pulled similar moves in the past, Pepper was inclined to agree but then he remembered: What was he going to do about Eric? Eric would not leave Flo's side without a fight. Pepper had to convince him that it was in Flo's best interest to stay here and be safe.

Quickly he formulated a plan: to tell Eric that, although Flo would be safe here, he couldn't guarantee the safety of Eric's adoptive parents. As strongly as Eric felt about Flo, Pepper gambled that he would feel duty-bound to go on the mission to protect Kath and Mitch.

"You seem to have everything covered," Pepper said. "Is there a chance you could spare a couple of those rifles for me and the boy? You seem to have quite a few."

Frank exchanged a glance and a nod with Debs before saying, "As we may be in your debt for the warnings, I think we can make that happen, although the accuracy of your intelligence is yet to be confirmed."

Finishing her drink and getting up to leave the table, Debs nodded to Frank. Then she said to Pepper, "We leave at seven o'clock in the morning. Don't be late."

"Yes, sir," he said sarcastically. He decided to have one more drink with Frank before he left as both the alcohol and the rebel leader were growing on him. But it would have to be his last drink as he still had to brief Flo and then convince Eric that they were leaving early in the morning. "Shall we have one for the road?"

"If I didn't know any better, I'd think you were

trying to get me drunk," Frank laughed as he poured the last drinks.

"Maybe some other time," Pepper said mischievously. With that, he finished his drink, winked and left.

27

ZAP MEETS KARLA

12 September 2202

Zap arrived at the pits at 3pm as arranged. Angus greeted him with a smile. "I'm glad to see you came, Zap. Were you followed?"

"No, no, I wasn't followed." Zap thought that Angus seemed a bit paranoid but maybe this was just Zap's sheltered upbringing.

"Good. The decisions you make today may determine how long you live. I apologise if that seems cryptic but for the moment, that's all I can say."

Zap was unsure of what Angus meant. Following Angus up to the top of the stadium, he remembered similar climbs he'd made to watch the fights with his stepfather. These steps were not the same plush carpeted steps designed for the elite though: they were narrower and well worn. He also noticed that the walls were damaged from the impacts of who knew what.

At the top of the stairs, as the stadium opened out into a wider area, it was like coming out of a dark tunnel into sunlight. At the far side of the space was a large wooden door, which was ajar. Zap recognised the two fight instructors sitting outside it.

They nodded to Angus but didn't get in his way. Angus led Zap into an office with a large wooden desk prominent at the far side. Sitting behind the desk was Karla, with Miyamoto standing by her side. The bodyguard looked Zap up and down, perhaps assessing whether he was any kind of threat. Zap assumed that, going by his reputation, if Miyamoto had sensed any danger he would've dispatch Zap ruthlessly and quickly.

"This is Zap," Angus said to Karla.

"Hello, young man," she said emerging from behind the desk and offering her right hand. Without a second's hesitation, Zap offered his own hand in return. He was unsure what else to do.

"Make yourself comfortable," she said as she gestured for him to take a seat. He followed her advice. "Has Angus told you why I asked you to come here?"

Zap paused, looking from Angus to Karla and back again. "He said that you needed my help and that it could be dangerous but, other than that, nothing else. Oh and he also told me to make sure I wasn't followed."

"Very good," Karla said. "Caution is always a good trait in anybody I deal with. For one so young, if you want to live as long as me, I would suggest that you continue to be cautious. I know that you have done some work for us in the past, gathering information through your position in the Company. Angus tells me that the information was useful and for that I am very grateful."

Unsure how to respond, Zap stuttered, "Thank you."

"Things are changing rapidly in the Sanctuary," Karla said. "But before we proceed, I want it to be clear that by coming here today, you are showing you are prepared to work with us. There is rebellion in the wind. The people are starving and unrest is growing. The greed of the elites has never been this bad. The shortages of food are a fabrication devised by the elite. With your access to intelligence, I am sure that you are already aware of this. If not, I am sure that you can confirm I am telling the truth in your own time."

Zap looked at her and tentatively nodded.

She continued, "We are sick of living under the yoke of such tyranny. The supreme leader Brand is a savage murderer with no respect for the lives of the Norm class. He sees our lives as a mere distraction and places little value on them. We have a choice: we can continue to be treated like cattle and live only at the whim of the elites or we can fight back. Although Brand is just a psychopath, the rest of the elite under him are downright greedy. They have more than they would ever need to survive, they have a hundred times more than anyone in the Norm class, but they still want more. They continue to reduce food supplies so that they can sell their excess on the black market."

Karla's voice was getting louder and she paused to keep her passion in check.

"If they actually increased supply, there would be enough food for everybody. Their privileged positions are safe. Even without these extra profits, they would never want for anything and nor would their offspring. Since the Water Wars, the elite have lived in luxury while the disparity between the classes continues to grow to the point that it has become unsustainable. All I am asking of you is to get me some information. Information that you have access to because of your position."

"That doesn't sound too hard," Zap said cautiously.

"You need to understand that you will be in danger. I'm not asking you to fight or to carry weapons. From the outside it will seem as though your life hasn't changed but, if you are caught, you will be tortured and then killed."

This seemingly offhand remark caught Zap by surprise as he recognised how serious his situation was.

Knowing the effect she had had on Zap, Karla said more softly, "To help the people, the resistance needs to overthrow the elite but in a sustainable way. That is why we need information. Just destroying the gel plants would not help the starving masses. If anything, it would make matters worse. To really change things, we need to know where all the food supplies are and we need figures to determine the best strategy and timing for our plans."

From Zap's limited responses, Karla was concerned she was overwhelming him. "Do you understand what I'm asking of you, Zap?"

"I think so. It's just a lot, a lot to take in all at once."

"I understand − I was young once too. But this is important work and I wouldn't ask you if there was another way." She had considered this over the last couple of days and this did seem to be the only way to get the information she needed quickly.

Zap reflected on the rumours that Karla had originally been married to Dave, the previous boss who ran the pits and all its criminal activities. Dave had recognised her talents and had put her in charge of his books. According to the rumours, he had cheated on her many times and hadn't anticipated that she would be even more ruthless than him. Unbeknown to Dave, she had built up her own power base, which people said had led to both Dave's untimely death and her subsequent rise to power.

Of course, these were only rumours. Few people knew the full facts and those who did would never talk. Whatever the truth, one day Dave had disappeared and Karla had seamlessly seized power.

Most murders in the Sanctuary resulted in the bodies disappearing into the gel plants. It was irrelevant how she'd come to power because she was definitely in charge now. Zap realised that she was not somebody to be crossed.

"What information do you want and when?"

"After today, you will deal directly with Angus," Karla said. "It's too dangerous for you to be seen with me on a regular basis. But everybody already knows Angus is your trainer, so it shouldn't raise too much suspicion. On each of your training sessions, Angus will brief you on what is required. You need to be very cautious – get the information in small amounts. As you are more technically minded than me, I'm sure you can cover your tracks.

"I am aware that you can provide more valuable information than what you have given us so far. I understand that you also have control over some of the electronic security measures, especially around this complex, that will be useful when the time is right. I trust Angus and he says that he trusts you. Are you willing to work with us for the freedom of the people?"

Zap had never been a fan of the current inequalities. Yes, he enjoyed his lifestyle but he hated seeing the poverty elsewhere. From the statistics he'd studied, he knew enough food and resources were available for everybody. He had often wondered what his mission in life was, always wondered how he could use his computer skills to help others. His training in the pits was primarily for self-defence but, given the chance, he liked to defend others from bullies and the state was the ultimate bully.

Although he felt like shouting, "Yes, yes, yes" to Karla's request, he chose his words more carefully. "I do not agree with the way that the Company treats people. I have seen the brutality, but I never thought I could do anything to change the situation. I'd always thought that I was destined to work for the Company until I was no longer any use and then would end up in the gel plants, like everyone else. You have given me a lot to think about. I need to go away and figure out how I can put this plan into place, but I accept your request for help and I will do whatever I can."

Zap was surprised to see a slight smile on Karla's face. For someone with such a ruthless reputation, the person in front of him seemed quite pleasant. "Well, young Zap, I'm glad to hear that. For the rest of today I want you to continue with your normal training session. Don't change any of your routine and over the coming days Angus will brief you. One thing I'd suggest is that you start to increase the length of your training sessions. This way it will not look out of the ordinary for you to be spending more time with Angus. Have you any suggestions on how to get the information to us securely?"

"I can bring the information in a digital format."

"We do not have a need for advanced electronic

equipment in the fighting pits. However, some of our trading partners have access to certain Company resources as required. Let Angus know what you require and we will source it."

Ideas were rushing through Zap's head. "Yes, we will need a computer or some way for me to transfer the information. I will have a better idea tomorrow about what is required. "

Karla motioned that the meeting was over. "Angus, take the boy and train him. Perhaps go easy on him today as I think he's already had quite a workout, albeit mental."

As Zap was going back down the narrow stairs, he suddenly thought that it would be hard for a lot of people to get up here at once. He wondered if he was already starting to think like a resistance fighter or if he was just feeling claustrophobic.

28

WILL'S VIEW OF THE ATTACK ON THE REBEL STRONGHOLD

12 September 2202

Will was respected and feared as a hands-on commander who normally enjoyed leading his troops from the front. Today he was using technology to save him driving for days to initiate an attack on the rebels. Will smiled as he mused that he could get used to this.

Despite the perception that the Company had resources that dwarfed those of the rest of the kingdom, its bomber planes were limited in number. It was only because this target was seen as strategically important that he could use two bombers this time.

The images on his monitor were not as crisp and clear as the ones that the Company transmitted on the evening newscasts. This discrepancy was due to the distance over which the planes were transmitting. It was rumoured that, before the Water Wars, mechanical satellites had been in the sky, allowing crystal-clear signals to be sent from one side of the planet to the other. Those satellites had apparently been destroyed during the Water Wars and so he had to make do with the technology at hand.

He had sent a dozen scouts ahead with the devices that would mark the targets for the aircraft. This strategy would leave plenty of spare troops in case the scouts didn't all make it. A mission this large would have normally required a larger strike force but, with the current unrest in the capital and other areas of the Sanctuary, deployment of troops for internal security was the higher priority. Although he was high up in the military food chain, Will still had to take orders from the civilian bureaucrats.

They had already lost contact with some of his scouts but that was to be expected. That his scouts might be killed concerned him less than that they might be captured. In the brutal southern outlands, lawlessness was part of daily life, so even his best-armed scout could fall foul of a large group of bandits.

An estimated six hundred plus rebels were in the stronghold. It was a sizeable force to engage but it also made it easy to infiltrate a spy into their midst.

The most recent message that he had received from his spy was that the rebels had split their forces in half and that he was travelling with one group to the Farm. The Farm was the secondary target as its destruction would deprive any surviving rebels of food and also of the crops they used for their biofuels. This would limit their mobility and reduce the threat for his Company forces.

Even with only half the rebel forces at the Farm, the number of Company troops in the area would not be able to win a ground battle. As soon as Will received the intelligence, he adapted his plans. He changed his timetable so that his troops on the ground would immediately take out the infrastructure at the Farm. They would also damage important resources such as the biofuel processing plant. The area was too large to destroy with only ground forces. For this reason, once the aircraft had struck the rebel compound, they would carry out a bombing run with their remaining cargo to decimate the Farm crops on their way home. The fuel bombs, as they were known, were different to the kind of bombs that would hit the rebel stronghold.

The strategy in attacking the rebel compound was to use the density of the buildings against them. A well-placed bomb full of explosives and shrapnel would inflict the most damage here. For a wide-open space, such as the Farm, one well-placed shrapnel bomb might take out the leadership, but to guarantee maximum results they would need a different type of munition.

Will had dispatched a hundred fighters to attack the Farm. Although he would have no view of the Farm until the bombers arrived, he had given control of the assault to one of his most trusted lieutenants. Dennis was certainly capable of the attack and, with a hundred troops under his control, he would have an advantage in numbers of an estimated three to one.

That was Will's initial plan and he'd had confidence in it until he'd learnt of the rebel convoy heading to the Farm. That was the last message that he'd received from his spy. If the spy was now dead, Will's only concern was that he might have told the rebels of the attack plans first. Should the rebels arrive at the Farm before his forces, the odds would swing in their favour and then they would be the ones with the three to one advantage. He had to accelerate his plan.

His troops needed to complete the assault and escape before the rebels arrived. He would have to wait for the aircraft to pass over the Farm before he could see if all of his plans had been successful. Hopefully the rebels would arrive at the same time and he would see them burned by the fuel bombs.

In preparing for this mission, he had looked at pictures of the rebel stronghold. A compound that housed over six hundred people was more like a village than just one group of buildings. Although the construction had clearly been designed strategically, they had most likely expected an attack from ground forces. This was one of the main reasons for using the aircraft. The pictures had shown a limited number of tall buildings, which apparently had several levels below ground as well.

When he'd begun planning for the task, he had been concerned that the rebels in the hidden levels would survive the attack. But his spy had communicated that the underground fortress had no external exit. When they brought the main buildings down, they would turn the stronghold into a tomb. Any rebels that didn't die in the initial assault would be buried alive under tonnes of rubble, giving them a slow and painful end.

As the planes got closer to the targets, the monitors showed Will what the bombers were seeing. It appeared that at least some of the scouts had been successful. The monitor displayed three digital signatures that were painting the targets for the bombs. He could hear chatter between the two pilots.

"Red dog, this is Blue dog. Do you see the three signals, over?"

"Hello Blue dog, this is Red dog. I see them, over."

"Red dog I will set two frags each to track frequency 56 and frequency 59, over."

"Blue dog, understood. I will set two frags to track frequency 47, over and out."

It always amazed Will how important these bombers felt that they were. In truth, they were hardly real soldiers, flying around the sky like birds and pressing a few buttons, killing people from a distance. These so-called commanders, who were revered by the elites, would probably vomit at the sight of some of the blood and guts that he had experienced in real combat.

Their communications sounded overly formal, remnants from a time before the Water Wars. It seemed was only natural that, as well as techniques, systems and some of the manuals for servicing the vehicles and planes, communications, protocols and tactical books had survived.

"Blue dog, weapons hot, over."

"Red dog, weapons hot, over."

"Blue dog, bombs away, over."

"Red dog, bombs away, over and out."

The signal on the monitors switched from an overview display showing the digital signatures of the targets to the view from the cameras of the actual bombs. Even though the images seemed a little shaky, it only added to the feeling that Will was riding the bombs down to the targets. The cameras showed a bright-green light on the ground. This was the work of the scouts: these lights painted the targets and allowed the bombs to automatically navigate straight to them.

After the bombs hit, the monitor switched again, this time to the high-level view of the targets from the cameras on the outside of the planes. On this first pass, it was hard for Will to distinguish the buildings but, when the first bomb hit, the explosion could be seen from the plane's 30,000-foot perch. On the second pass, the planes approached lower and observed the damage they had done.

With a limited supply of bombs, the pilots would only drop an extra load if they felt it was required. The point of using the marking technology, though, was to complete the task with the first load.

The monitor now gave a short close-up of the devastation below. The scene looked like a huge rubbish pile. From what Will observed from the planes' two passes of the compound, very little was left of the buildings below. Later he would be able to review the damage on the video images from the ground scouts, if they returned. For the moment, his main concern was to ensure that rebels hadn't escaped in large numbers.

The planes completed one last pass of the surrounding area, checking for any vehicles exiting it, but could not pick up any sign of them. The images on the monitors changed again, giving a view similar to the initial images that had displayed the markers to guide the bombs.

This time the blips on the screen had numbers next to them. This was a confirmation signal from the scouts on the ground. As well as transmitting a signal for the bombs to follow, the equipment could transmit a confirmation signal. Its information was limited but was enough to tell the pilots the bombs had been successful and it was not beneficial to waste any more munitions on this target.

It felt like today was going be a good day. Will was looking forward to reporting the successes to Brand. In his eyes, the compound was the more difficult target and the Farm was more of a nice to have. All the same, he was cautious not to get ahead of himself, knowing Brand was not the forgiving type.

Will was still concerned that the rebels might have reached the Farm before his troops had left. He'd had no communication with them since they arrived and, although he trusted Dennis's skills, he was aware that anything could happen. An old saying he remembered as a young child press-ganged by the Company had been drilled into him years later during his training for the officer elite: "No plan survives first contact with the enemy!" He wasn't sure who was supposed to have said that – the Company claimed it was one of the heroes from the Water Wars – but, whoever the phrase came from, Will found it apt in any battle.

"Red dog, this is Blue dog. Heading for secondary target, over."

"Blue dog, I'm right behind you, over and out."

With that, the screens switched to images of forests and open grounds and Will decided he'd seen enough. It was going to take the planes at least another hour to reach the Farm so he decided to have a break.

On reflection, Will thought he would report his success to Brand. He felt it was worth getting ahead of events. After all, giving Brand good news now might give Will a chance to delay reporting any potential bad news later.

He turned to the analyst who was sitting by the

monitors. "I will only be gone for a maximum of thirty minutes but if the planes arrive at the Farm early or if there are any issues at all, I want you to beep me. Do you understand?"

The analyst nodded. "Yes, sir, of course, sir."

Will looked at his name tag. "Jerome. I'm very good at remembering names, Jerome! How old are you, Jerome?"

Jerome stammered out, "Twenty-two, sir."

"Twenty-two. You could have a lot of years still ahead of you. If anything happens with those planes, anything at all and you don't contact me, you will not see your twenty-third birthday. You will take an early trip to the plants." Will let that statement hang in the air as he left to brief Brand.

Visibly shaking, Jerome vowed to himself that he would not take his eyes off the monitors until Will returned.

29

FRANK'S VIEW OF THE ATTACK ON THE REBEL STRONGHOLD

12 September 2202

The warning from Flo had given the rebels time to escape. The Company's plan to replace ground troops with an aerial attack had also worked in the rebels' favour.

Zap had been able to access the information on the assault. The knowledge of when it would come allowed the rebels to escape the stronghold while making it seem as if it was still manned.

The main strategy was to make it look like all of the rebels had perished during the aerial bombardment. When Frank had first heard of the attack, he wasn't sure if it was true but when the girl had read his mind, he started to take notice. Even with the advance notice, booby-trapping the buildings to make it hard for the Company to determine if anyone had survived was still a big task to finish in the time available.

Frank's knowledge of the hidden exit from the

underground levels had been a secret held only by him and a trusted few.

After the convoy had left for the Farm, he'd started to prepare his strategy in earnest. Apprehensive as he was and wanting to believe that this was all just a nightmare, his suspicions weren't enough for him to sacrifice his people.

His increased patrols had captured another six of the Company scouts, but even if they'd got them all, he assumed that the planes could still hit their targets without the guidance systems.

If the bombs came on schedule, he would have his fighters slip secretly below and begin the evacuation as the first bombs fell. He already had rebels moving stores and vehicles to a secure place outside the compound. The vehicles were in a location chosen for its ability to be camouflaged from above.

Although he hadn't experienced an aerial assault before, he had set up this external staging post when rumours of aircraft attacks had spread through the rebel community. As with the underground exits, the location of the staging post was known only to a select few.

With Zap's advance warning of the planes leaving the Sanctuary, Frank had been able to schedule evacuating his people. They had strategically placed dummies and other fake figures out in the open in the hope that it would fool those watching from the planes. It was doubtful that the Company would have other troops in the area to check on the results of the attack.

The main plan was to disappear unnoticed because, if the planes pursued them, they could wreak havoc from above.

Interrogations of the scouts had gone well. They

hadn't known how many other scouts had been deployed but this was consistent with the usual strategy for scouts. If they didn't know something, they couldn't give up the information if they were caught.

Frank was more interested in the information they had divulged about the technology that they carried. He now knew that it was only accurate when it was within five hundred metres of the target. True, it may have operated over a longer distance but he was sure that the scouts would want to ensure the success of their mission. He imagined how someone would feel after carrying this equipment for days, evading capture and possible death, only for their mission to fail because they were fifty metres or so too far away. No, these scouts would get as close as possible to their targets.

He had therefore placed his own sentries as lookouts in the main areas that he expected a scout to be located. He didn't expect to find all of the scouts and, although he hadn't been trained by the Company, he had been involved in enough battles to develop his own tactical skills.

It was clear to him that the scouts would wait until the last possible minute to set up their equipment. It would be a balancing act between being exposed for too long and getting within five hundred metres of the compound before the bombers' arrival. Frank hoped that this would work in his favour. At the first sign of any of the scouts near the compound, the last rebels who were above ground would deploy to the lower-level chambers.

He'd briefed everyone that remained after the convoy left for the Farm. It was a simple plan and, because so many resources had to be loaded into the trucks, he had to tell them what was going on. They trusted him and it was obvious to everyone that their choices were limited.

He now had fifty fighters hidden in the woods, guarding the trucks to keep their escape route secure. If the trucks were discovered and destroyed by the planes, it would leave them out in the open without transport or resources and vulnerable to attack.

One of the men guarding the vehicles had even captured a Company scout. His fighters were on high alert. Having stood guard himself in his youth, Frank knew that over time a sentry could become lax and complacent. Fortunately, as this was only the first day of their duties, his fighters were fuelled with the adrenaline that came with a sense of potential death.

Following a thorough interrogation, the scout who they had captured had stated that the Company was unaware of the vehicle stash. This information could be unreliable, coming as it did from an interrogation. Even so, given the Company surely assumed its attack would be a surprise, it would have no reason to expect the rebels to initiate an escape plan like this.

As the aircraft approached, the alarm was raised through hushed voices and hand signals.

The secret exits had always been covered for security reasons and, once that Frank was sure that an attack was imminent, he had tasked them with uncovering the doors. It was back-breaking work to quickly remove the stores that had camouflaged the exits.

Once through the first doors, his fighters would use the tunnels that led to the vehicles. It was expected that the tunnels were deep enough to withstand the bombardment. His main concern was that if the fighters weren't in the tunnels when the planes arrived, the weight of the materials from the collapsed buildings would cause the other areas to collapse and stop them from reaching the tunnels in time. But, supposing they got there as planned, they would wait in the tunnels and would not breach the final exit doors until Frank ordered.

"What do you see, Flo? What do you hear?" Frank asked hurriedly.

"Zap is working at his terminal. He is saying that the planes are transmitting a signal and he has managed to hack into it. They are very close!"

Frank trusted Flo's intelligence but he still took the extra precaution of deploying some of his people to watch out for the scouts.

"Okay, Flo, it's time to head to the tunnels."

As Frank would be one of the last to enter the tunnels, he had kept her by her side to receive intelligence for as long as possible. Although he was unsure how this mind talking or whatever it was called worked, he assumed that being in a deep tunnel might block the signal.

Now the benefit of up-to-date intelligence seemed to be outweighed by the imminent risk.

Flo ignored Frank for a minute to say a silent goodbye to Zap. "Please don't worry if you can't communicate with me. I am heading to safety but we may not be able to talk for a while. As soon as I can feel you in my head, we'll talk again."

Zap was preoccupied watching the monitors, while trying to simultaneously communicate with Flo. For a split second, he took his eyes away from the monitor, concentrated and tried to send Flo warm, safe thoughts.

He was trying to stop her feeling scared, being in no hurry to repeat the paralysing experience he'd had the last time she was afraid. He was taking a big risk here and his chances of discovery would be even higher if he was suddenly immobilised.

Flo felt the warmth coming from Zap and said "Thank you" in her head. Taking the hand Frank was offering her, she allowed him to guide her down to the tunnels. He was almost dragging her and she struggled to keep up.

The tunnels were a hive of activity. Multiple trolleys were being pushed towards the tunnels entrance and everyone was moving with purpose. Few were talking as no one was sure how much noise would travel to the outside. They needn't have worried, though, as the walls and the outside doors were thick and solid.

Once he reached the entrance to the tunnels, Frank bellowed upwards, "Okay, this is happening."

He had left only fifteen fighters upstairs. Soon only two would remain, looking for the planes through binoculars.

The thirteen stragglers followed Frank down to the tunnels. As the last of them arrived, Frank addressed his three lieutenants. He had already briefed each one but at this final check-in he could communicate the latest intelligence.

Each had their tasks, with a third of the survivors in their charge. They also had a hierarchy in case Frank hadn't made it to the tunnels in time. The plan was for them to stagger their convoys to avoid presenting one huge target on the road. This last brief was all the more important as they had no idea what was waiting for them outside of the tunnels.

"Okay, get among your people and reassure them. Let them know that we expect the bombs imminently and it's going to get noisy in here. I don't want anyone panicking once the bombs arrive. A stampede will result in casualties and the plan is to avoid that. Let them know that we have a plan and it will work."

With that, the lieutenants went to their task quickly. Although Frank was unsure if the tunnels would withstand a bombardment, he couldn't let his people know that. He had to exude confidence so that they could in turn brief the others with confidence. A panic in this confined space could be fatal.

Frank walked towards the tunnel exit, firmly grasping Flo's hand.

Being close to the exit would increase his own chances of survival but he was more interested in being there so that he was ready for any contingencies. For all he knew, the Company could already be aware of the exit and have troops outside waiting to ambush them.

Once the bombs fell, there would be nowhere else to go so Frank needed to be at the front to assess the threat in real time.

Suddenly the earth shook around them. Even though the ceiling above them stayed in place, the air was filled with dust. Some of the fighters had fallen over as the ground was moving, pretty much like earthquakes Frank had experienced in the past. He guessed this was the first bomb: the noise was muffled below ground, but the loud bang had been unmistakeable.

Five or six further bangs followed. They were so close together, it was hard to tell if they were landing consecutively or if more than one bomb had hit at the same time. It was all over within about five minutes.

They had not had time to receive a signal from the two spotters above, who were unlikely to have reached the tunnels in time.

Unfortunately, conflicts always brought casualties. If these two were the only people to die today, Frank would see that as a huge bonus. Still the safety of all of his fighters was always on his mind, which is why he was respected.

After the last loud bang, he waited a minute or so and then flew into action.

"Okay," he said to the fighters next to the doors. "You all know your positions."

Twenty fighters were standing with their weapons aimed at the door. The exit was a choke point and Frank realised that, if the enemy were waiting on the outside of these doors, their chances of survival were severely limited. Whatever came next, he wasn't prepared to walk out with his hands up and be slaughtered.

As he nodded, two large men rolled back the huge exit doors. The sunlight that burst through the doorways was broken up by shadows. The exit had been positioned so that anyone escaping would emerge under a canopy of trees. Although the trees' natural camouflage disguised their position, it could also be an advantage to potential ambushers.

Frank lowered his arm and the first group of fifteen fighters rushed out and took up positions in a protective arc, surveying their surroundings for potential threats. Nothing happened for a full ten minutes, as Frank had planned. He doubted that any potential Company ambush would have such patience.

Next he sent out a group of fifty fighters. This group

leapfrogged the fighters already there and took up a deeper defensive position.

The fighters guarding the vehicles had been waiting for Frank's arrival. The leader of this group had been briefed on where the rebels would exit and the six scouts that he had sent to welcome them were waiting in the trees as lookouts. They had been there for a couple of hours and knew to wait ten minutes after the first group exited before signalling their own people.

The front man in the reception group gave the agreed raised-fist signal and the lead man of Frank's group gave the same response back. Once the all clear was confirmed, Frank took charge of the initial fifty fighters outside of the tunnel and led them to the vehicles.

As soon as he reached the vehicles, Frank began to instil a sense of urgency. He placed Flo in a vehicle with two guards so that she could concentrate and gather new intelligence.

The rest of the group left the tunnels in staggered groups of thirty. Within an hour, the tunnels were deserted and the first convoy was ready to leave.

To balance the needs of exiting the compound as quickly as possible and maintaining a strategic spacing between the convoys, Frank had scheduled a tight timetable. Although the situation could all change in an instant, at the moment things were going to plan.

Frank hoped that the planes would stop circling after an hour or so. They may have initially stayed behind to check that their bombs had hit the buildings but Frank figured that, unlike the biofuel he used in his trucks, aviation fuel for planes would be in short supply. If they were concerned to avoid wasting fuel, they would not want to stay in the area for too long. Although he wasn't sure how many planes had been deployed, Flo's intelligence had been that there were only two.

He assumed that these two planes had other targets to hit and that would also affect their time in the area. Conscious that the Farm wasn't far away, Frank hoped that his fighters had been able to get there first so that they could provide the planes with a welcoming committee.

Frank waved to Ramirez in the front vehicle of convoy one. When Ramirez waved back, Frank took this as confirmation that no changes in the plan were needed and the first vehicles left.

Frank had been making final checks before he was due to leave and next headed to the jeep where Flo sat.

"Have you received any further messages?" he asked as soon as he opened the vehicle door. "What is happening?"

She paused before saying almost under her breath, "They've hit the Farm."

"What do you mean, they've hit the Farm?"

"I mean that the bombers have hit the Farm. They dropped some kind of bomb that burnt the whole place."

"Were my fighters there? Did they kill them? What happened? Tell me." He realised that he was shaking her and forced himself to stop. It was unlike him to lose his cool. She was not in control of the information, but the possibility that he might have sent half of his fighters into an ambush made him feel sick to his stomach.

"Zap could only relay what the planes saw. Lots of people were burnt alive but he didn't know how many survived." Flo replied before going silent.

His mind went into overdrive. Maybe that was the Company's plan all along? Maybe they expected him to send troops to the Farm and were waiting for the troops to arrive before they killed them all. Frank needed to take a minute. He didn't want to stop, he had to decide fast. The plan had been for them all to head to the Farm but he now needed to change that. He had to contact the first convoy.

As his vehicle had been set up as a command vehicle, it contained one of the few long-range radios that the rebels possessed. Quickly picking up the handset and pressing the send button, he shouted down the line, "Ramirez, Ramirez, this is Frank, are you listening? Are you listening?" He released the button and waited for a response.

Almost immediately, a crackly voice came back, "Yes, Frank, this is Ramirez. What's wrong?"

"Stop heading for your current destination. As soon as you can get to cover, stop and wait for my next message," Frank said. "Do you understand?"

With the overgrown roads and unkempt wilderness, they were never far away from cover.

"Yes," Ramirez replied. "We'll take cover very soon. What is going on?"

"The Farm is compromised!" Frank didn't have time to use a code. "Do you understand? The Farm is compromised."

Ramirez replied solemnly, "I understand."

Frank wished he had an alternative but they couldn't stay here and they were running out of options. There and then he decided to trust Flo's intelligence.

Ramirez had brought his convoy to a halt and had deployed sentries to the front and back of the convoy.

Shortly afterwards, he heard Frank on the radio again. "Ramirez, can you still hear me?"

"Yes, Frank. What's the plan?"

"We are heading north. Do you understand this instruction?"

After a moment's reflection, Ramirez replied, "Confirm that we are heading north and not to the Farm?"

"Yes," said Frank. "That is correct, do not head to the Farm, I repeat, do not head to the Farm."

"What's up north?"

"We are in a fluid situation. Wait an hour before you hit the main road north and we will meet you on that road. I will explain the plan in person but keep listening to your radio."

"Understood," Ramirez said. "Safe travels."

Grabbing his driver, who was loading stores into the back of the vehicle, and another man nearby, Frank addressed them both together. "I need to go instruct the convoy leaders of the new destination and I need you to man this radio right now. If either of you hears a message on the radio or if this girl tells you she has a message for me, one of you is to come and get me right away. The other must stay with the radio and the girl. Do you understand me?"

Both men nodded. Recognising the situation was dangerous, they believed that their best chance of survival was to follow Frank's orders to the letter.

Frank was thinking on his feet, relieved to have a contingency plan. He knew that this contingency plan wasn't known to Debs. From Flo's intelligence the Farm was already lost.

He felt as though he was abandoning Debs but had

to trust that she would do what she could for any survivors under her control. This plan was risky: they had no idea what resources were in the north and, with over three hundred fighters, their current supplies would not last long.

Frank took it as some consolation that Debs might be able to forage something from the farm and that his convoys wouldn't be putting further strain on those supplies.

They only knew of this back-up location because of the intelligence Flo had passed on. She had been told about the crossing point near the border. Supposedly endless resources were on the other side of the border. Any resources of this nature would surely be controlled by the Company but the rebels had always fought the Company for their survival.

They were not supposed to need a contingency plan. At the compound, their main contingency had always been to regroup and fortify the Farm if the compound fell. They had assumed that a ground attack would struggle to overwhelm such a large area and they had always expected a ground attack. Even an aerial attack of shrapnel bombs was thought to be of little threat to the wide-open space at the Farm.

Apparently he, like the others in the compound, had been wrong. They hadn't even known of a type of bomb that could burn large areas of ground. He knew that he could only work with the information he had but he felt that this was no excuse and his mistake could have cost his fighters dearly.

When he got back to the vehicle, Flo was still sitting motionless. Although they had no choice but to implement this plan, he decided on one last check.

"Okay, before we head off, I need to ask you, are you sure that we will be safe if we head north?"

"He told me, he told me," Flo repeated. "The Company has a staging post near the border where they store their vehicles and resources to deploy south. Any major attacks down here are staged through there. For some reason, it is not well manned. They feel safe."

Frank's ears pricked up at this information. "Why would they feel safe enough to have only a small number of troops guarding valuable resources?"

Was another surprise waiting for them in the north? At the moment, his priority was to get his people out of this area and assess things when they were away from the immediate risk.

He had no doubt that the Company would follow up on its assault by sending someone here to check on their success. If they found that the rebels had escaped, they would deploy ground forces or planes to pursue them and hit them on the road.

For the time being, Frank could only use his fall-back plan and hope that this was enough.

30

THE SECOND RESISTANCE COUNCIL MEETING

17 September 2202

It had been ten days since the first resistance leaders' meeting. As chair of this next one, Hubert began. "Thank you for coming. I know we're all busy people. I also know the risk involved in us all being together in one place. If we agree today to proceed with our plan, we are not going to be safe for some time. Before we continue without any predetermined rules, by a show of hands, how many of you are willing to proceed with this plan? I'm not asking you for unconditional support, I just need to know if you are committed."

Hubert looked round the table. Karla was the first to raise her hand, followed by Spider, Hook and finally CT. He felt relieved.

"Okay, so in principle we agree to proceed but practically, what can we do?" CT asked.

"First," Karla said, "I have secured a source of intelligence that I think will be very useful. Without revealing my source, I can say that we will have access to information relating to the schedules of the Company troops, their numbers, deployments and the distribution of resources around the Sanctuary."

This announcement raised a few eyebrows around the group, but she continued. "Although we all have our own methods of gathering intelligence, I think we can all agree that Spider is the master intelligence coordinator. I therefore propose that Spider and I work closely together to determine what information we need. I will then source this intelligence. Does that make sense to you, Spider?"

"I am willing to at least entertain the idea," Spider replied. Although at this stage the source wasn't important, he would want to verify any information from it through his own network of spies. Still, if she did have such a source, it would be very valuable to their cause.

"Now that we have decided to proceed, I need to share one more piece of information," said Karla. "My source has informed me that five or six hundred rebels are heading north. They may not reach us of course but they are on the other side of the wastelands and getting closer."

"Why didn't you open with this information?" Hubert asked.

"All I know for sure is that the Company forces destroyed their compound and that they are desperate. I don't know if they will even reach us but my source is in communication with them and they may be of some use. I am telling you this because we may have some back-up but we can't count on them."

"Okay, for the time being let's plan as if this band of

stray rebels doesn't exist. If they at some stage are here and we can use them, that will be amazing. For now, we're on our own. I assume that you will keep us updated with any progress of these rebels?" Hubert asked.

"I will of course let everyone know if there is any chance that we can get some support from them. To the matter at hand, I believe that if we are going to do this without being discovered, we need to act now. I propose that we set our sights on the upcoming festival. As someone that has prepared for many of them, I have an eye for detail and working out timetables and schedules. So I could put together our timetable, counting down to the festival. Does that sound like an idea?" As Karla looked around, the others nodded.

Spider spoke clearly and precisely, "What we are proposing here is a huge endeavour in only a short timeframe. It will require planning and coordination. We need to trust each other and work together but we also need to work smart. I suggest that, going forward, we restrict the number of large meetings like this. It will be safer for us to meet in smaller groups, even just in pairs."

"Agreed," murmured the other four almost as one.

It was CT who spoke next. "Clearly we need to turn the people against the Company. Although it may seem against our interests, I suggest that we reduce our black-market prices for gel packs and food supplies. Hubert, you and I are the biggest suppliers of food and drink to the masses and the elites. If we want to get the people on our side and be seen as saviours, we cannot continue to bleed them dry. If they see us as being as bad as the elites, when the time comes they may turn on us."

Hubert agreed. "We knew that this would require some sacrifices. I am willing to use up the bulk of my supplies to try to reduce the starvation. If we do not support the masses now, nobody will be left to revolt."

Hook offered his own perspective. "Another matter to bear in mind is the supplies to the troops. My contacts can help but if Karla's intelligence source can provide timetables, quantities of Company weapons and store replenishment details, we can intercept some of those resources. This has two benefits: we can deprive the Company of valuable resources and supplies, while helping to arm the people's army."

"That makes sense," said Hubert. "CT and I meet often because we are in similar trades. We will take on the plan for distribution of extra food rations to the people. Karla, if you can provide us with some extra security so that our charity is not in vain, that would be much appreciated."

"Of course."

Hubert continued to assign responsibilities. "Spider, you and Hook will be our tacticians. Determine what information is required and liaise with Karla to ensure it is supplied and utilised in a timely manner. Does that all sound okay?" Again, they all nodded in agreement. He was surprised how easily this seemed to be coming together. Of course, this journey was going to be anything but easy but at least they had established a starting point.

Having been thinking of little else since the last meeting, however, Hubert wasn't finished yet. "We have a maximum of just over a month to turn the unrest into an uprising. We cannot be seen to be behind this. Although it is obvious that the Company spies will know something is going on, we need to make sure that our hand in this is not seen."

"How do you propose we do that?" Karla asked. Now that she was committed to this venture, she was keen to insulate herself.

"I know of an organisation," Hubert said. "It was set up to support injured Company veterans, so it actually gets a small amount of funding from the Company. As you'd expect, the funding is not enough. I have the contract to clean the filters in the gel plants and, although this is an unpleasant task, it does supply some additional sources of nutrition."

This description almost turned CT's stomach. Although he had come from modest beginnings, since his rise to power he ate food far superior to the gel packs of the masses. He didn't like to even think about the residue after the gel packs had been made, consisting of hair and nails and other nasties. Most people had managed to turn a blind eye to the reality that eating gel packs made them cannibals but the idea of eating leftovers from the bottom of the filters would still be disgusting to some. Of course, that was only the people who had the luxury of having full bellies.

Hubert continued, "This organisation is known as SUP and supplies injured veterans and the spouses of dead troops. Because I supply them with the residue from my cleaning, they also supply certain other dependants. If any of my own people die because of the Company, I use SUP to look after their families. I believe we can filter our donations through this organisation to give us some deniability. Because it is in effect a Company organisation, it can operate under their noses.

"I like that plan," Hook said. "I like the idea of using their own service to feed the masses."

"Then it is agreed. We all have our own tasks to do. Before we leave tonight, if anybody needs to schedule your next smaller meetings, I suggest you do that now. This is the safest time to do it in person, to avoid using go-betweens that could be intercepted by the Company."

As Hubert finished, the room was suddenly filled with multiple conversations about specific timetables and resource deployments.

31

DEBS MEETS WITH THE SCOUTS NEAR THE FARM

12 September 2202

Frank had trained Debs well and she had adopted some of his cautiousness. She'd sent scouts ahead rather than have a horde of over three hundred fighters suddenly arrive at the Farm, uninformed and unprepared.

The twelve scouts had deployed in three vehicles ahead of the convoy. As trading partners, the rebels knew the layout of the Farm and the scouts had been briefed to approach from three prearranged locations. Their instructions were to observe for an hour and then return to the convoy. If they identified any Company soldiers, they were not to engage.

It was important to her that they witness the situation on the ground and report back with the intelligence she needed to get an overall view of the Farm. To keep the information up to date, only two of the vehicles would return to the convoy and the third group would remain in place to observe.

When the scouts returned, they were in a solemn mood.

"What did you see?" Debs asked.

After a pause, Jones, a female scout, said, "When we arrived, the troops were already there. We stayed up on the high ground and observed. We could see bodies laid in front of the buildings. Although we didn't witness the killings, from the positions of the bodies it looked like they had been lined up and executed. The Company set fire to the buildings and I estimate they had around one hundred soldiers there. There was nothing we could do to help."

"Did you see any survivors or any prisoners?" Debs asked.

"They spared nobody. The Farm is lost," Jones said sombrely.

Debs had a decision to make. The briefing from Frank before she left had included an initial plan to reach the Farm and fortify it. Although the Company had destroyed the buildings and killed the inhabitants, the Farm was still a valuable resource. That plan still stood. Frank and the rest of the fighters would be a day behind. The attack on the Farm validated their intelligence. Therefore the intelligence that the compound would be attacked was also highly likely to be correct.

If the compound was attacked, any of their people that managed to escape would head to the Farm. This would be their refuge. They could start with rudimentary buildings and they had plenty of fighters and lots of trees nearby. They might not have an abundance of artisan tools but they could make do.

There would be food in the fields and something to rebuild.

The next thing to consider was a contingency, in case the troops were still at the Farm when they arrived. It was a fair assumption that by destroying the buildings the Company was tipping its hand and showing that it had no intention of staying. The buildings were a strategic asset for any force mounting a defence; their destruction signalled that the Company was preparing to leave.

Debs had staged her vehicles by the side of the road in order to meet with the scouts. She had to plan for an assault in case the troops were still present but she also needed to avoid blocking the Company if it was leaving.

Her three staggered convoys had converged on this rendezvous point and were now resuming their separate formations. This location had been chosen because it was close enough to deploy an assault with all of her force at once, yet far enough away to avoid Company scouts.

The rebels had always had contingency plans for assaulting the Farm. As a valuable resource, it had been open to the risk that its guards would be overrun by a larger hostile group. If the Company troops hadn't left, they would feel the full might of these plans. The plans had assumed that the rebels would have to assault fortified buildings but the Company had made their task simpler by removing those buildings.

The family and the workers had been under the protection of the rebels and they'd had around thirty of their own fighters stationed at the Farm. The loss of Kath, Mitch, the workers and their own fighters would be felt as a big loss to their ranks but this was not the time to mourn. Although this had to be verified, she expected that the Farm would have put up a spirited defence. Even if the Company had managed a surprise attack, she was sure that it would have also incurred major losses.

The three columns would approach the Farm from different directions. The scouts had already left to return to their locations at the Farm and brief the other scouts. Each scout unit would link up with one of the convoys, prior to the assault.

"We must remain fluid. There may be surprises for us at the Farm so keep vigilant," Debs said to the group of leaders in front of her.

Pepper was impressed by the respect that the woman inspired in the people around her. Many of them were bigger and older than her but all clearly deferred to her instincts.

Eric was not present at the briefing. Pepper knew that, once he found out about the fate of his adoptive family, he would be hard to control.

"There's every chance that by the time we reach the Farm, the troops will have left," Debs said. "If that is the situation, we will not pursue them. It is important that, as we approach the Farm from three directions, we do not impede the Company convoy. Therefore, we will leave the northern route open." Debs showed the plan on the map so that everybody was clear what was required.

Once the briefing was over, everyone returned to the vehicles and their tasks at hand.

The command vehicle was to contain Debs, Pepper, Eric and three more fighters. Eric was already waiting inside when Pepper got into the vehicle. Pepper decided that the best approach was to get ahead of this and tell Eric what had happened.

"Eric, I have something to tell you."

Eric looked at him suspiciously. He had only recently begun to grant Pepper a tenuous trust at best. "What's happened? Is Mitch okay? Is Kath okay? Tell me, tell me!"

"We were too late. The Company has already arrived at the Farm."

"What are we waiting for? Let's go and rescue them," Eric said excitedly.

"We cannot just go in without scouting first. And this will not be a rescue mission." Pepper could see the rage in Eric's eyes.

"What do you mean, this will not be a rescue mission? Why will we not rescue my family?"

"Because they are already gone," Pepper said solemnly. He watched Eric deflate before his eyes. It was as though someone had stuck a nail in a tyre. All the air and energy seemed to disappear from Eric instantly.

He looked away from Pepper momentarily and then looked back, tears welling in his eyes. "What do you mean? They can't be gone. I only saw them a couple of days ago. I should have stayed there, I shouldn't have left them. I could've saved them."

Pepper tried to put his hand on Eric's shoulder but he brushed it away. "Eric, if you'd been there, you'd be dead too."

"If I hadn't been able to save them, at least I'd have been able to die with them. They were my family, my only family."

Pepper said calmly, "Flo is your family. She's your

family and you need to keep yourself safe for her. You're all she's got now."

For a moment, the thought of Flo seemed to calm Eric down. Then the angry boy inside him erupted again. "I'll kill every last one of them. They won't get away with this, I will kill every Company man I see. I will rip them apart with my bare hands."

Pepper realised that it was going to be a long journey to the Farm. He might also need all of his strength to restrain Eric when they got there. Debs, who had been paying close attention to this conversation, met Pepper's eyes knowingly. There was no need for words.

When they stopped for the final check-in with the scouts, Pepper and Debs would need to have an uncomfortable conversation. In the meantime, as their vehicle started up, Pepper was grateful that Eric had resorted to silent rage.

32

WILL BRIEFS BRAND ON THE FIRST PLANE ATTACK

12 September 2202

As usual, Will was frisked thoroughly before entering Brand's office. He had to relinquish his pistol, magazines and everything in his pockets – a metal pen, a lighter and even his notebook. Although these items might seem innocent to anyone else, Brand was not anyone else. Being paranoid was how he'd survived so long.

Brand wouldn't even let his female companions wear hair slides or sharp jewellery as he didn't discount anything from being a potential weapon.

He wasn't afraid of the Norms. Brand viewed the poor masses as he would a piece of dirt on his shoe, there for a short time but easily removed. His main concern was the other elites, knowing that, like him, they felt superior to everyone. They believed that they deserved all of the power. As with Brand, they had more things and pleasures than they would ever need, yet still wanted more. They believed they were invincible and that made them dangerous.

Greed and an ever-growing lust for more was what had led the world to the Water Wars. The ultimate resource all the elites desired was power. In the Sanctuary, Brand was ultimate power. He tried not to broadcast the fact that he was the supreme leader. Most of the people saw him at events, but only as a figurehead. Thanks to the propaganda machine, the council appeared to be the cause of any ills while no responsibility fell on him. Although this ruse worked with most of the masses, however, the resistance leaders and certain other individuals were aware of his position.

He was happy to remain behind the scenes while maintaining the seat of power. Power, not adoration, was the real reward. Just by clicking his fingers, he could achieve the death of anyone in the Sanctuary. The other leaders on the council were aware of this reality and they were afraid of his ruthlessness.

The council had enough political power to pass laws or edicts that would benefit them. Yet not even the combined power of everyone on the council could remove him. He had spies everywhere, including among some of the council members' lovers and confidantes.

With his web of spies, Brand would be aware of any proposed coup, as his rivals knew. Although they wanted more, none was prepared to risk everything for the chance to take over his position. This would just make them the next target for such a coup.

After Will had been kept waiting for ten minutes, a female assistant opened the door to Brand's office. She was a beautiful young woman, wearing nothing but a thin robe.

Although her skimpy garb was to allow him access on a whim, it served another purpose as well. The simple robe had no pockets, making it difficult for a potential assassin to hide a weapon. All Brand's women assistants were forced to undress and don these robes before entering his office. Will was one of the trusted few who was allowed to remain dressed.

Brand was sitting behind a large desk, playing with a sharp knife that he was using to prune his fingernails. In anyone else's office, this could have been an ornamental letter opener but Brand preferred a more deadly tool.

Although the masses didn't get written mail, any communications between council members would be written on paper and secured with a stamped wax seal. A letter opener for Brand was actually superfluous as, although the committee sent messages to each other, they wouldn't dare disrespect Brand with a letter.

Brand's spics let him know all that was actually going on, but he liked the fact that the council members had to submit weekly reports in person. These reports were rarely negative as they all feared the consequences of angering Brand.

As soon as the doors closed, Brand wanted answers. "What are you doing here?"

"I've come to report our success," Will said, reflecting that perhaps this was not such a good idea after all.

"Our success?" Brand said. "You mean my success?"

"Yes, yes, your success," Will said hesitantly.

"So we have killed all the rebels, destroyed the compound, destroyed the Farm. There are no survivors? Is that correct?"

"No, not exactly."

"No!" Brand replied loudly. "Then why are you here and why are you calling this a success?"

"The first half of the plan has been executed successfully. I thought that you would want an update."

"Give me the information and I will tell you if it's what I want to hear," Brand said impatiently.

"I watched the bombs fall from the planes onto the compound. Three of the scouts had successfully marked the buildings. The bombs hit with perfect precision and devastated the whole location. There were no visible survivors from that part of the assault."

"I sense a BUT coming here," Brand retorted.

"Before our attack commenced, my spy with the rebels informed me that they had received advance warning of our attack. A woman turned up at the compound, matching the description of the girl that we are hunting. She had an audience with the rebel leader and told him of the attack. My spy was not present during their conversation but she apparently convinced the leader of the threat. He sent half of his forces to the Farm."

Brand was quickly absorbing all of this information, analysing it and formulating various scenarios. Before he addressed Will, his thoughts went to the boy Ethan. Dick had told him about Ethan's dreams of communicating with the girl and this was too much of a coincidence. Someone with access to this information and communicating with somebody else had leaked a warning, almost in real time. Angered by this brief reflection, he quickly returned his attention to Will.

"It appears that you have stolen defeat from the jaws of victory. We have no confirmation that you managed to kill all of the rebels at the compound and you are here to tell me at least half of them have already escaped."

Will realised that it had been risky to present this report. He had been hopeful that his initial perceived success at the compound would temper Brand's anger from their previous meeting. And anyway, if anything the blame was partly on Brand. Will had wanted his mission to be a search and kill for the girl, but Brand had insisted on her safe capture. If she was a threat and Brand had stopped him from neutralising the threat, that wasn't Will's fault.

Of course, he daren't voice this to Brand. Instead, he moved on to some more hopeful news. "The rebels have headed to the Farm. They no doubt expect to have a ground battle on their hands. When the planes arrive, I am sure that they will provide a few surprises and another successful aerial assault. As soon as I heard that the rebels had intelligence of our plans, I expedited our ground assault on the Farm. By now everybody there should be dead and our troops should be heading home. The rebels will arrive just in time for our bombers, believing they have escaped the compound, but they will be consumed by fire."

Brand's spirits seemed to rise. "It appears that you are not totally incompetent. Thank you for the update. Go away and the next update better include the news that all of the rebels are dead." With that, Brand gestured to his assistant to open the door.

Will was glad of the opportunity to leave the room. He nodded respectfully to Brand and headed back down to the command centre as quickly as his legs would carry him. In his head, he was praying that his next report to Brand was not his last.

As Will was leaving, Brand removed his jacket. He was frustrated from that meeting and decided to use the assistant as a distraction to clear his head.

33

FLASHBACK TO PEPPER'S BASIC TRAINING

12 September 2202

As they got closer to the Farm, Pepper was pondering on his history with the Company.

He had always hated bullies and there were no bigger bullies than the Company. His mind flashed back to a time during his training after he'd been press-ganged into the Company forces. The training had created many painful memories that were burnt into his mind forever.

They had just returned from a forced march in the freezing rain. As usual they had very little time before the next punishment began.

The Company called the punishments training but the instructors seemed more interested in inflicting pain than training the best troops.

The recruits had no privacy during their training either. They slept in long huts with twenty beds to a hut. The beds were so close that if you stretched out your arm at night, you could touch the person in the next bed.

There were no doors on the toilets and they washed in long communal showers.

Even during shower time they were harassed. On the day Pepper was remembering, he was showering while one of the instructors, Rob Strong, was walking up and down the centre of the showers shouting profanities.

The recruits were all naked but Strong was in the customary grey overalls of the Company. Even though Pepper was quite tall for sixteen years of age, Strong towered over him, a giant of a man, bald and rippling with muscles.

Strong suddenly stopped inches behind Pepper. Pepper just wanted to get this shower over with and avoid engaging with Strong at all.

Unfortunately, if an instructor addressed you, they couldn't be ignored.

"Are you enjoying your shower, Taylor?" Strong pronounced his surname deliberately, speaking slowly but loud enough for the whole shower block to hear him.

This question had no correct answer. If he said yes, he might be banned from showers for a week, or worse. If he said no, he could be punished for being ungrateful.

"I'm grateful for the warm water that the Company provides for me, sir." He hoped this diplomatic answer would suffice.

"You like warm water do you, Taylor? Are you gay, Taylor?"

Homosexuality was a crime in the eyes of the Company. Like most crimes it was punishable by execution, after which your body was shipped to the gel plants.

Even the suspicion of homosexuality could get you twenty lashes of the whip, which had killed some recruits.

"No, sir," he said, knowing that this was the only reply that would be accepted.

"How do you know you're not gay, Taylor? Have you ever been with a man?"

"No sir, of course not."

"I've been with a man, Taylor, and I didn't like it so I know I'm not gay."

A cold shiver ran down to Pepper's spine. The instructors had been known to beat recruits to death as they faced no punishment for their indiscretions. The Company saw the recruits as expendable during training. If they could be killed, Pepper reasoned, they could be raped too. The fact that homosexuality was illegal was giving him no comfort whatsoever.

"Speak up, Taylor. How do you know you're not gay?"

"Because it's illegal, sir."

"So you always abide by the rules, do you, Taylor?"

"Yes sir."

"Well, that's interesting because I have it on good authority that you broke curfew last night."

Pepper had to think on his feet. He was in a precarious position, standing naked in front of an instructor who was looking for any excuse to dole out punishment. He was trying to both work out who had informed on him and find a way out of this. Yes, he had broken curfew but only because he knew that one of the boys in another hut was about to get a beating from some bullies.

Pepper had gotten the better of the three bullies but Strong was their squad leader and he was looking for revenge.

Although Royston, Pepper's squad leader, was reasonably fair to his squad, he clearly wasn't prepared to tangle with Strong over a recruit.

"Get out of the shower, Taylor."

Pepper went to grab his towel.

"No, Taylor, you don't need a towel as you are about to get wet again. Get outside onto the square."

As Pepper walked out into the freezing rain, he was followed by Strong who had grabbed a thick raincoat and a large whip before exiting the building.

All of the other recruits were now stuck to the windows to see what would happen. Some of them had grabbed their towels and others hadn't even showered yet. They knew they were required to watch and they did so for fear of suffering the same punishment.

"Go stand by the post. You know the drill. You've seen this before."

There was nothing he could do. Shivering with the cold, he walked to the post and placed his arms through the shackles. It took only seconds for Strong to secure the restraints and then he stepped back.

He heard the first crack of the whip before he felt the searing pain on his naked back. The first couple of hits seemed like agony but by the time of the tenth and final lashing, he had collapsed into unconsciousness.

He was left bleeding and hanging from the restraints by his arms for over half an hour. He was fortunate not to die of pneumonia or some other complication from his punishment but he used the power of hatred and anger to survive.

After the instructors brought him inside, they had poured vinegar over his open wounds and allowed him to don a set of overalls. That was the extent of the first aid they administered.

The wounds eventually scabbed over through the night but over the next few days they opened up on several occasions. Pepper remembered that the recruit he'd saved from the beating had sewed his wounds with a darning needle and thread. It could have been a lot worse if the wounds had been left open any longer.

This was Pepper's first public flogging. Although it wasn't to be his last, for him it was the most memorable.

The message of ruling by fear was instilled by all levels of the Company forces, the council, the Company leaders and even low-level leaders like Strong.

With life seen as worthless, there was no freedom or justice to be had.

His mind skipped on to exactly two years after the flogging. That was the day he had escaped from the Company. By that time Strong was no longer just an instructor at the Academy; now he was a commander in charge of field troops, including Pepper.

When Pepper refused to massacre unarmed children, he had been marked for death. He took some pleasure from the fact that he had personally killed Strong during his escape.

Unfortunately this pleasure was short-lived because to this day the Company forces were hunting for him.

34

WILL VIEWS THE ATTACK ON THE FARM

12 September 2202

Will stormed into the command centre, livid with the way Brand had treated him. Brand was known for treating people cruelly but Will had fought his way up the ranks and believed he was entitled to some respect.

He sought out the analyst, Jerome, remembering the special punishment he had promised him if he hadn't kept Will informed.

Glancing at the monitors and then back at Jerome, Will snapped, "Give me an update, now!"

Since Will had left, Jerome had only taken his eyes away from the monitors for a second or two, and that was to make briefing notes. He wanted to have an update ready as he knew his life depended on it. "The planes are still twenty minutes away from the targets," Jerome answered.

Will took a breath. "Why didn't you get me? Why didn't you call me?"

Jerome knew that silence was not an option. "I'm sorry sir, I thought you told me to call you when they were fifteen minutes away."

While realising he himself was being unreasonable, Will needed to take his anger out on someone and Jerome was an easy target. "Are you questioning me? Are you saying that I don't remember what I said to you?"

Jerome kept quiet, aware that the next few minutes could seal his fate.

"Have we heard anything from our troops at the Farm?" Will asked.

Jerome shook his head slowly.

"So we will have no idea what has happened at the Farm until our planes arrive. Communications!" Will stood up and addressed the whole control centre. "Communications is your one job. All you have to do is to ensure that my troops can communicate with me, when they are away assaulting and fighting the rebels. Is that not clear? That is all you have to do yet you managed to lose communications with over a hundred of our fighters. For all we know, our soldiers are currently getting slaughtered by the rebels."

Will's anger was building to a crescendo. "I suggest that you find some way of communicating with my troops at the Farm. Whatever you do, do it quickly. If I'm not getting an update from the commander at the Farm in the next ten minutes, every person sitting here now will be heading to the gel plants before the end of the day. Does everybody understand?"

Nobody looked away from their monitors, nobody dared engage with Will. This made him angrier. "Am I talking to myself? Am I talking to myself? I will take your silence as a sign that you are working so hard you don't have time to talk. That's fine, you only have ten minutes so I suggest you use them wisely." Will walked out of the main area and into his own office, where a fresh jug of coffee was waiting for him He slammed the door shut and poured himself a cup.

He felt the anger and the guilt flow out because he knew that his future with Brand depended on the success of this mission. He hated the fact that his future was in other people's hands. They had to re-establish communications as he could do nothing while he was blind to what was going on at the Farm. He sat down and took a gulp of the coffee to centre his thoughts.

After a couple of minutes, he was more composed. Opening his office door, he headed back to the monitors.

The monitors were displaying the view being transmitted from the plane's external cameras. As the ground below passed by, time seemed to pass slowly but he needed to know what was going on.

Suddenly over the speakers came Dennis's voice. "Hello command centre, this is assault force, over."

Sparked into action, Will launched himself at the nearest handset and keyed the mike. "Hello assault force, this is command centre. Give me an update – now!"

"Hello command centre, we have left the Farm," Dennis said. "We have killed everyone there, torched the buildings and left before the rebels arrived."

Will visibly relaxed, his shoulders dropping. The first part of the plan was working. His troops had carried out their part of the assault and had escaped before the larger rebel force had arrived. If they'd stayed, they could have inflicted some casualties on the rebels but that wasn't the plan.

His convoy was heading back to the border while the planes were going to complete their task at the Farm. All Will wanted was for the rebels to arrive before the bombers dropped their cargo and he could have a total success.

The next ten minutes were excruciating for Will. He was constantly looking at the monitors, hoping to see the Farm's buildings. Through intelligence gathered from previous aerial passes of the Farm, he knew what the area immediately around it looked like from the air. Unfortunately that wasn't enough information for him to identify how close the planes were now.

The planes were flying at 30,000 feet. He could still see some of the ground below but very little movement.

"Hello, Red dog, this is Blue dog. Five minutes out, starting descent, over."

"Red dog, right behind you, over."

"Blue dog, weapons hot."

"Red dog, weapons hot."

For the next few minutes, Will's eyes were glued to the monitor. On the ground below he could see some people moving like ants. It was hard to distinguish numbers but he did know that his troops had left no one there alive. The people on the monitors were clearly the rebel forces. He thought this was going to be a very good day. His plan was working perfectly.

He expected the rebels to arrive and find the buildings burning. Although they might approach carefully, they would hope to save some of the bodies. They wouldn't know that an aerial assault was imminent.

They would likely aim to fortify the Farm in case his troops came back. How wrong they were!

"Blue dog, bombs away, over."

Red dog, bombs away, out."

The planes were approaching lower than they did at the compound. They had no markers on the ground here to hit specific buildings. These bombs were designed to destroy the maximum area, leaving no crops or other resources behind and denying the rebels anything that they might use for the winter.

He could see movement more clearly now —these were definitely people, not animals. Suddenly the first bomb impacted from the rear. The image switched to the rear cameras on the plane. As it flew away, the whole screen was consumed by the flames. The bombs landed one after the other. Initially he could make out separate balls of flames; within seconds, the whole area was one large inferno as the flames joined together. It was like watching a river flowing across the land, a river of fire.

The planes made one last circuit, following the mission plan. Within the boundaries of the Farm, all that could be seen from the cameras were flames and blackened earth.

"Red dog, this is Blue dog. Heading home, over."

"Blue dog, this is Red dog. Right behind you, out."

With that, the mission was over. Will took a moment to analyse what he had just seen. Through his decisive actions on hearing that some of the rebels had escaped the compound, he had diverted his troops with perfect timing. His troops had completed their mission and left before the rebels arrived. Springing the trap, the planes had destroyed the Farm and with it the remaining rebels.

Of over six hundred rebels initially at the compound, he had destroyed half of them with the compound and now the other half with the fuel bombs. This was a good day for Will, a very good day. He was looking forward to briefing Brand.

His only concern was that he had no confirmation on the number of survivors. He could have turned his troops around en route to the border and get their confirmation that there were no survivors. Fuel was a consideration here as he was unsure how much his troops had, even though the plan was to refuel with the Farm biofuel. If they were close to the border, sending them back seemed like a waste of resources.

He grabbed the radio handset again. "Hello, assault force, this is command centre, over."

"Command centre, send, over."

"Do you have enough fuel to go back to the Farm, estimate the damage and still return to the border, over?"

"Command centre, say again, over?"

"Do you have enough fuel to go back to the Farm, ensure that there were no survivors and still drive to the border, over?"

"The biofuel at the Farm isn't running too well in our vehicles so it is doubtful we can do that. Is that our next mission? Over."

Will thought for a split second of Brand's earlier words about stealing defeat from the jaws of victory. "No, head straight to the border, confirm this order: head straight back to the border."

Of course, Will was gambling that the mission had been completely successful. Brand would ask if there had been any survivors and he needed a plausible answer. The option to send his troops back to the Farm to confirm success was one of his considerations when he had revised his plan and despatched them to the Farm early. That part of the plan had depended on the biofuel and had failed.

Judging by his earlier encounter, it was clear that Brand only wanted to know about total successes. Any variables would just make Brand angry so Will determined on the story he would tell. He decided to wait at least an hour so that he could practise his brief. He needed to ensure he was prepared for any questions.

Brand's first question would be, "Did you get them all?" and his second, "Can you confirm this?" Will had to provide an answer that would also allow him some flexibility should any of the rebels have escaped. The key was to divulge a few minor escapees, without seeming incompetent. A dozen survivors out of over three hundred seemed like a reasonable number so that was what he settled on.

If Brand's spies heard of people escaping the assault, he had not lied. If he told Brand that everyone was killed and it turned out just one person had escaped, Brand would catch him out for lying and that could cost him his life.

35

DEBS AND PEPPER ARRIVE AT
THE FARM

12 September 2202

Debs had met up with one of the scouts above the Farm. The other two convoys were also stationed outside the Farm, waiting for orders. They had all been briefed on their staging points and had stopped as planned.

Debs' first question was, "Has the Company left?"

"Yes," the scout said. "From our vantage point, it looked like all the surviving Company troops drove away, heading north."

"Have you heard from the other scouts?" Debs asked.

"Yes, they all reported the same news from their locations. Between us, we estimate that they had between a hundred and a hundred and twenty troops when they left. It was hard to get an exact number because we were all viewing from different directions."

The news of the Company's departure was better than Debs had expected. As they had already left, her plan for the ground assault was no longer needed. That was an advantage. However well prepared the rebels were, if she had needed to attack the Farm, she would have lost some fighters. As a good leader, she cared for her people. Another consideration was that with the recent Company attacks, skilled rebel fighters were becoming harder to find.

So now they would switch to Plan B. She had already briefed the convoy leaders at the last position. All she had to do was confirm the next move.

Debs grabbed the radio again. "Hello convoys two and three, we are going to Plan B. Do you understand? We're going to Plan B."

The radios squawked twice in succession. "Convoy two, understood, Plan B."

"Convoy three, understood, Plan B."

Debs nodded to her assistant Kegan and he left to brief their convoy.

Plan B was relatively simple. Thirty of her fighters would head north to shadow the Company convoy. She had despatched the vehicles with the most fuel so that they could travel the furthest but their orders were to only observe.

The main purpose for this tailing force was to locate the Company base. A bonus was that they would provide advance notice if the Company returned for a ground attack on the rebels. The other two convoys were each to send thirty troops to scout out the Farm.

Debs was suspicious that the Company may have set traps at the Farm. She wouldn't put it past them to booby-trap the bodies and there was no telling what other surprises were waiting for the rebels.

The two groups of thirty fighters would approach

the burning farm buildings at intervals. They were not just searching for traps but also looking out for any Company troops that may have been left behind on a suicide mission. A secondary mission was to check for any friendly forces who had survived the executions, but this was only a long shot.

Debs had heard stories about how, days after a mass execution, somebody had crawled out from underneath a pile of corpses. All life was valuable to the rebels and even one survivor would be a bonus.

It took around fifteen minutes for the scouts to form up, ready to enter the Farm. "Convoy two scouts you are good to deploy," Debs said over the radio.

"Convoy two, deploying scouts now."

Debs's plan was to stagger the advance. Sending in all sixty scouts could provide superior numbers for an attack in an open field. The problem was that if the Company had left traps or even suicide snipers behind, the more rebels she deployed, the more targets that she would be providing.

The first scouts reached the farm buildings unhindered, without a single explosion or a shot fired. Instead, an eerie calm hung over the area.

"Hello, Convoy three, you can now deploy your people," Debs said.

"Convoy three, deploying scouts now."

The first group had crawled quite a bit, looking for cover while they searched for potential hazards at the same time.

Although still cautious, the second group approached a little faster, walking in tactical formation, as they headed to the smouldering buildings.

The first group had already checked all of the bodies. "Any survivors?" Debs asked over the radio.

Convoy two's scout leader stated gravely, "No, sorry, everyone is dead."

It still seemed crazy to Debs that the Company had destroyed the buildings, killed the people and left all the valuable resources intact. Of course, potentially they had deployed poison or something. The good news was that it looked like the Farm had enough resources for them to survive the winter.

Debs was preparing to give those remaining in the convoys the order to move in on the Farm. She had planned to stagger their approaches so that each one could set up a defensive position before the next convoy moved in. The last convoy would remain ready to provide a rear guard, giving the others more time to fortify. There was still a chance that the Company convoy would return unexpectedly.

But then she heard a droning sound from above. Although she didn't fully recognise the sound, considering the warning of an aerial attack on the compound, it seemed obvious what they were and that the Farm was the next target. Was this part of the plan? The Company had baited the Farm and was now about to bomb it, hoping to catch as many of the rebels in the bombardment as it could. Somehow it knew that her convoys had headed to the Farm and they had planned for this occasion. She didn't know how many planes were coming or how many bombs they carried but she hoped that the wide-open spaces would favour her people.

She quickly got on the radio. "Hello, all troops on the ground, all troops on the ground, this is Debs, we have bombers incoming, I say again, we have bombers incoming. Get away from the buildings, get away from the buildings, and get into the fields. If anyone is close to the tree line, get into the woods. Get under cover now!"

From her vantage point, she could see the fighters below. Jolted into action, fighters were running in every direction, trying to find any modicum of cover. She expected shrapnel bombs to finish off the buildings. Why they would waste munitions on this was unclear – the fires had already done most of the damage. Perhaps they were trying to deprive the rebels of a foundation for rebuilding.

Whatever their strategy, she needed to get everyone to cover. "Convoys two and three, if any vehicles are not under cover, move them now," Debs shouted into the handset. "Camouflage as best you can, take cover, we do not know what is coming. Do you hear me, over?" She was talking fast, barely breathing.

"Convoy two leader, message received, all under control."

"Convoy three leader, received all messages and understood, enacting now."

At the same time as Debs was on the radio, she was directing her immediate forces. As soon as she released the button on the radio, she shouted frantically, "Disperse the vehicles, and get them under cover."

Luckily most of the vehicles had remained back in the cover, but a few command vehicles were together out in the open. The drivers quickly gunned their engines and darted under the trees.

The droning got louder and louder, like a huge swarm of bees. Suddenly a new sound, a whistling sound, started up. Debs had an ominous feeling in the pit of her stomach. More whistling followed.

Eric looked visibly shaken: he had heard bombs before and they always brought death. Seeing his fear, Debs said, "Although these bombs may do some damage, the wide-open spaces will limit it. Our fighters are spread out and we will survive this."

She wasn't prepared for what happened next. The first bomb hit, exploding into a fireball near the house. The already smouldering buildings now became enveloped in an inferno.

Debs reacted instinctively. Grabbing the radio, she shouted, "Get out of the fields." It was now obvious to her that the targets were the valuable crops, but her fighters were in grave danger. "They are using firebombs. Get under water. If you are near any river or water races, submerge yourself. Do not stay in the open fields, I repeat, do not stay in the fields – try to reach the woods."

The heat was suddenly unbearable, the effects devastating. People weren't merely running around burning – it seemed as though they melted where they stood.

The two planes flew side by side, leaving a line of devastation behind them. When the fire trail reached the woods, they too exploded. Even being wet from the autumn rain was not enough to protect the trees or the troops they were sheltering against these hell bombs. The fire raged on seemingly unhindered and the flames spread rapidly through the whole Farm area.

Debs had considered ordering her fighters to open fire at the bombers but they had not had time to deploy heavy weaponry. Any attempt to damage the planes with small arms would just draw attention to themselves. After the planes' first bombing run, they circled round for another pass.

She launched herself back into the truck to grab the radio handset. "Anybody who's not undercover, take cover now and then do not move. They're looking for survivors. Do not make yourself a target." With that, she crawled away from the vehicle in case it was the next target.

The planes seemed to be mainly concerned with surveying their success, however. Before long they headed off northwards.

Debs was devastated. She had sent her people into the fields, making them easy fodder for the fire. The flames had taken over sixty good fighters. All of the scouts around the buildings were gone plus some other fighters who had been waiting to deploy in the woods. Frank had trained her to expect losses during fighting but this wasn't fighting, it was a massacre. Just plain murder.

After she was sure that the planes were not returning and the fires had left nothing but a scorched piece of earth, Debs decide to make her move.

She called on the other convoy leaders to come to her location. They had to discuss their limited options. Their initial plans had literally just gone up in smoke and she needed to take control and lead the shocked survivors.

36

DEBS BRIEFS THE REBELS FOR THE JOURNEY NORTH

12 September 2202

The mood in the clearing was sombre as Debs prepared to address the convoy leaders. They sat on their packs, waiting for her to speak.

Slowly and deliberately she began. "It is clear that we cannot stay here. The Company knows of this location. Even if we were to rebuild and fortify it, they could just as easily return and in a few minutes burn this place to the ground. Before today, I had never seen bombs that could create such devastation. I have now and we need to take them seriously."

Pepper watched the leader of Convoy two get to his feet. He was older than Debs and quite a bit taller. "What can we do? Where can we go?"

"That's a good question, Cenk, and I'm just about to explain," Debs said impatiently. "Before we left the compound, I had a long discussion with Frank. We talked about our options and discussed worst case scenarios. Most of the plans involved fighting the Company for the resources at the Farm. If the worst happened, he trusted me to think on my feet. I believe you'll all agree, we've reached the worst case scenario."

"Clearly no resources are left here, so what do you suggest?" Cenk asked in a challenging tone.

"Before I explain my plan, let's take stock of our situation. How many fighters do you have left?" she asked the convoy leaders.

"I have seventy-six people alive, of whom twenty are badly injured," Cenk stated coldly.

"I have eighty people left alive. Eight of them are badly injured and another five in critical condition," replied Lacey, the leader of Convoy three.

"With my eighty remaining troops, that brings us to a total of two hundred and twenty fighters capable of fighting and twenty-five injured. And before anyone speaks, I have not forgotten that we have lost over sixty of our brothers and sisters today!" Debs let those numbers sink in.

"We will head north and meet up with our scouts that are trailing the Company convoy. We will follow the convoy to its base and plunder it for its resources. My plan is simple but is not without risk so I am open to any other reasonable suggestions."

Debs had only just finished when Cenk countered. "So to clarify, your plan is to follow a heavily armed convoy belonging to the Company, which has just defeated us, and attack it in its own base?" he said incredulously. "Why not head back to the compound?"

Debs was prepared for this suggestion. "We left the compound because we had intelligence of proposed attacks on both the compound and the Farm. The attack on the Farm supports our intelligence, so the compound is believed lost. Frank and I discussed the option of returning to the compound after an attack and he believed that the risk of returning to an ambush was too high. As with this location, if the Company is aware of the compound, it is not safe. The convoy will not expect us to follow them though. They will expect us to cower under rocks. We will surprise them. We will go on the offensive." Debs' voice, which had been gradually getting louder, was resolute as she finished.

"The reason they don't expect this plan is because it's a crazy plan!" Cenk said. "It's suicide to attack their base. They are better armed and better supplied."

"With the addition of the scouts ahead and the element of surprise, we have a better chance there than staying here and starving. Once Frank knows what has happened here, he will also head north to bolster our numbers."

"Why don't we wait for Frank to come here?" Cenk asked.

Debs was hesitant to identify Flo as an intelligence source but needed to convince them to follow her. "The intelligence that warned Frank of the attacks will have updated him on our situation. I cannot divulge Frank's sources as the Company has spies everywhere, but I think we can all agree, the intelligence has been reliable."

Cenk murmured under his breath but didn't say anything further out loud.

"We will leave ten fighters from each convoy here to care for the injured. Although there are not enough resources for us all to survive, they should be able to scavenge enough for the smaller group. We will also leave any stores that we can spare for their immediate survival. We'll plan to return for them once we have more resources but a small group will make less of a target and they could survive even if we fail." Debs waited for any feedback but the group around her remained silent.

She continued, "I want you to go back and prepare your people. I have been in constant communication with our scouts and the convoy is still heading north. I am currently confident that we will not be heading into an ambush but want to head north before our scouts are too far away for our radios to reach. We will travel in the same convoys as when we came here. I will lead and then Cenk and Lacey will follow at thirty-minute intervals.

"Yes we want to avenge our losses but the main reason for the assault is to get the resources that will help us survive the winter. I want constant communication between our convoys."

"What about the chances of the Company intercepting our signals?" Lacey asked.

"I am prepared to risk that as I believe the risk is greater if our convoys are separated – we are a more powerful force if we consolidate our numbers. I realise that this is a desperate plan but our options are limited. This is your last chance. Has anyone got any better suggestions?"

Pepper looked around the group and noted that no one voiced any objections. He wondered how he had ended up here.

He was now part of a group of freedom fighters, where the dangers just kept on increasing. He longed for the simpler time, as a lone wolf, when he could hide in large groups. Blending in was a tactic he had used time and time again to escape the Company. It was hard enough for someone of his size to avoid standing out, but this group of several hundred fighters that he now belonged to would be much more visible.

37

WILL BRIEFS BRAND ON THE ASSAULT ON THE FARM

12 September 2202

This was the second time today that Will had stood in front of Brand. At least this time he felt he had better news.

"Have you news of complete success? Have you got good news for me or do I need to replace you with someone who can succeed?" Brand asked.

Will was cautious. Brand could be joking about replacing him. But the best way to survive with Brand was to treat nothing he said as a joke. Brand loved his own jokes, but they were his jokes and nobody else was allowed to take part in that comedy.

"We have successfully destroyed the Farm. The firebombs burned all of their resources, including food supplies. When the bombers arrived, the rebels that had escaped the compound were already at the Farm. I had the planes fly over for a final pass after the bombardment and the rebels that had been seen moving before the bombs were dropped, moved no more. There was no visible movement whatsoever from the planes." Will stopped as he could see Brand was about to respond.

"So you are telling me that not one rebel has survived? We have killed all of them, both at the compound and now at the Farm."

"I cannot lie," Will replied. "There may have been a negligible number of escapees. Maybe a dozen in total."

"You do well not to lie to me," Brand said, "because if I find you are lying to me, you will not be living much longer."

"I value your trust in me," said Will, "and that is why I am being honest. In such a large area, the odd person may have avoided detection from the air. The firebombs did exactly what we expected of them. The burning buildings and the bodies of the Farm residents drew the rebels into our killing zone. The firebombs finished off the buildings and everybody in those fields would have been turned to ash. Those bombs create so much heat that it can melt steel girders. Blood and bone stand no chance against that heat."

"I suppose you expect some kind of reward, some kind of congratulations for doing your job?" Brand said briskly.

"No sir. I serve at your pleasure. I just wanted to ensure that you received a report of the results of the assaults in person and in a timely manner."

"As soon as you knew that the results of the assaults were successful," Brand said with a wry smile. "That's okay, I appreciate that you are bringing me good news for a change. For this, you don't just get to live another day. As a display of my trust, I have another task for you. Captain Smit seems to be having some trouble controlling the Norms living in the capital. Riots and disturbances are becoming more and more frequent. I realise that policing is not the best use for your particular talents so I am tasking you to evaluate Smit. I have told Smit that some of your elite forces will be supplementing his security forces around the capital."

Will took this in. "As you wish."

"Your men will be primarily protecting the council buildings but you will personally observe Smit as he carries out his other tasks. You will spend a couple days with him and will then report back to me with suggestions on how we can improve matters. Look at his subordinates and let me know if you think any of them could do a better job. I am not prepared to throw resources at Smit if he is going to waste them.

"The masses are not a real physical threat to the elite. However, incompetency such as Smit is displaying could make matters worse and impact on their revenue streams. None of the council leaders would defy me openly, but any opening in which they can feel emboldened could inconvenience me. As you are aware, William, I do not like to be inconvenienced."

"I will task two of my troops to immediately bolster the guards in the council buildings. At the same time, another troop will be tasked to accompany me with Captain Smit, giving me oversight and also ensuring that I do not meet some kind of freak accident."

"Yes," Brand said. "Take precautions. Smit may be incompetent but he is not stupid. He will see you as a threat and, like any cornered animal that is when he is at his most dangerous. He won't openly shoot one of my representatives but if a simple accident were to befall you, he would get rid of the oversight that you are providing and blame you for your incompetence. And by proxy he would try to push back and blame me".

"My troops are loyal to you, sir," Will replied. "They will be briefed on the potential threat from Smit and he will not be given any opportunity to hurt you or myself."

"Good to hear. I'm glad we are on the same wavelength at last. I require an update from you in three days – that's seventy-two hours. Do you understand?"

"I will have my first recommendations for you within seventy-two hours," Will stated. It wasn't long but for once Brand seemed in a good mood and this was not the time to sour it.

"Just to show you that I do reward loyalty, I have a gift for you." Brand gestured towards a female assistant. This was a different woman from Will's earlier visit. She wore the same plain robe but had a much curvier body and filled it out well. "You will be starting the task tomorrow morning but tonight, as a reward for today's success, you have the company of Lola. Lola, you belong to William for the evening. Do whatever he says and I will see you back here tomorrow evening," Brand said casually to the woman.

"Thank you for your generosity, sir," Will said as he exited the office with Lola.

Will knew there was always subterfuge in Brand's decisions. To anyone else, this might seem like he was being given a simple reward of a woman to use for sex. But everybody Brand employed spied for him. Will would have to be cautious in taking Lola to his quarters. He wasn't stupid enough to have anything incriminating left out in the open but anything could be misconstrued and lead to his demotion or execution.

He was aware of the possibility of being drugged by

such a tantalising companion. He would be sure to pour and monitor any drinks that they consumed and before he retired to go to sleep he would get Lola escorted from his apartment. He didn't believe he spoke in his sleep – he had recorded himself sleeping on several occasions to verify this – but one could never be sure what minor piece of evidence could incriminate you.

Of course, Will wasn't plotting against Brand but in order to survive in the political environment of the capital, he had to keep some secrets. Information is power and, because of his proximity to Brand, he was sometimes rewarded for favours from the other council members.

Currently nobody had the power to rise against Brand but if at any stage one of them saw weakness, and an opportunity to take down Brand, this would put Will in danger.

Hedging his bets was a very dangerous game to play, but the capital was also a very dangerous environment. It was not just dangerous for the poor, who were treated like cattle and fed to each other. It was also dangerous for any elite who displayed weakness. All of the other elites were like vultures looking for the next carcass.

38

DEBS' CONVOYS HEAD FOR THE BORDER

16 September 2202

Debs and her convoys had been following the scouts, who had been following the Company forces for the last three days. They had maintained a safe distance from the scouts while remaining in radio contact.

The radio began to squawk. "Hello, Convoy one, this is Forager."

Debs grabbed the handset. "Hello, Forager, this is Convoy one. Send your message."

"The Company forces have disappeared. I say again, the Company forces have disappeared."

"Please confirm: have you lost contact or have you lost the Company forces?" Debs asked.

"We have arrived at the toxic wastelands and there is no sign of them. Do you want us to continue into the wastelands?" The scout's voice wavered.

After quickly analysing this information, Debs issued

her orders. "Find cover and wait for us to reach your location. Do you understand?"

"Message received and understood. We are still on the same road so just continue to head north and you will see us."

"We will be with you in approximately thirty minutes," Debs said. She'd heard of the toxic wastelands before. Supposedly it was a remnant of the Water Wars, the old border area between what had been the two countries of Canada and the USA, now scarred by nuclear and chemical fallout.

If the Company forces had disappeared in this area, they may have taken a safe passage she was unaware of. Until she had a chance to observe this for herself, she was not going to put her scouts in harm's way. Having determined her next moves, she had to brief the other convoys.

"Hello Convoy two, this is Convoy one."

"This is Convoy two, send your message."

"Convoy two, I am heading for a rendezvous with our scouts, I need you to halt at the next safe location you find, take cover and wait for my message. Do you understand?"

"Loud and clear, we will find cover and wait for your call," Cenk replied.

"Thank you, stay safe and we will talk soon."

Debs next called Convoy three with an almost identical message to Lacey.

Lacey, having listened to her conversation with Cenk, had already begun searching for a safe location to park his fighters.

"We're just coming to a halt now," Lacey told her.

"Thank you, stay safe and we will talk soon."

Debs pondered that it was fortunate that she thrived on a challenge. Every time she thought she had prepared for the next eventuality, things changed. She looked around at the other occupants in the vehicle. Eric was asleep but Pepper was listening intently.

"What's this toxic wasteland?" Pepper asked.

"It's a place that was destroyed during the Water Wars. It's said that this area used to be a border between the two countries of Canada and the United States of America. It was bombed from both sides to stop their opponents using it as a staging post for attacks. Any plants and wildlife that live there are deformed or toxic."

"I have to admit that I've never been this far north before. Not even when I was a Company trainee," Pepper said unguardedly.

"You were a Company trainee?" Debs asked suspiciously.

"I was with the Company but then they decided that they preferred me dead. As I preferred me alive, I decided that we should part ways," Pepper said with a smile.

Debs seemed to accept this on the surface but still eyed him with some wariness.

"It's strange," Pepper said. "We are supposedly heading to a toxic wasteland, yet the wildlife and the vegetation seem a lot more vibrant the further north that we go.

"I know," Debs agreed. "It is a bit of a conundrum. I've noticed some birds overhead and the headlights have reflected off the eyes of several critters during our night drives. Why would there be more wildlife heading to a wasteland than further south?"

"Maybe because fewer predators are up here?

Humans can't survive in the wastelands, but maybe smaller animals can?" Then he smiled. "So do you still want to go north?"

"I don't think we have much of a choice. Our resources are running low and we need to find out where the Company troops have gone. Hopefully we can still locate their trail and follow them."

"Hello Convoy one, this is Base one over." Debs was amazed to hear Frank's voice over the radio.

"Is that you Frank?" Debs blurted out without any thought of security.

The voice that came next seemed quite jovial. "Yes, yes it is I! We heard your messages a while back but for some reason you couldn't receive our transmissions."

"Where are you?" Debs asked.

"It seems like we're heading to the same location as you."

"I have so many questions but that can wait until we meet. For now, where will we rendezvous?"

Frank was cautious as he understood that this channel could be monitored by the Company but the main thing was that they were alive. "We have no maps but we have intelligence and if you are heading on the main north road, we'll meet you at the border. As we get closer, I'll contact the scouts if I need further directions."

"Okay, see you soon." Debs was elated. Although she had competently taken on the role of leader, it was reassuring to know that she would have Frank's support going forward.

Even Pepper seemed to perk up. "Wasn't that a nice surprise? It seems they weren't all killed at the compound."

"I wonder how many of our people survived," Debs said more solemnly. "We'll have to wait and see. It's not safe to pass that kind of information over the radio but at least we know that we have some back-up on the way."

Eric had been listening quietly to the exchanges. "Ask him about Flo. Is she okay?"

"We need to restrict chatter over the radio, we'll see them soon," Debs countered.

Eric didn't reply but it was obvious from the way his shoulders sank and the look on his face that he wasn't satisfied with the delay.

The rendezvous was set but Frank left the bulk of his people under cover along the route. He had them prepare two defensive positions in case they had to suddenly retreat. Not knowing what they were heading into, it was nice to have his own back-up plan, should they suddenly be pursued by a Company convoy.

This plan was okay to take on a ground assault but it was hard to fight death from above.

At the clearing, the wheels on Frank's Jeep had hardly stopped turning before Eric came bounding forwards. He yanked open the door and threw his arms around Flo.

"Are you okay? Are you hurt? How are you?" Eric said, like a mother worrying over her child.

"I'm fine," Flo said. "But you're crushing me." Eric realised then that he was exerting a little too much pressure. He eased off slightly but still held her close.

Behind Eric, Debs and Pepper were walking towards the vehicle at a more rational pace.

"Well hello there," Pepper said to Frank. "You are looking well for a dead man."

"I could say the same about you," Frank said. "Rumours of my death have always been an exaggeration."

Trying to seem unemotional, Debs held out her hand, but Frank clasped his arms around her tightly. Their eyes locked and they both felt her relief as she handed back the leadership role.

"You have done well, young lady." Frank knew that Debs had stepped up but he was still her mentor and was determined to provide her some comfort. After a few moments of silence and reflection, it was time to take control. "How many of our people survived?"

"We lost over sixty at the Farm. They dropped some kind of firebombs. We didn't stand a chance: the fields were engulfed in flame and all of our scouts that had gone to try to help the others disappeared in a river of fire. It was awful." She was almost in tears.

"It wasn't your fault. Flo received info about the firebombs but too late to alert you. I could only hope that you would arrive after the bombs had been dropped. There was nothing we could have done. You managed to save some – how many?"

"I left thirty of our people at the Farm to tend to another twenty-five that were either injured or dying. They should be able to scavenge enough to survive if we don't return. I have a total of one hundred and ninety-five personnel spread over three convoys and another thirty scouts that we will rendezvous with here. How did you fare at the compound?"

"We were very fortunate. Most of our people were down in the tunnels, as we'd planned. We lost a few spotters because the planes came in too fast. A few minor injuries from small roof collapses but the underground caverns stood up pretty well. Flo told us that the farm had been lost, which is why we headed North instead of to the farm. I didn't want to put any further pressure on any limited resources you had left."

"I understand. You taught me that we have to remain flexible, which is why I ordered my fighters to follow the Company forces."

"So our combined strength is now over five hundred strong." Frank was relieved that so many had survived.

"I have about a third of my forces here and the rest waiting in two groups further south."

"Great minds think alike. I have the same configuration of our forces," he said smiling, proud of his protégé.

"The scouts were following the Company convoy at a safe distance yet, when they arrived here, they found no sign of the Company vehicles. It makes no sense."

Frank was looking out at the fences. "Considering that these fences and their warning signs are supposed to be very old, they appear well maintained. Does that seem right to you?"

Debs thought for a moment before replying, "No, it doesn't. Why would the Company have people risk exposure to the wastelands just to maintain warning signs?"

"Exactly," Frank said. "The Company doesn't care about the lives of the Norms and a pile of rotting bodies would be more of a deterrent than a few warning signs. No, something is not right here and I intend to find out what it is."

Frank remembered what Flo had told him: that this was all a façade. "This is all a lie. The Company wants us to think that this is dangerous but in reality, this is just a smokescreen. Flo has intelligence that the Company regularly fuel-bombs this area to make it look more devastated. At the other side of those hills are stockpiles of resources. There is a border post so it has security but with our numbers we should have the advantage."

Ever the pragmatist, Pepper did not hold back. "Hold on a minute. We are looking at a burnt, desolate landscape. The only things surviving out there are warning signs, telling us if we go any further, it's at our own risk. Telling us it is toxic and our chances of survival are next to zero. The signs are pretty explicit:

CONTAMINATED LAND! ANYBODY PASSING THESE SIGNS DOES SO AT THEIR OWN RISK. YOU HAVE BEEN WARNED. NOBODY WILL HELP YOU WHEN YOU DIE IN THIS WASTELAND.

Doesn't sound very friendly."

"It's not designed to be," Frank said. "The idea is to scare off the uninformed, but we are informed and we have intelligence, don't we Flo?"

"I agree that we have trusted her intelligence so far, but this a big leap of faith. To suddenly head out into a toxic wasteland, in the hope that we can find a battle at the other side, isn't my idea of safe."

"You don't have to come with us," Frank said. "However, there will be no reward for you if you don't." And with that he smiled.

Although Pepper tried to project a mercenary image, someone who only cared about himself, Frank felt that he was wearing Pepper down. He was starting to exhibit more empathy and humanity. There was even a chance that this was the early stage of a friendship.

Frank addressed Debs. "We need to get the rest of the convoy here. I want to have a discussion with our leaders and all of our people. If they are to risk their lives, they need to know exactly what risks are involved. I am not prepared to lead our people blindly into the wastelands. We are perhaps the largest rebel force in this kingdom. The Company has recently been wiping out our brethren and if it was to wipe us out too, it would be a large blow to the Norms."

"I'll go spread the message," Debs said.

"We'll convene here again in two hours," Frank said.

39

THE SUMMONING OF SMIT

16 September 2202

Smit had been standing in Brand's office for over ten minutes. Since the moment that the scantily clad woman had escorted him to stand in the far corner of the room, Brand hadn't even acknowledged his presence. He felt like a recruit at the Academy being called to the commander's office.

The security detail outside had thoroughly searched him. He had been forced to strip to his underwear and he'd not even been allowed to keep his wristwatch. He felt vulnerable and, after recent events, he knew this meeting was not going to be a congratulatory one.

Brand was reading through William's report. Even though William had briefed him in person the day before, he always demanded a written report. He was glad that as usual this one was well written and detailed. It was apparent that Smit's troops were loyal to him, which is why William had not replaced him in front of them.

Will had arrived to report on Smit shortly after the recent riot. Even though Smit had lost soldiers in the riots, those who did survive attributed their survival to him. This was why they remained loyal to him.

It was clear that Smit had lost control over the Sanctuary's security. The current unrest in the Norm classes was reaching boiling point. It was not lost on Brand that this was mainly the fault of the elites. The amount of profiteering brought about by their greed amazed even him. Restricting food supplies so the black market price would rise might have initially been a profitable strategy but they had pushed it too far.

Starving people were harder to control if you didn't feed them occasionally. He would have to address this at the next council meeting, but for now he needed to portray strength. He couldn't let the rank and file of the Company troops know this was the elites' fault. He needed a scapegoat and he had chosen Smit.

He threw the report on the desk. "Captain Smit, come and stand on the red line in front of my desk."

Smit approached slowly, to avoid being perceived as making any sudden movements. He wasn't sure how much trouble he was in but his situation was clearly precarious. The last thing he wanted was to provide a reason for his own execution.

"I have summoned you here to explain yourself, Smit. It seems as though you have lost control of the capital. The recent riot at the distribution point is just one in a number of events that make me doubt your abilities. Do you remember the last time I summoned you?" Brand waited for a reply.

"Yes sir."

"Good, then you will remember that it was to discuss

your inability to stop some of my valuable soldiers being killed by rebels at a checkpoint. Because of your incompetence then, I had to send a message by killing some valuable pit warriors. I told you at the time that I expected to see improvements. Instead you have gotten worse! I like to think of myself as a fair man so before I decide on your fate, I'm going to let you give me a reason for not having you immediately taken out of this room and straight to the gel plants for processing. Do you understand the gravity of your situation?"

Smit felt sick to his stomach. During the previous riots, he had seen his own troops ripped limb from limb. At one stage it seemed likely that the crowd would overwhelm his location and also tear him and his surviving troops apart. He had felt less scared then than he did now.

His fate might depend on his next few words. There was every chance that Brand had already made a decision, but if Smit had any chance of saving his own hide he needed to do it now.

"You will see from my report on the riots that some of my troops did not follow their orders. The troops near the gel distribution tables pre-empted their orders and they paid the ultimate price. Their commanders on the ground survived and I punished them immediately. After the riots, they were sent straight to the gel plants, as an example to the rest of the troops."

Brand picked up another sheaf of papers from his desk and brandished them at Smit "Yes, I read your report. Although I have been known to read fiction for distraction, this is not the kind of fiction that I enjoy. According to your report, your failures are due not to your incompetence but to that of your soldiers! I am a firm believer in accountability but if your soldiers are at fault, this brings up the question of leadership. Do you not believe that a leader is responsible for the actions of his troops? As you punished some of your own troops for the actions of their subordinates, surely I should punish you for their actions?"

Sweat was running down Smit's face even though he was wearing very little and it wasn't overly hot in the office. He was trying to think fast while keeping his eyes on the leader. Brand held the arm of his chair with one hand while the other was still brandishing the sheaf of papers.

"I have served the Company well for the last fifteen years," Smit said. "I have no family, no partner, my whole life has been devoted to the service of the Company."

Brand immediately pounced on his words. "So what you're saying is that you have had no distractions. Which means you have no excuse for your incompetence. If you had stood here and told me that you had a wife who had just died in labour, leaving you to bring up six children alone or any of the feeble excuses that people usually try to use as mitigation, you may have stirred up some sympathy. But what you're telling me is you have no excuses and you are no longer of any use to the Company."

A lump had formed in Smit's throat. He was finding it hard to talk but he realised if he didn't defend himself, his life would be forfeit straight away. "No sir, no sir, I am not saying that. The people are starving, they're becoming more and more desperate. If I had more resources, I could quell the uprising. We need to seek out the leaders of this uprising, and if I was given more troops, I believe I could do this." Smit was trying to formulate a plan, any plan, just to stay alive.

Brand also noted that William's report identified issues with the potential uprising – that somebody seemed to be agitating the crowd and escalating the unrest. For the moment, this didn't matter. Smit had already been replaced in the time it had taken him to enter the council buildings. When Smit had been summoned, he had left his troops in William's hands.

In his turn, Will had installed his own soldiers in temporary control and had left Dennis in charge. He trusted Dennis, who had proven himself with his successful assault on the Farm. As a reward for his success, the moment his convoy cleared the wastelands he had been brought back to the capital by helicopter.

Smit hadn't noticed Brand pushing a discreet button in the armrest of his chair. So he was startled when the doors behind him opened and several armed men entered. The men lined up against two of the walls – three men either side of him, their weapons drawn.

Smit hoped that they would not shoot him straight away, not so much because he felt his life was worth anything but more because he thought Brand wouldn't want to mess up his office. Realising that he was out of options, he dropped to his knees and raised his arms in the air. "Please, sir, I have given my life to the Company. I know I can do better. Please just give me some more resources." Smit resorted to crying as his final option. He didn't expect sympathy from a man with Brand's reputation but he had no other choice.

"Please, please, I'm begging you. I know I can quell the rebellion. I just need some more manpower."

While he was whimpering on the floor, he noticed

the presence of someone else in the room. Standing nearby was one of his most trusted lieutenants, Jason – Jason River.

"Lieutenant River," Brand said.

River stood to attention. "Yes sir"

"I have some questions for you and I want you to think very carefully before you give me your answers. As Captain Smit's second-in-command, I believe you're the ideal person to answer these questions. Do you believe that Captain Smit is incompetent?"

River hadn't known why he'd been summoned to the supreme leader's office. But he did know anybody who entered this room was in danger. He had come prepared to do anything possible to leave the room alive. He decided to play for time. "Sorry sir, I do not understand the question."

"Well, that doesn't bode well," Brand said. "I had hoped that you had more potential than your boss. He seems to be incapable of maintaining the security of the Sanctuary and the capital. This was his only job, a job that he has held for some time. He has been happy enough to accept the benefits of the position. He has had more luxuries than most of the capital residents could even dream of. Do your troops trust you, River?"

"Yes sir." Surely that was the only answer that Brand expected. After fluffing the first question, he was determined not to make that mistake again.

"Let's start again. Your troops trust you. Do you trust Captain Smit? Is he a competent leader?"

River had to make a decision quickly. As much as he liked Smit, it looked like his leader was done for. For his own survival, River had to consider denouncing his boss. This was not personal, just survival.

"He has made some mistakes, sir."

"Honesty at last, I do like honesty. And what were these mistakes?"

Thinking frantically, River decided to focus on leadership. "His orders were not clear during the recent riots. We lost soldiers and, with better leadership, those soldiers might still be alive."

He was hoping that he would get away with not having to provide too many details on the riots. He assumed Brand had already been briefed. He wished that this would all be over soon. If he could just talk himself out of the situation now, he might live another day.

"So you do think that your boss is incompetent – that's fine, as I agree. If you were to be promoted and replace your previous boss, do you think you could do the job more competently? Think carefully before you answer."

River realised that his boss was lost. The supreme leader had clearly written him off. The only question now was: would River's words save him or seal him to the same fate as Smit's? His survival instincts kicked in. "Yes sir, I know that I have the experience to progress. I believe I deserve a promotion and I know that I can learn from Captain Smit's mistakes."

Brand enjoyed seeing people squirm and suffer – it was one of his main pleasures. He nodded to the armed men and they all raised their weapons, aiming at both River and Smit. "I'm a man who believes in loyalty, River, and what you have just said concerns me. It seems that you do not have any loyalty to your boss. I'm sure you'll agree that is rather disturbing. How do I know that, once you leave this office, you will be loyal to me? I need to see something to show me your allegiance is not with your previous boss but with the security of the Company. Is it?"

Seizing on what he thought was an opportunity, River replied, "Yes, I am loyal to the Company."

"You and I have both decided Smit is no longer worthy of your loyalty or the Company." Brand looked River in the eye. "Are you willing to prove your loyalty?"

There was no going back now. "Yes, I will do whatever it takes."

"I like that, I like that we have something in common. We are both prepared to do whatever it takes. Something Captain Smit was not. What have you done to contribute to the Company?"

Not knowing where Brand was going but realising he needed to provide an answer, River blurted out, "I have performed well in the Company sports teams."

"Not really what I had in mind." Brand grabbed the knife that was sitting on his desk and tossed it to River. Although the move was unexpected, River managed to catch it without losing any of his fingers. Now that he was in possession of a weapon, all of the soldiers aimed their weapons at him. Each one of them had their finger poised on the trigger. To a man, they knew that if anything happened to the supreme leader, they would be dead before the end of the day.

"Time for you to prove your loyalty. I have just given you a knife. If you want to take over from Captain Smit, I need you to dispose of him."

A shocked look came over River's face – although not as stark as the pain that Smit's face now showed. No longer grovelling to Brand, Smit turned his attention to

River. He was still on his knees with tears streaming down his face.

"River, have I not treat you well? You know I am not a bad person. Please don't do this, don't do this."

They were his last words. Without further hesitation. River plunged the knife deep into Smit's throat before withdrawing it just as quickly. A gurgling sound followed and the blood began to gush through Smit's fingers as he grabbed for his throat.

"Excellent. Now throw the knife on the floor, over there." Brand said pointing to the left-hand corner of the room next to one of the soldiers.

River automatically followed instructions and tossed the knife away. The fact that River had obeyed his order without a second thought and killed his old boss to prove loyalty was not lost on Brand. It was best that he didn't retain his weapon.

Abruptly, Smit stopped twitching. Although most of his blood now covered the wooden floor, the floor had several layers of varnish. Once the body had been removed, the cleaning crew would make the floor seem good as new in a very short time. This was not the first time somebody had been killed in this office.

"Well, River, I'm glad to say you have passed today's test. You are now the leader of the internal security for the capital and the whole of the Sanctuary. When you return to your new office, you will find Mr Spears is keeping your seat warm. Mr Spears works for William, who you will have no doubt noticed accompanying Captain Smit for the last few days. I expect a seamless handover. Here are the written orders for you to give to Mr Spears. You can choose your own subordinates.

Spears was one of those who suggested you for the promotion so ensure you treat him well."

Brand had prepared two sets of orders for Spears. The first set, which he had just handed over, was to tell Spears that River was now in charge and that Spears and his troops no longer needed to stay as Sanctuary guards. They could return to their usual duties.

He had created the second set of orders in case things hadn't worked out as he anticipated. If he had needed to kill both Smit and River, these orders would inform Spears that he was to consolidate his position and, until further notice, to keep the position of Sanctuary security leader.

"Well, Captain River, I'm sure you have lots to do in your new role. Go away and do it but be aware that next time you are in this office, I expect you to bring me good news. Use whatever means necessary but I want this uprising quashed, do you understand that?"

Even though he was still in shock, River composed himself and stood to attention. Looking straight at the supreme leader, he said loudly, "Yes sir, I understand. I won't let you down."

"Good. Now get out."

River turned and left, trying to remain as composed as possible. After leaving Brand's office, he headed back to Smit's old office. He needed to come up with a plan fast. Word would get back to the troops that he had killed Smit. A lot of the soldiers liked Smit. River had to take charge – he needed people to be loyal to him. So he needed to spread the word of Smit's failures.

He would build on Brand's narrative that Smit was incompetent. It was Smit's fault that his troops had been killed at the food riots. Smit had been warned in advance. This story was coming straight out of his head but it seemed a reasonable explanation.

Nobody could prove or disprove what Smit knew in advance. River was going to make it about the soldiers. Let them believe that it was to their benefit to get rid Smit.

He had decided that his first task was to pick the most violent men and form them into a squad, a death squad that would instil fear in the population. Brand wanted results and River was going to give him results. He didn't have Smit's leadership experience but he definitely had a violent streak.

River assumed that the fear he had felt in Brand's office was so strong that it would work on the masses. Although this might have been true in earlier times, the current climate indicated more brutality might actually infuriate the masses. If so, the resistance in their plan could stoke up revolution. This was a Lesson River would learn on another day.

"Get that out of my office." Brand pointed to Smith's carcass. "Take it down to the basement and put it on the next shuttle to the gel plants."

He had hardly finished talking when two cleaners entered with a tarpaulin. They rolled the body up and carried it out. Brand was already off to another appointment before the body had even left his office.

40

HEADING INTO THE WASTELANDS

16 September 2202

Frank had gained agreement from the convoy leaders. Even though Cenk was initially reticent, he seemed to realise this was the only option. The next step was to gather the forces. They had chosen a place close to the border with as much cover as possible. This would be the only time that they were all in the same place and at their most vulnerable.

But on this occasion Frank wanted all his people to hear the briefing. Now they were all gathered in front of him, while he stood on the top of a vehicle.

After an eerie quiet, he began in his deep voice. "Most of you have known me for some time. Some worked with me, some lived in the compound long term and some were just trading partners until the Company attacked.

"Since we learnt of the bombardment, some of you went to the Farm and we all experienced the devastation. Over the years we have all lost many friends

259

and colleagues at the hands of the Company, including in the recent attacks. I am grateful that you have trusted me with your safety so far."

He took a deep breath. "The next step on our journey is extremely dangerous and I want to ensure you all know the risks. It is my intention to follow the Company convoy into the wastelands. The signs say it is toxic but we have intelligence that this is all a façade designed to discourage people from going through." Looking around, he could see fear in some of their eyes but not one person was speaking.

"Our choices are limited. Winter is coming and the resources that we had stockpiled, both at the Farm and at the compound, are no longer an option. We have intelligence that lots of resources are on the other side of the wastelands. So far we have survived because of our intelligence and that is why I believe we should continue to rely on it. If it wasn't for this girl," he pointed to Flo, "coming to warn us of the Company attacks, most of us would not be here now." Frank let that sink in before continuing. "Some of you may not know that since our two convoys re-joined, she also detected that Pence was spying on us for the Company. It was he who told the Company that some of us were heading to the Farm. He was responsible for the deaths of our fellow fighters but he has passed his last message.

"I trust the intelligence that there are resources at our destination. I am also certain that without replenishing our current supplies, we will not make it through the winter. Attack is risky but if we run away, that is even riskier. I'm sure you will admit that it is a novelty to be the attackers instead of playing defence but we don't know exactly what is waiting for us. Our intelligence indicates that we have the greater numbers and we have the element of surprise. If anyone wants to opt out and turn around, that is your choice and you will not be judged. Before you make your decision, though, also consider that if you turn round now you will be deciding to spend the winter hunted by the Company, with no safe haven and no resources." Again Frank paused.

"If you choose to take on this challenge, we are going up against a well-armed enemy and I cannot guarantee we'll all survive. What I can guarantee is that I will be with you one hundred percent. I will be risking as much as you for our survival. If we relieve the Company of these resources, we should have enough to survive on through the winter. If we do not attempt this, we will not survive the winter. I have only one question for you all: who is with me?"

After a moment of quiet, almost as one, the men and women around him shouted, "I'm with you, I'm with you, I'm with you." It was a moving sight, even to Pepper. Any thoughts he'd had of abandoning these people were now gone. This display of trust from Frank's people went a long way to instil confidence in him.

Not one person was still, everyone was raising their fists in support. After the cheering had reached a crescendo, Frank signalled with his arms for quiet. Eventually silence again fell across the people. "I am humbled by your confidence in me. I will not let you down. Now that I know that this is what you want, we will implement the strategy. Go back to your vehicles and prepare. Your convoy commanders will be with you shortly to brief you. We are going to strike a deathly blow to the Company, we will get some revenge for our fallen friends and at the same time plunder resources to help us survive the winter. This is for our survival and we are survivors."

With that, Frank jumped off the back of the vehicle and hurried back to his own Jeep, keeping Flo close. Eric, Pepper and Debs followed.

The next few days were going to be busy. He had got as much information as he could and he felt confident that they had the element of surprise. Whoever their guardian was that was supplying the information to Flo, he hoped to get the chance to thank him some day.

41

THE ATTACK ON THE BORDER POST

18 September 2202

The graveyard shift was one of the hardest for the guards to stay alert for. Stretching between 1 and 4 am, it was late enough in the night so that you're shattered but too far away from morning for your body to be alert the next day. Marvin and Leo still had two hours left of their shift.

Very rarely did anything happen at this time of night on the border posts. If they were lucky, they got to see some jackrabbits having sex under the tower downlights, not that this was much of a distraction. Games like betting on how many rabbits they would see provided a slight break from the boredom.

The three-month tour on the border post always followed the same routine. In the 24-hour period of quick reaction force, they remained fully clothed in their gear, ready to deploy in five minutes. After that was a 24-hour period of enhanced readiness, where they needed to be ready to deploy within an hour. Those two periods alternated until, for just one 24-hour period every week, they were on a leisurely four-hour readiness to deploy – but that just never seemed to come round soon enough.

They were constantly tired from the physical activity on the day of reduced readiness and there was little to challenge the sentries on the border. The rough roads that they navigated during their patrols across the border point jarred your bones to increase fatigue without keeping you fully alert.

At 2.15 it was time for Leo to start the rotation. Whoever had come up with the brilliant idea of the sentry rotation clearly never had to do it themselves. Each of the ten sentry towers was manned by two sentries. The technique was that at fifteen minutes after each hour, one of each of the sentry pairs would leave their sentry tower and walk to the next one. It took approximately 30 minutes to walk between each tower.

The theory behind this rotation was that not only did it give them somebody on the ground as a roving patrol, it also prevented any pair of sentries from lying down in their tower and going to sleep.

Someone always seemed to be moving around and the constant requirement to reset your night vision (between roving out in the dark and manning a well-lit tower) made it hard to identify changes in the environment around the guard posts.

Leo had just got to the bottom of the guard tower ladder when he thought he heard something. Although the sentries were supposed to keep in contact by radio, it was rare to hear voices on any radio as the sadistic sergeant on that shift punished anybody he believed was messing around, making them run around the next day with a large log above their heads. Rather than risk becoming a victim of this punishment, Leo decided to have a look for himself to find out what the noise was.

The towers were situated in an arc. With this design, they didn't cover as much area as they would in a straight line but the area between the towers that the sentries patrolled was more evenly spaced.

Leo decided to continue on the arc while at the same time keeping alert for anything out of the ordinary. Within five minutes of leaving the base of his tower, he heard some rustling nearby. As he had not been provided with night-vision goggles and with only a small moon tonight, it was hard to discern shapes and the source of the rustling. He eventually realised that he had encountered two rabbits copulating and instinctively stopped to stare at them.

For this reason, Leo failed to notice Pepper's silent approach. In one clean motion, Pepper seized him from behind, clasped his hand over Leo's mouth and at the same time slit his throat. Leo emitted less noise than the thumping of the rabbits and nobody else noticed this confrontation.

This was not the first night that the rebels had observed the guard posts so they were well aware of the rotation of the sentries and timed the attack accordingly. At the same time as Pepper was dispatching Leo, Frank and several other rebels were ambushing the other sentries moving between the towers.

In the overcast night, the downlights of the towers still did not really help the sentries in the towers to distinguish between their comrades and potential enemies. The border post had never been attacked so the guards in the tower rarely glanced at the patrols.

As each of the sentries lifted the hatch to let their comrade into the tower, they were met with silenced pistols and dispatched quietly into the night.

Even in the quiet of the night, the silenced pistols emitted scarcely any noise, alerting no one to the fate of the sentries. All in all, the rebels took out a section of ten linked guard towers, leaving a gap in the defences for the several hundred rebels to pass through. No alarms were sounded.

Those manning the towers waited until the majority of their fellow rebels had passed through this gap. Then they followed, taking with them the radios from the sentries and any weaponry or other resources that they could strip from their bodies.

When the rebels came across the main guard compound, it was obvious that security there was an afterthought. The Company had been more worried about an attack from the Sanctuary side of the border than from the southern side. The bogus warning signs and other camouflage, designed to make the wastelands look dangerous and inhospitable, had served the Company so well that it had become complacent.

Around three hundred sentries were stationed about the border outpost – not a huge number but the Company believed that it was under little threat. A quick reaction force was also on standby to bolster those numbers via helicopter. It would be limited to the number of troops the helicopters could carry so effectively was more of an afterthought.

Taking out the communications was the first task. The rebels made short work of the antennae and satellite dishes, stopping communications to any potential assistance.

The only people awake at this time were the workers in kitchens and other support activities. Most of the soldiers were sound asleep in their beds and that is where most of them died.

The guard towers had been equipped with breathing apparatus and gas masks, along with gas canisters designed to use against any potential attackers. Pepper and the rebels had taken the masks and deployed the canisters against the compound.

The sleeping troops were oblivious to the release of the gas. Had this happened at a different time of day, they might have had the time to don their own gas masks and survive. The element of surprise favoured the rebels and the whole assault was over in less than an hour.

42

PREPARATIONS FOR THE FESTIVAL

21 September 2202

The aging ceremonies routinely happened every month but the festival towards the end of each year combined the coming winter months of aging ceremonies into one big event. This ritual had come about because the elites wanted to retire to their secure compound for the winter but did not want to miss out on the entertainment that attending ceremonies offered them. The days of the festival were also a chance to show off their finery.

It was little concern to the elites that by combining several ceremonies they were robbing some of the masses of months of their lives. Anyway, the extra fights they enjoyed as part of the festival were a way to placate the masses as well.

Winter seemed to arrive earlier each year, with the effect that the elites took longer and longer holidays at their secure compound hideaway away from the capital.

This year's festival was scheduled for the middle of October. That was only a month away.

Karla had to prepare for three days and three nights of fighting at the pits as well as the activities that she was working on for the resistance.

Angus had been giving her daily updates from the boy Zap. When she learnt of the rebels' successful assault on the border, she'd informed the other resistance leaders immediately. It had been only a few days since they had last met but already their initial plans were starting to take effect.

The extra food was getting through to the masses, emboldening them to strengthen their rebellion against the Company.

Stoking up the people was a great start but the extra rebel troops would help to do some real damage.

When Zap arrived for his daily workout, Angus brought him to Karla's office.

"Hello Zap. I just wanted to thank you for all the good work that you're doing. Have you spoken to your friend who is with the rebels today?" Karla asked.

"Yes, they are making good time on their way to the port."

"I want you to liaise with Angus and keep updating him. We will arrange for someone to rendezvous with the rebels when they reach the other side of the water. With your skills, you are the one person who can make this happen. This could be critical to our survival. Are you up to the task, young man?"

"I will keep communicating with them for as long as I can draw breath," Zap replied.

Karla lifted an eyebrow in the direction of Angus,

prompting him to comment, "He's a good lad and I trust him to do the right thing."

"I'm glad that you are committed to the cause and I will not hold you up any further. If there is anything at all that you need, tell Angus and we will do everything possible to get it for you."

"Thank you Karla. I realise that we are all in danger until this is finished and I won't let you down," Zap said.

With that, Karla dismissed them and moved on to more pressing matters.

The current plan was to launch the rebellion and the attacks on strategic targets in the days leading up to the festival. To hide this plan, however, Karla had to act as though the festival was going to take place.

She had over thirty fights to schedule as well as gel distribution, elite seating and all of the extra security precautions that an event like this required.

Already the volume of food delivered daily to the pits had increased to help build up the warriors ahead of the games. The extra food would continue to arrive right through the festival, when it would also be needed for the people attending.

The elites supplied this food as they wanted a good exhibition from the warriors. One added advantage this year was that if the rebellion did go ahead, the warriors would be able to fight against the Company instead of for it.

Keeping up the pretence that the festival was going to go ahead had another advantage. If the rebels failed and the festival went ahead, it would give Karla some plausible deniability of ever being involved. And then, of course, she would actually be prepared for the festival too.

43

ZAP IS SUMMONED TO BRAND'S OFFICE

25 September 2202

Zap had been around the council buildings before, but he had never been summoned to see the supreme leader.

Rumours were that when people went into his office, they never came out. These could have just been horror stories designed to scare people but, whenever anyone spoke of Brand, it was only in whispers.

Even the most senior people that Zap worked under seemed scared to talk about Brand. He knew Dick had visited Brand's residence on a technical callout and so he asked him what he was like.

It turned out that Dick had not met Brand in person on that callout. He said that Brand lived in a suite in the council buildings known as the big house. Even the surroundings of his home had been imposing and he got the impression that Brand was someone to be wary of.

With only this limited information, Zap found himself standing outside the supreme leader's office, waiting to be ushered in. For twenty minutes, he fidgeted and paced nervously, still wondering why he had been summoned. No matter how hard he tried, he couldn't come up with a harmless reason for him to be here today.

The only thought that comforted Zap was that, if the supreme leader suspected him of wrongdoing, the troops would have abducted him and taken him straight to the gel plants already. An early trip to the gel plants was the ultimate fear of most Sanctuary citizens. Stories of disappearances were increasing. Even innocent people went missing at all times of the day.

If the supreme leader wanted to see him, it could be a lot worse.

When the office doors finally opened, Zap was greeted by a young, good-looking woman, wearing nothing but a thin gown. He had seen good-looking women before but he was taken aback by her beauty as well as by her revealing clothing.

Expecting the security to be extremely tight, Zap was surprised he hadn't been searched yet. As he approached the doors, he lifted his arms, expecting a thorough body search. One of the guards seemed ready to begin the search before a taller guard shook his head at him. This was confusing because, even though he wasn't a threat, Zap hadn't expected such easy access to the supreme leader.

As hesitant as he was, he let the woman lead him into the huge office. At the far end was an enormous desk with a well-dressed man sitting in the only chair. The man was picking his fingernails with a large knife and smiling. This was unsettling. Zap hoped the smile was a good sign because he had never been so scared in all of his life.

He was having problems just walking behind the woman. Placing one foot in front of the other suddenly seemed alien to him.

The man stood up and put the knife on the desk and picked up a sheet of paper. "Come and sit," he said, while perusing the paper. "Ethan, is it? Or do you prefer to be called Zap?"

Zap was taken aback and unsure how to answer.

"Come on, speak up," the man said.

"My friends' call me Zap," he managed to stutter out.

"Well I assume you'd like to be my friend? So I'll call you Zap. My name's Brand but you can call me sir. Take a seat, Zap."

Zap did as he was told. Sitting in front of Brand, he suddenly realised that in his efforts to please his host, he hadn't noticed that they were alone. When had the woman left the office? Was there a different exit he hadn't noticed?

"You are probably wondering why you were summoned here?"

Zap was unsure how to answer this question. He didn't know why he had been summoned but he knew he was scared so he decided it was best to say nothing here.

"The reason you are here, Zap, is that it has come to our attention you have been communicating with a fugitive outside of the Sanctuary."

At those words, a chill ran up Zap's spine and he felt the blood drain from his face.

He'd heard that Brand had spies everywhere but the

only person he'd told about his dreams was Dick. Dick was his friend though – maybe their apartments were bugged?

What had he said? When had he said it? What had they heard? He had a million thoughts running through his head while he tried to maintain his composure on the outside.

"I'm not sure what you mean," he replied quietly.

"Come now, come now," Brand said. "Don't be shy. You should be proud of your skills. I'm aware that you can communicate with this person through your mind. What you may not be aware of is that she's an enemy of the state. Are you a patriot, Zap? Do you care about the security of the state?"

"Yes, yes, of course I care about the state," Zap said desperately.

"Great, because if you care about the state, you'll be glad to know you can help. We've been searching for this woman for some time. The first thing you need to realise, is you must not believe anything that she tells you. She is a master of manipulation and she will get you killed. Are you are aware that she has killed before?"

Zap was unsure whether this was a question or a statement. Before he had the chance to answer, he heard a voice in his head say, "How did I sire such a snivelling wretch."

The voice was Brand's. For a moment Zap was confused, he'd only heard Flo's voice in his head before. It now seemed that he could read others thoughts. Quickly regaining his composure, he decided to hide this skill from Brand as he tried to determine what was going on. What was Brand talking about? Who was he talking about? Was this man saying that he was Zap's father? That made no sense.

Zap had always thought that his real father was someone powerful – but the supreme leader? One thing he was sure of: whatever he was feeling or whatever was happening here, he mustn't let Brand know that he could read minds. That was far too dangerous.

"I didn't know that she'd killed anyone. She seems so innocent," Zap said.

"What has she told you? Do you know where she is?"

"We don't have normal conversations, it's more like feeling each other's thoughts. It's stronger when she is feeling strong emotions, like when she's scared."

Concerned not to divulge too much, Zap wracked his brain, trying to remember what he had said to Dick that Brand might have overheard. He'd told Dick that Flo was outside the Sanctuary and that she'd been attacked. He hadn't mentioned that she was with the rebels and that they were on the way here. It struck him then that this might be the only reason he was still alive.

"So where is she?" Brand prompted.

"All I know is that she is not in the Sanctuary. I have no idea how close or far away she is. Whenever I've felt anything from her, it's been mostly fear. I think she has been in danger a lot. I understand now how dangerous it is outside the Sanctuary, just as the Company has told us."

"It is good that you realise how dangerous it is outside the Sanctuary. It is good that you realise how fortunate your current situation is. I want you to ask her for some information. Will you do that for me, Zap?"

"I will try my best." Zap replied. Clearly, saying no was not an option.

"That is all I ask of anybody, that you do your best for the Company, the people of the Sanctuary and the state. I want you to find out where she is and who she is with. Can you do that for me, Zap?"

"I'll try," Zap said. But while his voice was agreeing, in his mind he'd decided not to help Brand. He realised that his fate was now entwined with Flo's. Once Brand had Flo, Zap may no longer be of any use to him. Also, having powers that the Company couldn't control would make him a threat – a situation he doubted they'd allow to continue.

"Do you enjoy your life, Zap? Do you enjoy the luxuries that your job provides?"

"Yes sir," Zap replied cautiously.

"You know that there are people starving in the streets? You've heard of the riots and how dangerous it is outside your secure complex?"

"Yes, I've heard things," Zap answered, although he thought the questions were rhetorical.

"Good, I'd hate for you to lose your job and your accommodation. I wonder how you would fare on the streets? Even worse, I'd hate for you to take a one-way trip to the gel plants," Brand said with insincere concern.

Zap was confused. If this man was his father, why was he treating him so cruelly? Was this really his father? He decided to feign compliance. "Is there anything else you need me to find out?"

Again he heard Brand's thoughts. "Are you really grovelling or are you trying to play me? Perhaps you have got some of my genes and the son is trying to outfox the father? I will keep a close eye on you and see if you can prove yourself worthy enough to be my son. Let's wait and see what the girl has to offer. Females can be more devious than the males. If your sister is the stronger, she may be the one that I let survive."

Zap found it hard to hide his emotions. While he was scared rigid, his mind was also racing to take in the news that not only was Brand his father but also Flo was his sister. He tried not to react as Brand spoke.

"No, for the time being just find out where she is and who she's with."

"I will do my best, I promise sir."

"How often do you communicate? When will I have an answer?" Brand asked abruptly.

"It depends on where she is. If she is somewhere quiet, it is easier for us to converse. Sometimes it might take a day, sometimes it might be two or three days before I hear from her. It is not a regular communication, it's not like the way we're talking now. It depends on how strong her emotions are at the time, I can't command it."

Zap was playing for time. He knew the rebel attack was getting closer. He didn't want to expose this, and he needed to remain free for as long as possible to keep giving them information.

"I'll give you the benefit of the doubt," Brand said. "You have two days. In exactly two days' time, I expect to hear from you. I expect you to bring me some answers, do you understand?"

There was no point in contesting this matter. Zap had tried to gain some time, and had maybe bought himself an extra day. "I will come back in two days and I will bring you all the information I have gathered."

Brand perceived that Zap's posture seemed to have become more comfortable as they talked. He continued to look him up and down.

Again Zap heard the voice in his head. "Maybe you're not such a wimp after all, maybe you're not your mother's son." Yet again, Zap had to fight to hide any sign of emotion. This was so much information in such a short time, he had to get away as soon as possible.

"If it's okay sir, I'll go now. I'll find somewhere quiet straight away to try to communicate."

"Okay go now. I will send someone for you in two days. Be ready."

With that, Zap turned and left the office. As soon as he was outside the building, he started to move fast. Initially he just walked rapidly so as not to draw attention to himself. His speed continued to increase until he was sprinting. He wanted to get home to the safety of his apartment but after what he'd just heard, that didn't feel safe.

It was just after three in afternoon. He decided he needed to talk to Angus, so he headed for the pits. Normally he would go straight there but he had suddenly discovered paranoia and took a lot of twists and turns to check if he was being followed.

Confident that he had reached the pits unobserved, when he arrived he was breathing heavily. As always at this time, Angus was training warriors. Zap waved to him frantically.

It was unheard of for Zap to come to the pits this early on a weekday. Angus could tell from his face that something was wrong and he excused himself from the warriors.

"We need to talk," Zap said. "I've just been with Brand, the supreme leader."

At this, Angus grabbed him and took him to a room deep in the bowels of the pits, constantly checking for any watching eyes.

44

DECIDING TO HEAD TO THE SANCTUARY

19 September 2202

After the adrenaline rush of the victory at the border post, it was time to take stock of the situation.

Frank and Pepper were standing in the border compound's control room. Several maps were displayed on the wall. Some covered the areas on either side of the border but one was of an island location marked "Sanctuary".

It had taken the rebels a while to read through all of the information they had captured. The surviving Company troops had not been forthcoming in their answers and, rather than resorting to interrogation techniques, Frank tasked Flo with reading their minds and seeking clarification from her contact in the Sanctuary.

Pepper and Debs listened patiently while Frank laid out the questions to Flo.

"Have you managed to get through to your man in the Sanctuary?"

"He's called Zap," Flo stated indignantly.

"Okay, have you managed to get through to Zap?"

"Yes."

"And?" he asked impatiently.

"He confirmed what we have learnt here: that the Sanctuary has over eight hundred thousand inhabitants and a combined Company force of less than twenty thousand, including the security force."

Frank considered those numbers before he spoke. "Given that information, we have a few choices. We can take the resources that we have plundered here back to the Farm, we can stay here or we can continue on towards the Sanctuary. Staying here is not an option as the Company will eventually notice that it has lost communications with its people. Given the numbers you have all just heard, it would be suicide to continue towards the Sanctuary. That gives us only one option: the Farm."

The rest of the rebels seemed resigned to Frank's decision but Pepper had always questioned authority. "What makes you think it would be suicide?"

"Because it would take us almost a week to get there and we would be moving closer to an enemy with a superior force," Frank said off-handedly. "Anyone got any other questions before we brief the fighters?"

It was clear that Frank, who was normally so measured, was under a lot of pressure but Flo was fuelled with Zap's emotions. "No, wait, you haven't let me finish."

"Is there more bad news? Let me guess. An assault

force and more planes are heading here to finish us off!" Frank's patience was clearly fading.

"No, the news is that Zap has been working with the resistance. They are planning a rebellion in the Sanctuary. If we were part of that, we could take out the Company for good," Flo said.

"Suddenly the little girl has grown up into a tactical genius," Frank sneered.

"I'm just passing on the message," Flo said innocently.

"Don't be afraid, tell us the rest." Pepper had become almost a de facto parent by now.

"The people are starving and restless, they are ready for rebellion. There has already been rioting in the streets. Zap says that it will only take a little push for the people to overthrow the Company. They have the numbers but not the training. If we were to go and assist them, we could tip the balance in favour of the resistance.

Before Frank could answer, Pepper offered his initial opinion. "Before anyone gets any ideas, I have been on this journey with you people for a while now. I've been risking my butt for some kind of reward and I expect payment. I never signed up for a rebellion or to become a freedom fighter but as I've spent most of my adult life being hunted by the Company, it might be nice to be able to stop looking over my shoulder."

While Pepper had been talking, Frank had been weighing up their options. "So the story that you have for us is that there is a Company stronghold, which contains several thousand well-armed troops. The strategy for our redemption is to head towards this stronghold and assist a resistance movement and a mob of unarmed people to overthrow the leadership?"

Debs was the next to offer her opinion. "Frank. One thing you have taught me over the years is that strength of spirit and willpower can overcome severe odds. We all know that food supplies are getting shorter and people need food. When it comes to survival, people can be motivated by fear or hunger. No matter how many times the Company has beaten them down, if the people reach the tipping point where hunger overcomes fear, they have the numbers to succeed."

"So," Cenk said, "let's say the intelligence is good and you decide to go down this path. After travelling for several days, you manage to avoid being spotted and being killed by aircraft and you don't find a reception committee waiting in ambush. Do you think that the Company won't have noticed that they have lost communication with their border compound? Let's assume they don't notice, you join the resistance and succeed in overthrowing the elites. How do you feed the masses? If there is a food shortage, you have now taken charge and the masses are looking to you for food that you don't have! If that is your big plan, count me out!"

Flo almost shouted. "You don't understand, there is no food shortage. Zap has access to the information that proves it. It is just the greed of the elites that is creating the shortages. People don't need to be turned into gel. Plenty of food is available from farms and orchards and even fish off the coast. Just as they lied when the signs said that the border was contaminated, the one percent have been lying to us for years about the supposedly war-ravaged kingdom in the north. It is not as damaged as they would have us believe. This is all Company propaganda. If we distributed the resources evenly, we would have enough for everyone."

This piqued Frank's interest. Logistics had always been one of his concerns. Even with the winter gear and resources that they had plundered here, they were still in survival mode. The further north they'd gone, the colder it had become but heading south as the winter progressed wouldn't help much either. They had accessed a short-term fix but the outlook for their long term survival was bleak.

"What do you think, Debs?" Frank asked.

"It doesn't sound much of a plan, that's true. But we left the compound and the Farm because their locations were known to the Company. If we go back there now, we are heading back to danger with limited resources. Heading to the Sanctuary is risky but if we can break the Company for good, we are all safer in the long term."

Realising this was a risky option, Frank wanted everyone's counsel. "Well, Pepper, you've heard Debs' suggestion. What's your opinion?"

"Although I agree with you that this sounds like suicide, considering the potential rewards it might be worth the risk. If we could take out the Company once and for all," Pepper paused as he pondered his whole adult life on the run, "it would make my life a lot easier. I have spent years being hunted by the Company. It's hard for me to imagine those hunters being gone."

"So am I right in thinking that the plan to head to the Sanctuary appeals to you?" Frank asked.

"I wish we had a better option but if we have a chance of taking out the Company for good and getting to a place where food is plentiful, that is almost too good to be true. If I never had to eat another gel pack, it'd be worth it."

Frank turned to Lacey and Cenk. "This affects all of us. We are not attempting this new mission unless everyone agrees. What do you two think?"

Lacey stood up straight, "I've always been known as cautious, Frank, but we have been living under the boot of the Company all of our lives. Surely it's a risk worth taking?"

Cenk seemed reticent as he began, "I didn't want to come north, and I thought it was a crazy idea. This next plan seems even crazier! I have to agree though – we can't keep running forever. Our luck or the number of places to hide will eventually run out. If you choose to head to the Sanctuary, I'll back you."

"It sounds like we have a consensus," Frank said. "Debs, I want you to identify the communications protocols between here and the Sanctuary. Interrogate any of the prisoners that you want but we need answers in the next couple of hours. I need Flo near me but if your methods come up short, let me know."

"On to it," Debs said.

Frank continued, "Cenk, you take your people and prepare some defences in case the Company has already decided to send in reinforcements. Assume that, if they are coming, they will arrive via plane so if you can hit them before they land, that would be helpful. Brief me as soon as you are ready."

"Understood," Cenk said, leaving at a brisk pace.

"Lacey, start preparing for the move to the Sanctuary. Get an inventory of all of our stores and divide things evenly between the three convoys. Pepper, I want either you or Eric to be with Flo at all times. She is critical to this mission as all communications will be going through her. I'll give you a half a dozen guards until we leave but whenever we are on the move she is your responsibility."

"Understood," Pepper replied.

"As for you, young Flo, we are going to find you somewhere nice and quiet where you can get as much information about the Sanctuary as possible. I want to know what we are heading into and I want your friend to inform the resistance that we are willing to assist."

"Of course."

"It looks like the fun's just getting started," Frank said as the meeting broke up.

45

RIVER DISCOVERS THAT THE BORDER POST IS LOST

26 September 2202

Since the start of the assault on the border, Zap had been sending false signals to the central computer. He had hacked the system and was fooling it into believing that the daily reports were still coming from the border. This had delayed the Company's discovery that it had lost the border compound.

Some family members of troops on the border had complained that their communications had not been getting through, but these communications had always been sporadic. Extensions to border deployment and communications blackouts had just become a way of life.

The families of regular Company men got on with their own lives during such deployments, not because they felt abandoned but because they accepted it as a trade-off with regular food supplies and accommodation.

But when the number of complaints increased from officers' families, although they didn't have the same power as the elites, River decided to investigate.

Brand had given him blanket powers to quell the rebellion but, as unrest grew, his resources were becoming ever more stretched. The digital reports had still been getting through from the border but voice and video communications had been down for a while.

Unable to spare a gunship, River had despatched a small helicopter with his own pilot Dempsey and half a dozen troops as a reconnaissance.

To Dempsey, the border compound seemed a little quiet. However, as he came in to land, attendants stood there with fire extinguishers as usual. As his rotor blades slowed, several men in overalls approached. There seemed to be more ground crew than normal but that raised no suspicions.

He had seen that the antennae were damaged before he landed and assumed the breakdown of communications was a mechanical issue. The troops that accompanied him started to exit the helicopter. Hunched over as they were to avoid the blades, they never saw the ground crew drawing their weapons. Although Dempsey heard the muffled shots, he had no time to call back to the capital. He didn't even have time to work out what the sounds were before his head exploded with the impact of two bullets.

River was not having a good day. He'd lost communications with the helicopter he'd sent to the border and now he was having to visit the ports because one of the grain ships had been attacked. Normally River would've taken a helicopter to the port but the helicopter he kept on standby was the one he'd dispatched to the border. Reduced to driving, he'd now been travelling in a convoy for the last six hours.

As soon as he'd been notified of the trouble at the port, he'd sent reinforcements. With a security system that was woefully overstretched, his reinforcements had been nowhere near enough. The masses had overwhelmed the grain ship and he'd needed to deploy a gunship to prevent his reinforcements from being overrun.

Official Company food supplies in the Sanctuary were dwindling faster by the day. He had requested that the council increase the supplies but had received no replies. The rumours of black-market profiteering from the elites were running rampant. Other rumours were that the masses were being given food supplies freely. Someone was stoking resentment against the Company and setting themselves up as the saviour. All this and the breakdown in communications with the border post were giving River a headache.

Having seen the fate of his predecessor, he knew that Brand required rapid results. Determining that he needed to take drastic action, he'd deployed his specialist troops.

The specialist troops were known for their brutality and the people had started calling them the thug squad. Made up of rejects from other teams, in any traditional unit these people would have been sent to the gel plants for insubordination or overzealous violence. River had decided instead to deploy them and let them feed their base instincts. In areas of raised unrest, he sent them in to quash any thoughts of rebellion.

River had to be careful not to let them injure too many of the workers because the elites would not accept lower productivity on the farms or in the processing plants. All the same, there was plenty of the poor to go around so the elites would overlook the loss of some through brutality, within reason.

Lacking the finesse of his predecessor, River used a strategy to keep the peace that was actually counterproductive. Reports from areas where the thug squad had been deployed showed they had made the locals more irate and resolute.

Traditionally the masses were compliant at checkpoints, having learnt to work within boundaries, but now they were pushing back in these areas. Constant punishment for no reason created confusion and removed the deterrents against fighting back.

A certain look was developing in the eyes of these people – a look of desperation as though they had nothing to lose. But it was too late for River to change strategies now. He had decided to double down, increasing both the day and night patrols in the Sanctuary. As a result, he had fewer reserves but more Company troops were on the street at any one time.

Owing to the high value of grain shipments, the timetable and location of their arrival was a closely guarded secret. River wondered how the masses had found out about the shipment, but that was a problem for another day. His first priority today was to view the damage and see what could be salvaged from this disaster.

Even from a distance, he could see the smoke still rising from the port. This was not a good sign.

As they pulled in to the port area, he noticed that the sentries had their fingers on their triggers. These were his reinforcement squad as the original sentries had been overwhelmed.

The squad had not had time to remove all of the bodies around the barrier. They had put the dead Company troops under cover but the rioters who had been shot or trampled in the riot remained strewn out in the open.

At this time of year, the bodies were not going to rot and they would eventually be picked up and taken to the gel plants. His main focus was to confirm that the people presented no further threat. The clean-up could be sorted afterwards.

River had only just entered the port area when his vehicle was flagged down by Greg, the leader of the reinforcements.

"What have you got to report?" River had no time for pleasantries.

"Sir, we seem to have returned order to the ports."

"Returned order," River said, "and what do you think order looks like? Is it the sight of a grain ship smouldering in the harbour?"

"I'm sorry sir but we had no choice," Greg said. "We did not have enough troops to restrain the rioters. By the time we arrived, the masses had overrun the guards at the port. They were on board the grain ship, helping themselves to the contents and we had no way to retake it."

"You are telling me that heavily armed soldiers couldn't have scared off some unarmed idiots by firing a few rounds in the air?"

"No sir, this was not just a few people. Several thousand rioters had stormed the boat. Some fell in the water in the rush to climb on board but the others showed no mercy to them. These people are starving. How they found out about the grain ship, I don't know, but when we arrived it was a disaster. The boat was covered in feral people. It was all my troops could do to defend ourselves."

River knew that it had been out of their control but he wanted the man to expend all of his excuses before he responded.

"We put up a barricade to keep them away from the gates," Greg continued, "but in reality they just wanted to stay and gorge themselves on the grain. The sound of bullets did not faze them so, rather than trying to drive them off, the only thing to do was to let them stay on the boat."

"Yes, I got the report from the gunship," River said. "It was I who gave the orders to fire and sink the boat. This was a valuable shipment and the council is not going to be happy. Can you give me a reason why I should not relieve you of command and send you to the gel plants?" Like any Company commander, River was looking for a scapegoat.

Greg seemed to think before he spoke. "I was low on troops and I was low on resources. We have had many convoys of arms and ammunition intercepted recently. With a shortage of bullets for our troops, the choices were to sacrifice our soldiers for a boat-load of grain that was already lost or to sacrifice the grain and have troops left to fight another day."

River knew this was true but he couldn't show weakness. He could not show that he was resigned to this situation as well. "I will deal with you later. For now, get some trucks in here and see how many bodies that we can recover to the gel plants. The more gel we can supply, the less chance we'll have of more starving rioters."

Although it was obviously not a lack of food driving these issues, River couldn't admit this openly to his troops. Keeping control of the masses was hard enough but keeping control of his troops if they believed that he'd already lost control would be almost impossible.

The scene at the ship was one of absolute devastation. The shells from the gunship had made the boat sink fast. Overloaded with people as it had been, they also had no chance of escape, especially with the gunship strafing at anyone who managed to swim free.

River looked at the bodies half burnt and half drowned in the water, like something out of a nightmare. It seemed as if some people had almost managed to crawl out of the water but now had huge holes where their faces should have been. The gunship's high-velocity bullets made a mess of a body.

An acrid smell of burning flesh hung in the air, from where the phosphorus shells had turned the metal into a molten mess and the people on board with it. Even if they did manage to recover some of the corpses, River doubted much would be left over that would be useful for the gel plants. He was no expert on the process but the bodies seemed to have little value now that most of the liquid was evaporated from them.

River spent an hour walking through the debris taking notes so that he could not only produce a detailed report but also work out how he could shift the blame to the ship's crew.

In his mind, he saw Smit prone in Brand's office with his blood forming a lake over the floor. This was not the fate that River wanted for himself.

After reviewing the situation at the ports, he determined that his time would be better spent investigating the situation at the border than travelling in a convoy for six hours back to the capital.

He had the refuelled gunship land on the side of the jetty to pick him up. He was accompanied by two dozen of his specialist squad. Tactically they weren't well versed but in brutality they were unmatched. If he faced an issue at the border, these men were expendable.

Within an hour, they were approaching the border compound. From above, nothing looked out of the order. The helicopter he'd sent in advance was sitting on the landing pad, seemingly intact. So if it had landed, why had they lost contact?

Thumbing the microphone for his headset, River said, "Hello, Recce squad one, this is Blue leader. Is everything okay, over? I see you on the landing pad but have not heard back from you. Confirm this message, over."

No reply. As they got slightly lower, River noticed that none of the antennae for the compound was intact. Perhaps some kind of storm had taken them out, but these weren't broken masts – they looked to have been destroyed at their base. Something was wrong here.

He shouted to the pilot, "Do not land here. I want you to hover but keep at a safe distance. We need to see what is going on before we get any closer."

"Hello, Blue leader," came a crackly voice over the radio. "Do you read me, over?"

River was pleased to hear someone at last. He needed to confirm who it was but at least this was progress. The voice again came over the radio. "This is Recce squad one. Something is interfering with communications in the area. We are safe and well, over."

The voice on the radio was Tom's, the leader of Frank's rear guard. Initially his ruse seemed to be working.

Although River didn't know everyone's voices, he knew the name of his pilot was Dempsey and he decided to test the voice. "Hello Recce one, if this is the pilot, please confirm your name, over."

"Cwrzsasdd wdffffffff." The reply was garbled and impossible to understand. Was it a mechanical problem or a ruse to draw them in closer? River needed more information. They couldn't just leave now, but he was also cautious about landing. He could see his helicopter out in the open and it looked okay from this distance, but where were his troops? Not hearing the name Dempsey over the radio worried him.

Frank had left Tom with a contingent of forty fighters. They had expected Company at some stage and, although the rebels weren't large in numbers, they had captured quite an arsenal when they occupied this place. The border post was equipped with heavy weaponry designed to take out who knew what. Perhaps the Company had expected some kind of heavy truck to charge the compound.

Whatever the original purpose, Tom now controlled the weaponry and he decided using it was his only chance to take out this gunship.

If they could stop the gunship from communicating with other garrisons, it would buy them more time. The longer it took the Company to send reinforcements, the more time the resistance had to enact their plan and the better their chances of success.

Tom had tasked four of his fighters to take the shoulder-mounted rocket launchers to the roofs. They were to remain under cover until he gave the signal to fire.

As soon as Tom realised that the gunship was not going to come any closer, he decided the best option was to act now and use the element of surprise. He raised his arm and the signal was relayed to the rooftops. No radios were used to avoid the signal being intercepted by the gunship but hand signals were enough to get all four rockets fired at once.

The pilot noticed the first flash as River spotted the others. "Get out of here, get out of here," River shouted over the radio.

The pilot had logged many flight hours. Although he'd previously only been fired on by the odd rifle or pistol, he was fully aware of the danger. "Hold on tight," he shouted, pulling back on the stick to take the gunship straight upwards.

All four of the projectiles missed the gunship but the explosion of the last one was close enough to create a shock wave that made the pilot's flight harder. He did not wait for orders but headed away from the border to create a safe distance between his ship and these missiles.

Tom knew he had missed his chance here. All the same, their quiet capture of the first helicopter had been more than they'd expected.

Although this rear guard wasn't a suicide mission, it was still very dangerous. All of his fighters were volunteers, chosen as they were all single men with no families. Unlike some of the people in the convoys who'd formed couples and conceived the odd child, Tom's men had only themselves to live for.

They'd spent their whole lives in survival mode. If their actions helped the rebels' plans to succeed, it could change their lives forever. If they died here, at least they had chosen their own fates and where to make a stand.

"Back to the capital, head back to the capital now!" River shouted, shaken. The image of the burning wreck of the boat was still seared into his memory; the realisation that they had come close to the same fate in this gunship was almost too much for him.

He was not prepared to take any further risks. He could feel the anger and fear among the others in the gunship. Their anger was because they had just been fired at and weren't allowed to fire back. Their fear, because they were used to outnumbering and being better armed than their prey.

Encountering somebody that they couldn't beat with clubs and who could kill them without them having a chance to raise a hand made them feel smaller. Like most bullies, when confronted by force, they experienced fear.

River considered ordering the gunship to pass back over the compound and open fire but the risks were just too high. He had to go back and regroup. He had a report to write and there was every chance he was going to be summoned to Brand. What he was going to say and how he was going to squirm out of this, he had no idea. What he did know was that danger lay in his future.

46

THE REBELS RENDEZVOUS WITH HOOK

26 September 2202

Frank and the rebels had been hiding near the port for the last two days. They'd salvaged what winter clothes and stores they could from the Company compound but had left enough supplies for the rear guard to survive for an extended period. Frank hoped that by joining forces with the resistance, they could start the rebellion before the Company sent reinforcements to the border compound.

Even If his plan succeeded, his people at the compound would not receive relief for some time. They may have escaped the danger of bullets and bombs but, as winter was setting in, the main threat was starvation.

Some emergency supplies were available at the border: gel packs in the freezers and some small crops in greenhouses. This wouldn't have been enough for the original number of Company troops manning the garrison but It should last his rear guard a good while.

After allocating reserves for his rear guard, they had

pillaged the majority of the compound's food and fuel. With over five hundred people to keep alive though, Frank's reserves were dwindling and they needed new supplies.

Zap and Flo had been communicating regularly. Although it had been agreed that the rebels would join the resistance, they first had to find a way of getting over to the island on which the Sanctuary was located.

There were far too many people to carry on one or several small boats. Flo had informed Frank that the resistance had connections in the shipping ports so they were currently relying on their help in this matter.

Tonight was the scheduled rendezvous with one of the resistance leaders. From the description they'd been given of this man, Frank was fairly confident that he would stand out. His distinguishing feature was that he had a hook for a hand – which would be hard to fake.

Emerging from where they'd been waiting in the shadows, three men came walking towards the lead vehicle. Frank had positioned sentries ahead so, to have got this far, the men must already have been stopped by at least two of his guards.

All three of the men carried backpacks but no visible weapons; his fighters had been ordered to relieve them of any weapons before this meeting point. As they came closer, even in the rain, Frank could see the glint of the metal of the leader's hook.

Just to speed things up, Frank approached the men, flanked by Debs, Pepper, Eric and two other fighters. All of the rebels carried the standard silenced pistols and two fighters on top of the truck shouldered rifles. The rifles were a last resort as Frank didn't want rifle fire echoing through the night so close to the port.

The two groups stopped ten feet apart.

"I have been given a password," Hook said, "and I assume that you have the other half. The fact that we are here at this time of night makes it doubtful any of us are not the people we expect to meet. But just to give us all a warm feeling of security: there are fifteen boats in the water and there are fifteen trucks in the port."

Frank smiled and replied, "Fifteen boats plus fifteen trucks equals a hundred." He thought it sounded a bit childish when you said it out loud but Zap and Flo had decided on the code words. The truth was that it was pretty smart as the chances of somebody working out that fifteen plus fifteen equalled a hundred was very low.

Hook offered his good hand to Frank, partly as a sign of good faith but also because it left his razor sharp hook available if he needed a weapon.

Frank took his hand and shook it. "I'm Frank. My people have been waiting here for two days. Are we all set?"

"Yes," Hook said. "If we try to go through the front gates, the size of your force will attract too much attention. Instead, we can use a hole I have in the fence that is guarded by some of my people."

"What do your people do?" Frank asked curiously.

"I guess you could say that we redistribute things from the port."

"Smugglers and thieves," Frank said. "We are in good company."

Not sure if this was an attempt at humour, Hook replied, "I understand you stole the odd things from the border compound, including the lives of the people there."

For a moment, the smile left Frank's face. It was true

they had needed to kill for their own survival. He had been responsible for a lot of death over the years but he saw this as a necessary evil. He was accountable for the lives of his people and their safety was his only real concern.

"I guess you're right," Frank said, letting go of Hook's hand. "What do we do about the vehicles?"

"This is kind of a one-way trip," Hook replied "I myself have always tried to live my life with the hope of a backup plan but over the last few weeks it's become apparent that we are headed for only one of two outcomes. We will overthrow the Company and survive or we all die trying. I would suggest that your fighters hide the vehicles as best they can. Bring with you only what you can carry but do not expect to return to these vehicles."

Judging by the look on Frank's face, he wasn't happy about leaving the vehicles.

"I have made some arrangements on the other side," Hook said. "Smuggling you through the ports on both sides of the water is going to be difficult enough. Since the riots have begun, security in the Sanctuary has been increased tenfold. The good news is that increasing security has stretched the Company thin so its security net has holes. Should we fail in our tasks within the Sanctuary, I doubt any of you will survive to take a return boat journey. Before you come with me now, you need to decide if this is what you want. Once you board these boats, there is no turning back."

Frank would have preferred to drive his own vehicles onto the boats but understood Hook's point about the difficulty of smuggling a large group. There really was no turning back. This was all or nothing: he saw this as the future not only of his fighters but also of the masses.

Over the last couple days, he'd talked with Flo about the injustices and disparities in the Sanctuary that Zap had told her about. Even without the exact numbers, the intelligence was that the Sanctuary held enough resources for all of the people there but the insatiable one percent had chosen to hoard them while starving these people.

Frank had never really seen himself as a good man. In some ways, his forefathers would have seen many of his actions over the years as criminal. Since the Water Wars, humanity had changed a great deal. Grading someone as good or bad was determined by how high they were in the pecking order; if you had the luxury of being able to grade somebody, you were usually higher up.

"How long to the boat? And when do we leave?" Frank asked.

"We should have everyone on board within an hour," Hook replied. "I've had to split you into two boats. They should both leave about the same time and arrive about the same time. With this arrangement, we can use smaller boats so they are less noticeable but also, if one of the boats should be discovered, at least the resistance will have half of your force for the revolution. I hope you understand this."

Frank was pragmatic. The reason they were attempting this venture was that he believed his force could make a difference in the resistance's fight. Losing all of his fighters in one fell swoop would not help the people and so he resigned himself to this. "Debs, you and Cenk take half our people and brief them. Once they've unloaded, ditch the trucks. Be back here in ten minutes. You will be on the second boat. Pepper, you and Lacey get among the rest of our people, give them the same orders and high-tail it back here. You and that group will come on the first boat with me."

Hook was impressed with Frank's decisiveness, the way he accepted the situation and also the way he reacted to the information straight away.

He'd been hesitant when Karla had first briefed the resistance on the arrival of these rebels. They were an unknown quantity in an already fluid situation. On the plus side, these were battle-hardened people with nothing left to lose, which made them a valuable asset. If the Company were unaware they were coming, this was a surprise that could definitely make a difference.

"Flo, with me," Frank said. "I want you listening for info from Zap in case he can help us with any advance warning. Pepper, once you're back, stay by her side."

Before Pepper could answer, Eric said, "I'm coming with you."

Frank had expected no less. Since they reconnected at the border, Eric had not left Flo's side day or night. Whenever Flo had come to brief him on Zap's intelligence, Eric had tagged along. During one of the briefings Flo had divulged to Frank and Eric that the commander of the attacks on their compound, Paris's compound and the Farm was the right-hand man of the leader of the Sanctuary, an individual known as Will. Ever since then, Eric had been obsessed with finding more about this Will.

For all he knew, Eric slept at the foot of her bed like a faithful guard dog. This was fine: her security was important and having Eric around saved Frank from having to divert his valuable resources for this task.

True to his word, Hook saw them safely through the fence and the boats left on time.

A winter storm was churning up the waters, and the heavy downpour while the fighters were boarding had reduced the level of scrutiny of the boats' cargo. The sentries of the port seemed happy to stay in their little hut, rather than patrol in the rain.

Even though the Sanctuary have been experiencing unrest, it appeared the land on this side of the water had not suffered the same problems. These guards seemed unaware of any threats, reminding Frank of the complacency of the border sentries. He'd considered taking out the guards and bringing his vehicles along but he bowed to Hook's guidance as this was his domain.

The resistance in the Sanctuary trusted Hook enough to make him the liaison. He was putting his life and the lives of his own fighters at risk so Frank had to trust his strategy and stop second-guessing the plan. Trying to override the strategy would have just been something to feed Frank's ego and he was not prepared to risk over five hundred lives just so that he could feel superior.

It was clear some of his people had not been on a boat before. In truth, Frank hadn't spent much time on boats himself. As the boats tossed up and down on the churning waves, many of the fighters emptied the contents of their stomachs over the floor of the holds where they were hidden. These people had tough constitutions – they could survive on gel packs and anything else they could scavenge – but apparently being shaken up like a cork in a bottle was a little too much to stomach.

The smell of so much vomit was almost overwhelming. Everyone was happy to eventually reach the island port.

The storm had abated by the time they pulled alongside the dock. Frank had been given the courtesy of standing in the boat's cockpit. Looking down at the docks, he noticed a convoy of Company vehicles. Immediately he drew his pistol and aimed it at Hook. "What's the meaning of this? I thought you were on our side?"

"Wait, wait, wait," Hook said. "You don't understand, those are ours."

"What do you mean those are ours?"

"I realise that I haven't provided as many replacement vehicles as you left behind. I did tell you I had made arrangements and I believe that I also told you, I'd recently been redistributing quite a few things from the Company."

A ramp was dropped from the boat and the first truck drove on board. "Those are my crew driving those trucks," Hook said. "There is enough space in the back for all of your people and also a selection of Company uniforms. Not enough for everybody but enough that your fighters can pass as a Company convoy at first glance. I apologise for not warning you but I wasn't sure if the vehicles would make it."

"And what was your plan if they hadn't been here?"

"Remember what I told you about backup plans? They seem to have gone out the window lately. If they hadn't been here, we would have been in big trouble."

Frank almost smiled at this. The relief from realising

the trucks were friendly was easing the tension in his body slightly. If this smuggler had managed to steal so many Company trucks, perhaps this venture was not totally doomed.

He waved to the cockpit of the second boat as it pulled alongside the docks. Through his binoculars, he could see Debs and through a similar pair she was observing him. He pointed to the remaining trucks on the docks and gave a thumbs-up signal, which she returned. They couldn't trust electronic communications in case the Company was listening.

The second half of the convoy drove up the ramp onto the other boat. As the first vehicle on Frank's boat came to a halt, out jumped CT. "Frank, this is Clarence Thomas, CT to his friends. A man I have had to trust with my life recently."

CT smiled. "We have a farm outside of the capital that is large enough to accommodate you and your people. We will leave in two convoys, thirty minutes apart. If that is okay with you?"

Frank nodded and addressed Hook, "With your permission, I will take CT with me and we will brief the other convoy leaders."

Frank then turned to Pepper "It's going to take a little while to sort things out but we need to get out of here. I'll be back in twenty minutes. I need to ensure that Debs understands the plan and introduce her to her guide, CT. I assume you'll be leading the second convoy?" he said to CT.

"Yes that's the plan," CT replied.

"I'll meet you on the dockside, Pepper. I'm taking Flo with me but we will be straight back." Eric tried to object but Frank cut him off. "I understand, Eric, you don't want to leave her side but we need to move quickly and I need her with me in case Zap sends us an urgent message. Stay here with Pepper and help him load up our people."

He paused waiting for pushback from Eric but there was none. "Pepper, my people have come to trust you as one of their own so don't let me down. I'll be back as soon as possible. Cenk, you support Pepper – I want our people off this boat ASAP. Put armed men in each cab and find out who we can fit in these Company uniforms. I know it's distasteful wearing their clothes but this is not the first time we have used this subterfuge and it may keep us alive."

As promised, Frank returned to the convoy in less than half an hour. He jumped into the vehicle next to Hook and the driver, both of whom were now wearing the Company uniforms. Flo joined Pepper and Eric in the back seats of the double cab.

"I thought you were both going to be in uniform?" Frank said to Pepper.

"I'm sorry," Pepper said. "But young Eric here has a big issue with the Company and I thought it would be more expedient just to let him sit in the back, rather than fight over this. I wasn't sure how many dark skins there would be here in the Sanctuary so I thought it better for me to sit back here too."

"Okay," Frank said, "but if we come across any checkpoints, keep your heads down."

47

BRAND TAKES STOCK

26 September 2202

The thug squad had been neutralised. Some thought that it had been the work of off-duty soldiers. They had been ambushed when they had gone to employ their brutality tactics in an area inhabited by families of dead soldiers.

Brutality against the masses was one thing but brutality against your own side was not acceptable. Most of the Company troops didn't like the thug squad – some of them had previously served with squad members and had suffered at their hands. The problem with putting all the bullies in one place was they had lots of enemies and you created a focus for those enemies.

Some of the Company leaders had initially questioned the policy of creating the thug squad. River had ignored these concerns as he had Brand's backing and wanted to make a big impression. But once the squad started targeting the families of dead and injured troops, tensions with the other troops heightened.

It all started because the families were complaining that the Company had reduced their food rations. Now that the SUP had a secret benefactor that was not part of the establishment, the families' allegiances were being challenged. The military community was more of a family than most. Knowing that at any stage their own families could be starving, soldiers too began questioning which side they should be on.

It was surprising how fast the unrest had grown, even among the Company troops. The elites had miscalculated how far they could push people. Brand had even needed to attend one council meeting and lay down the law. He'd arrested two of the council members and sent them to the gel plants as an example.

Yet the elites had already committed themselves so strongly to their greed that they could not understand consequences. As far as they were concerned, they were above all rules and laws so consequences meant nothing to them.

Having never been stopped before, they thought they could just continue with the same actions. The disparity between the haves and have-nots had been going on so long that, in the view of the elite, the lives of the poor had no value. They saw to it that the poor were sent to the plants at forty-five, whereas they could die of old age if they chose.

Brand only became involved in the day-to-day running of the capital when things started to go wrong. And this time, things had really started to go wrong! As the situation spiralled, it was starting to affect Brand and anything that impacted Brand annoyed him. His spies had told him of the growing unrest. No matter how many times he tried to instil fear into these idiots, they just didn't get it. The situation had deteriorated to the point where they almost had a full-scale rebellion on their hands.

That imbecile River had been stoking up resentment and making the situation even worse. Brand was unsure if it would be a good move to replace River and his troops while still trying to quell a rebellion. He was himself a big proponent of brutality as a way of keeping people under control.

Yet using cruelty for no reason removed structure. If you didn't give the masses the structure they craved, anarchy could occur. The numbers were not in the elites' favour so they had to rule smartly. Apparently Brand was the only member of the council who got this message.

His spies had told him about the impending attacks. He didn't know where or when they would occur but he knew they were coming. All the troops were supposedly on high alert, but they were stretched thinly because of the approaching festival. River's strategy of increasing patrols was stretching the troops even more.

Smit may have had his failings but he understood strategy a lot better than River. He would not have made these same mistakes but unfortunately Smit was no longer around. It was rare that Brand admitted making mistakes, even to himself, but replacing Smit with River was something he was regretting. He would have been better off installing one of his own puppets to do his bidding.

Time was running out and Brand was making his own contingency plans. He had not survived as the supreme leader for this long without having lots of contingency plans. In this time of crisis, he had to consider his own survival.

48

ZAP AND FLO MEET

27 September 2202

F lo couldn't wait to meet Zap.

They had been coordinating between the rebels and the resistance in their minds but had not had a chance to talk socially, let alone meet in person. She had so many questions for him.

Frank was going to a meeting at a place known as the fighting pits. She had convinced him to take her along so that she could finally meet Zap.

Eric had tried to insist that he should come too. However, she sensed that he felt some jealousy towards another male in her life so she had convinced him to stay with Pepper and prepare for the coming battles. Pepper was working with Eric to develop his shooting skills, which at the same time was helping to break down any remaining animosity between them.

"I've been told we'll be with you in ten minutes," Flo said in Zap's head.

They had said that they would wait until they met to talk but Flo was too excited for that.

"I can't wait to meet you, I've got lots to tell you," Zap replied.

As Frank and Flo exited their vehicle, they were greeted by a man with one eye and a small serious-looking man.

"I'm Angus and this is Miyamoto," the one-eyed man said to Frank, offering him his hand. "The rest of the resistance leaders are already here, please follow us upstairs."

Frank shepherded Flo along with him, while taking in their surroundings. He had survived for a long time by being able to quickly size up a person and his instincts told him that his two guides were able to take care of themselves. Sending two such men to meet them served as reassurance that the resistance wasn't playing but also showed that they did not yet trust Frank fully.

As they reached the top of the stairs, Flo saw a young man who looked about the same age as her. Their eyes immediately locked with recognition.

Not prepared to wait any longer, she ran towards him as she felt the word, "Hello" in her head. Zap also started to advance and they met half way, both smiling delightedly.

"Hi, I'm Flo."

"I kind of guessed that," Zap said with a grin.

Frank had let Flo run ahead to meet Zap but had now caught up. "You must be Zap?"

Zap nodded, more reserved now.

"We've a lot to thank you for. If it hadn't been for your warnings, I don't know if I or my fighters would be still alive."

Zap blushed a little, unused to such praise.

Angus and Miyamoto were gesturing for Frank to follow them into the meeting room with the rest of the rebel leaders.

"This will probably take a while so take some time to get acquainted." Frank patted Flo on the shoulder and left them standing together.

"Are you thirsty or hungry?" Zap asked.

"It is a bit warm in here."

"Follow me."

Zap led her to a large kitchen-like room that had big containers of cold drinking water and tables full of fruit and other foods. "The elites are supplying all of this to feed the warriors before the festival. They like the warriors to be fit and well in order to put on a good show. Help yourself."

"Water is fine."

Zap poured a tall glass of cold, clear water and handed it to Flo. "Come with me. There's a small office just round the corner where we can talk in private."

Soon they were in a small room filled by four large, comfortable chairs. "Make yourself comfortable. I've so much to tell you," Zap said. "We've been so busy passing information for others but the things I have to discuss needed to be said in person."

"Tell me everything," Flo said impatiently.

"The reason why we are so alike is that we are brother and sister."

For a few seconds, Flo was speechless. "You're my brother? What makes you think this?"

"I can't remember our mother and until recently I didn't know that our father was alive – but recently I met him."

This was a lot for Flo to take in. "Our father, we have a father who's alive?" She started burbling, "I was only young when my mother took me away and I only recently found out that she was called Mary."

"That's a nice name," Zap said thoughtfully. "I wish I'd known her."

"What's our father like? Can we meet him? Is he close by?"

"He is relatively close by but you do not want to meet him."

"Why not?"

"Because if you were to meet him, you would be in danger from him."

"What?" All this was just too much for her. Now she understood why he had waited until they met in person. "What do you mean I'd be in danger from him?"

"He is called Brand and he is the leader of the elites. The true head of the Company known by some as the supreme leader."

"That doesn't make him a bad person."

"The elites treat everyone else as though their lives are worthless. Their greed is the main reason why the masses are starving. Yet, as bad as the rest of the elites are, compared to our father they would be seen as reasonable people."

"How do you know this?"

"I only recently found out that I can read minds. Can you do that?"

"My powers have been growing over the last year or so. I've progressed from reading people's emotions to also reading their thoughts."

"Before meeting our father, I had communicated with you of course but I didn't known I had other mental gifts. Then when I met our father, his thoughts started filling my head. Maybe it was the strength of his emotions but, whatever it was, he didn't seem to be aware I could tell what he was thinking."

"And what was he thinking?

"He didn't care about me or you, he just wanted to know which of us he could use best. His thoughts made it clear that he was happy to dispose of whichever one he decided to be of least use to him."

"Are you sure that's what he was thinking? Sometimes when I'm reading other people's minds, it's not that clear."

"I'm positive. As well as his thoughts, he threatened me with his words. I was supposed to report your location to him by today."

Flo was quiet for a few minutes but the excitement of meeting Zap overcame the news of her father. "We seem to be alike in our abilities. Perhaps it was because I was under stress that mine blossomed early but yours too will grow."

"The signal between us has been getting stronger," Zap said. "Perhaps our abilities are growing."

"Do you think there are more people like us?"

"I don't know. I only sensed you by accident. Maybe it's just because we are brother and sister that our gifts are strong or maybe we will get stronger and be able to sense others."

"Gifts, is that what you call them?" All this information was starting to wear Flo down.

"You can see it as a gift or a burden, depending on your frame of mind."

"What do you mean?"

"It's hard to trust other people if you can read what they're thinking. Most people tell lies, even small lies."

"So you do think it's a burden." By now Flo felt like crying. "I was kidnapped because people wanted to use me. Although we've been helping the resistance, it seems as though I am still being used."

"We have been willingly using our gifts for the greater good and if I had to choose, I'd say it is definitely more a gift than a curse."

"What makes you think that?"

"This gift has helped me reunite with a sister I never knew I had and has given me the opportunity to save people's lives. Hopefully we can be part of something great. Something that's going to stop the people from being downtrodden. To help them overthrow the greedy."

Listening to Zap, Flo was filled with a sense of hope. After they talked in the room for over an hour, they went back to wait for Frank outside the meeting room and talked some more.

When Frank joined them, it felt to them like they had only just begun talking.

"Can we stay here tonight? I've got so much more I want to find out," Flo asked Frank.

"I'm afraid not now, there'll be time enough for that later. I still need you to help us communicate with Zap for a little longer."

"How much longer?" Flo asked, echoing Zap's thoughts.

"Once we put our plans into action, it's going to get dangerous out there and this is one of the most secure places in the city. You'll be coming back here to stay with Zap then. Promise me you'll take care of her, Zap?"

Without hesitation, Zap heard himself say, "I promise."

"Good, I've come to think of this young woman as family and I can't afford to lose any more family," Frank said.

"Can we just stay a little longer, please Frank?"

"I'm sorry, just by being in the city we are putting ourselves and others at risk. We need to get back to the fighters and prepare for what's to come. It's been nice to meet you, Zap." Frank offered his hand.

"It was nice to meet you too."

"You have five minutes, Flo. Say your goodbyes and remember you're coming back soon."

The beaming smile that Flo had arrived with was fading. Feeling her sadness, Zap blurted out, "Don't be sad, you know we are going to have lots of time together when this is all over. Can you feel it?"

A small smile came over Flo's face. "Yes, I can feel it."

As she walked towards Frank at the top of the stairs, she shouted over her shoulder, "See you soon." At the same time, inside their heads she said, "I can't wait to come back and talk some more".

Zap shouted after her, "I look forward to your return. I've always wanted a sister."

With a start, Frank turned to Flo. "Sister!"

"I know, I only just found out myself."

He was suddenly speechless.

After Angus and Miyamoto escorted them back to their vehicle, Frank left with Flo to brief his fighters.

49

PREPPING FOR THE WARRIORS' ESCAPE

27 September 2202

As computer programmers in the central information unit, Zap and Dick had been working together for several years. Their computers weren't as advanced as the computers of a hundred years ago, but they did control a lot of the security and environment for the Sanctuary.

Over the last twelve months, Zap had believed that he and Dick had become pretty good friends but, all the same, he had held back from telling him about his interactions with the resistance and the warriors. At first it was because he hadn't wanted to put Dick in danger, even though Dick's input could have helped sometimes. But now that he knew Brand had placed Dick there to spy on him, Zap had an even bigger reason for not bringing him in on the secret.

When Dick asked Zap what his plans were for the evening, he wanted to say, "I'm helping to stop this system of useless mindless death for the fun of the elites." Instead he said he would probably stay home and play computer games. He could hear Dick's thoughts, "This will be the last time that you play games as I know what you've done,"

This was the day that he was due to report Flo's whereabouts to Brand and so Zap now flinched at any sound outside the door. Seeing Flo earlier that day had bolstered his resolve but he knew that the next 24 hours were the most dangerous for him.

Zap had known some of the people in the fighting pit for a while. These were the trainers, the medics and support people. The warriors themselves generally never lasted long enough for him to build a strong relationship with them.

Although the security systems around the warriors were mainly mechanical, the alarms, lighting and some electronics linked to the main stadium security were controlled by computer.

The plan was simple: at three o'clock tomorrow afternoon, he would disable the electrics and the external security locks so that the warriors could overpower the guards.

Finding people willing to guard the savage warriors wasn't that easy so the Company troops were only responsible for watching the outside of the stadium while the trainers and ex- warriors were expected to police the inside.

The Company security was always stretched and recent raids had further reduced the number of troops guarding the stadium. The warriors now outnumbered their Company guards on a scale of more than ten to one.

Through his dreams and mind contact with Flo, Zap

knew that there was more to the world than the Sanctuary. His access to intelligence had also shown him that the damage outside the Sanctuary wasn't as widespread as the internal media control would suggest.

Only the military were allowed to use or carry guns in the Sanctuary. This didn't mean that the warriors didn't have weapons. Although the warriors tended to fight hand-to-hand, they could use weapons for specific tournaments and bouts. Spears, clubs, hammers and rudimentary weapons could just as easily kill a sentry caught off guard as kill another warrior. The warriors in the pits had never imagined they would have a chance to escape. Once Karla outlined her plans to them, they gained some hope that they might.

Brand's recent show of power and the arrival of the rebels from the south had initiated the actions that were to follow. Zap's initial intelligence support was now being extended to technical support. He'd been asked to coordinate the power cut in order to increase the warriors' chances of success and accepted without a second thought.

The resistance had planned coordinated hits of the gel plants and the other key areas of the Sanctuary at the same time. This would give them the best – if not the only – chance of success.

Checking the system, Dick had seen that Zap had input the code that would disable the electronics and the lights of the pits at three o'clock on the afternoon of September 30th. Dick was ecstatic – what kind of rewards Brand would provide him when he turned over such valuable information?

Dick normally reported the information about Zap through an intermediary. However, once before when

Brand had wanted some more detailed personal information, Brand had summoned him to the big house. The cover story had been that Dick was going to sort out some computer issues. Given Brand's status, it was plausible enough that one of the best technicians in the Sanctuary would go to the big house.

However, just as Brand had his own spies throughout the Sanctuary, the resistance also had many ears and they had raised their suspicions of Dick.

Zap had been informed of these suspicions a few days before. Reading Dick's mind confirmed them. It was time to do a little misleading of his own.

Unbeknown to Dick, the attacks would actually be carried out tomorrow. Dick would pass on the wrong information to Brand.

Zap needed to reprogram the system after Dick had noted the initial settings. The resistance had provided equipment at the pits so that he could access the systems remotely. Now was the riskiest part of the strategy as he had to remain in his apartment until Dick reported on him.

The plan was for the resistance to apprehend Dick after he had passed on the information. Although Zap realised that Dick was endangering all of their lives, he was unsure how he felt about the death of somebody who he'd spent so much time with and had been one of his only companions for so long.

In the early days, Zap had taken some solace in having somebody to confide in. Unfortunately, this had led Zap to tell Dick about the female voice in his head and their communication through shared dreams.

Fate was a strange thing. Zap had told Dick about dreaming of a young woman who felt so comfortable and familiar to him it was as though it was himself. When Dick had passed on this information in his weekly report, it had seemed minor to him yet it was this information that had initiated the summons to the big house.

After reading Dick's mind, Zap learnt that this was the information that Dick had presented to Brand personally at the big house. It was this meeting that had sparked Brand's suspicion that the female was Zap's twin and perhaps still alive. The opportunity to have some kind of telepath at his disposal had been part of the reason why Brand had been searching for her in the first place.

Zap knew that he was playing a dangerous game by stringing Dick along. With the deadline to report to Brand now passed, at any stage the soldiers could bring him in for the report. With this false information about the attacks that Dick was passing on, Zap just hoped that he would be left under surveillance for a little longer, with Brand assuming he could learn more this way than arresting him three days before what Brand believed was the date of the attacks.

Dick and Zap were two of the few people allowed access to the system. For it to be monitored around the clock, one of them was usually on-call to fix any problems. If they both disappeared it was unclear who would check the system but the remote access would allow Zap to wait until the last minute to reset the system.

It was getting late and Zap's nerves were on edge. He hadn't heard Dick return and wasn't sure if this meant that he was coming back with an escort of Company troops or had been taken by the resistance.

A soft rapping on his door startled him. "Open the door," came the voice of Angus.

As Zap quickly opened the door, Angus and another man pushed Dick through the doorway ahead of them. He had his hands bound behind his back and tape over his mouth.

Looking into Dick's eyes, Zap could feel the hatred in him as he listened to his thoughts. "You idiot, you think that you are winning but I have told the Company of your plans for the 30th. The troops will be here for you in a couple of hours and you're screwed."

"He's given them the information we wanted and the Company troops will be here for me soon," Zap said to Angus.

Dick looked confused.

"If they're on their way, we need to get moving. We're going to take you with us and, if you behave, you may live. If you cause any trouble or try to raise an alarm, we'll still take you with us but we will be carrying your dead body," Angus said to Dick. "Do you understand?"

Dick nodded and produced a muffled sound that Angus took to be yes.

"If you are attached to anything in this apartment, I suggest you take it with you now as I doubt you are ever coming back," Angus said to Zap.

Zap had a small knapsack hooked over one shoulder. "I have some clothes and a few tools in here and that's all I need."

The four of them left the apartment, never to return.

50

ATTACK ON THE ELITE COMPOUND

28 September 2202

Frank's people had been chosen for the attack on the elites' winter homes. They had brought Flo along and, as was expected, Eric had insisted on coming too. It was quite a distance between the winter homes and the council buildings so they hoped for little interference from the Company.

With the Company forces already stretched thin in the capital, the elites relied primarily on their own security. Living in a gated compound also contributed to their safe keeping.

Lacey had been sent with some of the rebels to bolster the fighters in the capital and Pepper had volunteered to go with them.

The plan for the compound was relatively simple. For several weeks before the festival, the elites tended to retreat to their winter homes. This was a time when they carried out their final preparations for the winter but it was also a time for preening. Tailors visited the rich to create an array of amazing outfits for the festival. Of course, over the three days of the ceremony, the elites would require at least two outfits for each day. Only the lucky ones among the masses had a change of clothes at any given time of year.

A key part of the strategy had been for the rebels to get a large group of fighters to this isolated compound. Its isolation was one of its security strengths but also created a certain level of complacency.

For the last week or so, the resistance had set up their own food distribution point nearby, still under the guise of the SUP organisation so the elites would have found it hard to reject. In reality the elites didn't concern themselves with anything happening outside their compound. So it was of no concern to them that, as news of the daily free food spread, the size of the crowd grew steadily.

As with any routine, people came to depend on the daily food and if this supply was disrupted, trouble would ensue. Nobody had asked or cared about where the food came from. If the hungry people learnt that a new distribution point was now inside the elites' compound, they would accept it readily.

This was the plan. On the day of their attack, the resistance would spread the word of the new distribution point. This would create an extra strain on the security at the accommodation and also allow Frank's numbers to be bolstered by the crowds. With excessive stocks of food inside the compound, if the rebels could get people inside they would go on the rampage, gorging themselves on the surplus food.

Zap had provided Frank with schematics and plans of the compound. The numbers were in their favour but

Frank was still cautious. It was expected that several thousand of the Norm class would show up to storm this place. By breaking through the fences and approaching the main gates from behind, Frank's people would take out the defence force at the main gate and throw them open.

The unrest in the Sanctuary had been reaching fever point in the last few weeks as the shortages at the gel distribution points were becoming more and more common. Yet the level of hunger clearly varied between areas. On the farms, the workers had started to steal more food to survive. Urban areas had more of an issue with access to food and here it was becoming even harder to control the crowds.

Even in the capital, in effect, there were two groups of people. One group was being fed through the SUP and armed by the resistance, as well as receiving a briefing to create as much chaos as possible against the Company. The second group wasn't organised: they were the starving masses who were spoiling for a fight.

The strategic targets in the Sanctuary were the elites' winter accommodation, the council buildings, the garrison in the capital and the gel plants. Control of the gel plants was a key factor in the plan. The captured gel packs would be distributed as soon as possible to help placate the starving before anarchy took hold. Then the resistance could set up as de facto leaders.

The other garrisons weren't as much of an issue, thanks to Hubert's strategy of using the SUP organisation to supply food where the elites were not, so that the loyalty of even some of the troops was wavering.

Because of their lack of numbers, the resistance and

the rebels had to be smart. As soon as Frank's people had disrupted the elites' compound, they needed to head for the capital to support the fighters assaulting the council buildings.

During the assault on the elite compound, it was important for Frank's people not to be confused with the Company troops. They had abandoned the Company uniforms in favour of clothing that looked completely different. Although it was illegal for the Norm class to carry guns or any weapons, they were less fearful of punishment and repercussions now that they were starving.

As planned, Frank and his people cut a hole in the fence and headed through. Sneaking up behind the troops at the front gate had been easy. The guards had been preoccupied by the crowds outside and the noise of their shouting.

"We've been told the food's in here," one of the men closest to the gates was shouting.

"Give us food, give us food," the crowd had started shouting.

Frank could see the crowd was getting irate. It was touch and go whether the security guards would start firing warning shots into the air first or progress directly to shooting into the crowd.

It was clear from the numbers gathering outside the gates that these reasonably sturdy gates would not sustain the onslaught.

Before the guards had time to react, the familiar "Phut, Phut" of silenced nine-millimetre rounds came from the rebels' pistols.

The crowd outside seemed unsure what was happening. Surprised by the felling of the guards and not knowing if the same threat was also a danger to them, they took a few steps away from the fence. Suddenly the gates were thrown open and the cause of the disturbance was beckoning them inside.

"Help yourself, take whatever food and supplies you want," Frank said. "This compound is now the property of the people."

The crowd needed no further encouragement. They quickly swarmed through the opening and in no time at all they were ransacking the elite compound.

Now that they had set the crowd amok, Frank gathered his people to leave.

If everything went as planned, the crowd would overwhelm any minor resistance and devastate the compound. If there were any problems, it would be the masses and the elite among the casualties, not Frank's fighters.

He felt a twinge of guilt about using people as potential cannon fodder However, his concern as always was for his own people and after all, he reasoned to himself, their long term plan was to help the masses.

Heading to the capital, subterfuge was again their friend. The people in the front of the vehicles had now donned the grey overalls of the Company over their own clothes. If they encountered any checkpoints, their disguises should be enough to get them through an initial inspection.

Debs and the people she was leading had been hidden in the crowds in the capital. As Zap had been disrupted the security at the pits, the Company sentries there had been attacked from both sides as the escaping warriors surged out while Debs' team had hit them from the outside.

Hook had supplied guns to supplement the weapons of the warriors and Debs' fighters had their own guns. The combined forces of armed warriors and Debs' armed rebels were formidable even without the support of Frank's convoy.

Their next task was to take out the capital's exterior security from the inside and then join forces with Frank's people for the final assault on the council buildings.

Frank had passed through a few checkpoints on the way to the capital. When they reached the outskirts, however, they met with no resistance. The permanent checkpoints on the roads were no longer staffed, as they had been taken out by Debs and her people.

It had been decided that the fighting pits would make a great rallying point. If things went wrong, this would also be a good place for the resistance's last stand.

Hubert had sent any fighters he could spare to the gel plants to help Cenk and his people with the distribution of the gel packs. Hook had organised a strike at the ports, so the dockworkers had simply not turned up to work. Important supplies from outside the Sanctuary sat on some of the ships, unloaded.

This was yet another factor stretching the Sanctuary's security forces. Valuable military reserves were now employed as dockworkers, operating forklifts and other vehicles in order to unload the ships. With the current unrest, the Company soldiers did not have the resources to police the striking dockworkers at the same time.

Spider had been marshalling his spies and spreading the information and disinformation that the resistance wanted out. He had been partially responsible for convincing the masses to converge on the elite compound.

Everyone had a part to play in the assault today. CT had managed to sabotage the drinks supplies for the officers in the Company forces. He had not used deadly poison as this would have only raised suspicion and forced an investigation that could have exposed him. Instead, for the last week or so he'd been supplying them with tainted drinks, designed to make them gradually ill. It is hard for a leader in the throes of diarrhoea and vomiting to maintain command and control of a group of soldiers.

Having tasked reliable fighters to distribute food, Hubert now needed to rendezvous with the others. Once they overthrew the council buildings, they would take charge for an interim period. Each of them had been allocated a temporary position, which would be immaterial if they failed but they had to believe that the resistance and the rebels were going to succeed. Having a plan in place for what to do after a successful assault was necessary to fuel that belief.

Spider's first task would be communicating with the Company forces outside of the capital. They had already been spreading unrest within the Company. CT had weakened their command structure and, once the capital had fallen, he would inform the Company forces of the situation with Zap's help.

They hoped that they would be met with minimal resistance but the news that the resistance had disposed of the elites and were now in charge had to be handled delicately. The Company forces' initial reaction might be to fight so the message had to be that they had no one left to fight for.

As trained soldiers required a rank structure, if the resistance leaders took on that structure it would make a transition easier.

After some initial skirmishes, the resistance fighters were now consolidating. Karla and Hubert were standing in Karla's office and the plans were well underway.

They were reviewing plans of the council buildings that Zap had provided. Zap was now safely entrenched in front of a computer screen, looking at the trussed-up form of Dick in the corner of the office. He wished that things had been different but Dick had brought this on himself.

51

ATTACK ON THE GEL PLANTS

28 September 2202

Cenk's task was to take out the gel plants but first his team needed a way in. Zap had provided them with the location and the routes of the night patrol closest to the gel plants and this was at the core of their plan.

With their vehicles parked a block away, Cenk's team had waited in several houses along the same street until just before curfew. At ten o'clock exactly, Cenk and five of his fighters sprawled on the path, holding empty bottles as though they'd been drinking.

"Hello Bravo one, this is Bravo Two, over."

Carl keyed the mike. "Bravo one, send, over."

"Hello Bravo one, we have six men out after curfew. They're sitting on the ground and it looks like they've been drinking, over."

"Excellent," Carl said. "Where are you?"

"We are on the corner of Shortland Street and Lorraine Road, over."

"Okay we will be there in five minutes. Observe them but do not approach, over."

"Understood, out."

Carl arrived in the usual formation – positioning himself at one end of the road and Bravo two at the other. He stood in front of his vehicle with four of his troops and waited until his other five troops had formed up in front of theirs.

Clearly, this was going to be an easy takedown. The drunks were not armed so his men had only their clubs drawn. "It won't matter if the meat gets a bit battered tonight," Carl mused. Once they went through the gel plants, no one would know.

He loved the power that his position gave him. It allowed him many perks, including access to pretty women. In reality, though, the best part of the job for him was that he could break heads with impunity. This really was the ideal job for a psychopath.

He approached the group with four soldiers by his side while his other team advanced from the opposite direction. The five men on the ground looked to pose no threat. Although two of the soldiers in the other team had their rifles by their side, they were all preparing to use their clubs.

"Hi guys," said Carl. "Are you having fun tonight?"

One of the men, who seemed a little older than the rest, smiled as if in good cheer. Carl knew that was about to change shortly. "Do you guys know what time it is?" he said laughing.

"Bllr Zazaz." The older man muttered something unintelligible.

Carl saw this as an opportunity and moved closer to the drunks. Holding his own club at the ready, he indicated to his troops that the fun was about to start. Well, at least the drunks have experienced some fun for their last night on the planet, he thought.

"It's clobbering time!" he said gleefully.

Two of the men were lying on their fronts as if they were asleep. It was going to be less entertaining if they were unconscious already. Still, even if the patrol didn't get to enjoy cracking heads, this easy collection would add towards their nightly quota.

As both groups approached, they didn't even raise their rifles. The tired drunks seemed no threat at all. Suddenly the face of the older man seemed to change. Gone was the muddled look to be replaced by a more serious gaze and a more subtle smile.

This unsettled Carl slightly as he recognised the emotion in that face as the kind he normally felt before he did something brutal. Before he had time to react, however, everything changed.

The two men who had been lying on the ground rolled over in an instant and without any hesitation opened fire with the rifles they had been concealing. The two Company troops with their rifles by their sides collapsed.

Carl started to shout, "Ambush" but the words never left his lips. The older man had a pistol in his hand. "Let's not get cute," Cenk said, aiming at Carl's head. "Do as you're told and you might still live through tonight."

Like most bullies, Carl was also a coward. He raised his arms in the air and his troops followed suit.

"Do you realise who you are messing with?" he shouted with the last bit of bravado he could raise.

"Oh yes," Cenk said, "I know exactly who I'm messing with."

Cenk had been briefed that this convoy leader was well known for his violence. This man was responsible for the disappearance of Hubert's nephew. It had taken Hubert some time to find out who he was but he had his contacts. Other patrols had been within a similar proximity to the gel plants but Hubert had asked that they target this one for the added bonus of revenge.

The Company troops were taken back to their vehicles, stripped of their clothing and equipment, and had their hands tied behind their backs. The final act of humiliation was that they were shot in the street, naked. Their bodies were then bundled face down into the back of the trucks.

To some, this might have seemed cruel but Cenk's main motivation was to be cautious. If they tried to take the troops into the gel plants alive, the chance remained they could raise the alarm. Dead people could say nothing and they were not just piled up face down but had been shot in the face to avoid recognition.

He liked to minimise risks. When they had prepared the ambush in the street, he had twenty fighters secreted in the other houses nearby, who emerged as soon as he held the Company troops at gunpoint. This provided extra cover and made the job of stripping them quicker. He wanted to get out of there before another patrol came looking for the first one.

Cenk and nine of his fighters put on the Company uniforms. Two of the uniforms were a bit bloody but they could explain that with the bloodied bodies in the back. The rest of Cenk's fighters followed at a distance in their own vehicles. In all, he had sixty fighters under his command. Sitting in the front vehicle with him was one of the pit warriors to act as a navigator. As the rebels hadn't been in the Sanctuary long, it was helpful to bring some local knowledge along. The warrior sat in the back seat with his face covered by a hat to disguise his warrior's brand.

Reaching the gel plants, they slowed down to approach the barrier. The sentries didn't recognise Cenk but he and his fighters were in Company vehicles, wearing Company uniforms so the sentries were a little complacent. Who would have the power or the inclination to attack the gel plants anyway?

Taking the sentries unaware, the rebels disposed of them with their silenced pistols, "Phut, Phut". Two of Cenk's men in uniform got out of the trucks and opened the barrier. Once they had taken out the sentries, Cenk had the rest of his convoy enter the plant.

Although the plants were automated, other security guarded the expansive site. Even with sixty fighters, it was going to be a mission to keep control of this place.

The initial plan had been to destroy the plants but until other food sources could be distributed safely, these gel packs were a valuable resource. His first task was therefore to secure the food supplies and, if necessary, to be prepared to ship some of the packs.

His fighters had been briefed on the layout of the plants, the machinery was several plants but they were all located within the same compound. They were split into four teams, each with their own mission. A fifth team had already replaced the guards at the barrier. Their Company uniforms would pass first inspections and allow them to take out any unwary night patrols that turned up.

52

STORMING THE COUNCIL BUILDINGS

29 September 2202

Ever since the rebels had come through the main doors of the council buildings, River and his troops had been on the defensive. Their mission was to try to stop anyone from getting upstairs to the supreme leader.

Both Will and River realised that they were losing the battle and so ten minutes ago Will had left to check on Brand. Since that moment, River had started to ponder if he had been left as a sacrifice to enable Will and Brand to escape.

However, River was a soldier. If he was to die doing his job, then he expected to fight to the end because that's what he was meant to do.

He was almost surprised at the firepower that the rebels had in their possession. He had heard rumours of consignments of Company weapons going missing, but clearly the amounts had been downplayed.

In the past, the Company troops had always had

superior firepower when fighting the masses. Today, however, the weapons were fairly evenly matched and neither side had enough bullets for a protracted battle.

The news of the other attacks around the Sanctuary had filtered through but they were still given very little time to prepare for the attack on the council buildings. As the bullets ran low, pockets of hand-to-hand combat were breaking out. River's troops had been trained in combat but he recognised the W brands of the warriors from the pits and they were in a different league.

The troops were trained to keep the peace by means of superior firepower but the warriors survived each fight on their wits, treating every day as if it was their last and aggressively fighting to the death. River recognised that, as the warriors were openly displaying their brands, it was now open rebellion.

He checked his weapon: only five rounds left. The melee of battle within the twists and turns of the council buildings made it hard to determine which side controlled which bits of the ground floor. He motioned to two of his troops and they followed him up the stairs. They had locked down the elevators to prevent the rebels from using them as a way to get behind them so by going upstairs they would have command of the high ground.

By the time they reached the doors of Brand's office, River and his troops were breathing heavily. The rebels were hot on their trail and seeing the doors to Brand's office were wide open and the office was empty gave him little comfort.

Again River felt abandoned by Will and Brand and once more he vowed to put up a last-ditch defence.

They crouched in the alcoves as the rebels climbed the stairs.

Pepper and Frank were among the first rebels to reach this floor. Flanked by six others, the leaders going first wasn't a tactical move but Frank was determined to get his hands on Will as the man who killed his brother. Pepper had grown to like Frank and wanted to keep him alive.

Their intelligence from the resistance was that Will would be close to Brand. Frank had studied the picture of Will until the image was burned into his memory.

River's two troopers managed to take out two of the advancing rebels before they too were dispatched. River himself managed to hit a rebel in the thigh with his last round. Then, deciding that he wasn't ready to die after all, he threw out his weapon. "I'm unarmed, I surrender," he shouted out. "Don't shoot."

Frank had seen the Company man continue firing until he ran out of bullets and then attempt to surrender. He was in no mood for leniency but he recognised the rank slides of an officer and decided to see if he had any useful information. "Where's Will?" he shouted.

River saw an opportunity to be useful. "I can help you. They aren't here but I can help you."

Frank fired a bullet into River's right thigh, causing him to collapse to the floor, writhing in pain. "I am not in the mood to mess around. Where is Will?"

"I think they went upstairs, I think they went up," River said through clenched teeth.

By now more rebels had reached the top of the stairs and Frank tasked them. "Pepper, I'll take these two upstairs, and you and the rest search this floor for anything or anyone you think will be useful."

Pepper nodded and, holding his pistol in front, led the other rebels through the open doors into the big office.

Frank bounded up the steps flanked by his chosen rebels.

Frank and his fighters were cautious as they climbed the steps but not cautious enough. They had only climbed for around five minutes when a hand from above fired two rounds into the rebel to Frank's right.

Frank and the remaining rebel flattened themselves against the wall. "Stay where you are for a minute," Frank said. He eased his head out so that it was still mostly covered by the bannister and tried to see what was above.

Not being able to identify a target, he decided they had to move forward. "Keep as close to the wall as you can. I'm going to lead but if you see a target above, don't hesitate, just fire twice in its general direction."

As soon as they started edging upwards, there was a loud crack and a round from above bounced off the wall nearby. Without any hesitation, both he and his fighter fired two rounds in the direction of their assailant.

A pause in shooting was followed by the sound of a gun clattering to the floor. Frank was suspicious but they had to keep moving upwards.

Looking up, Frank saw an exposed leg behind a pillar. He held up his hand for the remaining rebel to hold off and, taking aim, he fired twice into the exposed calf.

When the trooper above crumpled, Frank finished him with a bullet to the head.

They encountered no further resistance until they came to a steel door labelled "Roof access only". Lying next to the door was a dead trooper, taken out by the chance ricochet.

Why would someone run to the roof? Frank wondered. Surely they were retreating to a corner with nowhere left to run.

Motioning to his escort to cover him, Frank grabbed the handle and threw the door open, ready for anything. The rebel with him wasn't as prepared and immediately fell forward with a hole in his forehead. Before the waiting assailant could fire again, Frank launched himself through the gap, diving for the little cover the bannister provided, while loosing off two more rounds in the general direction of their assailant.

Crouching behind the handrail for cover, he spotted a man above. It was only a short glance but he couldn't mistake the face – Will. They began to exchange bullets.

As he closed the distance between them, Frank saw a steel door not far above. He assumed that the door led to the roof. At the moment he was facing only one enemy but, not knowing what was beyond the door, he decided he had to act fast.

There was the click of an empty chamber as Will fired his last round into the stairwell. Frank was also out of bullets so he took this opportunity to attack.

Pounding up the stairs, he avoided a boot aimed at his head and managed to get Will in a bear hug. Will suddenly used the back of his head to smash Frank's nose.

This would have stunned a lesser man but Frank had withstood much harder hits during his tough upbringing and managed to keep hold of his prey. Will wasn't a small man though and, through a combination of strength and squirming, he levered one of his feet briefly against the railings in order to push Frank backwards. In no time, they were tumbling down the metal stairs, collapsing into a heap at the bottom.

During the fall, their positions reversed on several occasions. Although Frank landed on top of Will, his arm ended up underneath. Not only had his arms taken the brunt but the fall had dislocated his left shoulder.

Frank's right arm was still free but both men were moving sluggishly.

As the two men were struggling to gain some composure, Eric came into view. Since Zap had told him that Will was the man responsible for the deaths of his family on the Farm, he too had memorised his image and he too was out for revenge.

He knew that Will had controlled the attack remotely but his hatred for the Company only further fanned his rage. Seeing red, he charged forward without even waiting for Frank and Will to become untangled.

Eric began beating Will's exposed head, pounding him with punch after punch. Will's nose broke with a crunch but Eric continued until his whole face looked like a piece of raw meat.

The movement jarred Frank back to reality and he managed to extricate himself from the tangle of bodies. Although he still had one good arm, his attempts to pull Eric away from Will were unsuccessful.

Pepper came into view next and he immediately set to work helping Frank restrain Eric. Even though they were bigger, it took all of their combined might to get him off. Eric's commitment to killing Will had brought out the animal in him and they had managed to get him off just in time.

Will was still breathing but with only shallow breaths.

Pepper decided that as a prisoner Will could be useful. Once he'd determined that his injuries weren't life threatening, he turned him over and tied his hands behind his back.

"What's up there?" Pepper asked motioning up the stairway.

"I don't know, but this guy seemed keen to get there so perhaps it's some kind of escape route," Frank replied.

"You stay here," Pepper said. "You're not going to be able to do much with that shoulder."

"Then put it back in."

With a slight grin, Pepper said, "If that's what you want?"

He placed his left leg on Frank's ribs and took a firm grip on his left arm.

"We are doing this on five, one, two three." Pepper suddenly tugged on the arm and the shoulder popped back into its socket.

After the initial pain and a gasp, Frank managed to regain his composure. "What happened to five?"

If he hadn't just had his shoulder relocated, Pepper would have thought Frank was smiling. "If I'd waited until the count of five, you'd have been tense. I find it helps a shoulder pop in easier if the patient is more relaxed."

"So you've done this before?"

"Let's just say I've had it done to me a few times so you could class me as an expert. I still think I better lead until you get back to full fitness."

"Okay but we can't leave these two together. The prisoner isn't going anywhere so we take Eric with us."

Eric was still staring at Will on the floor. "Do as you're told and stay between us," Frank ordered.

All three of them carried silenced pistols, Frank's now restocked with a full magazine of bullets from Pepper, as they ascended the stairs. When they came to the steel door that led to the roof, Pepper turned to Eric. "When I open this door, we have no idea what's on the other side. I want you to stay low because you are shorter than me and that will make you a smaller target. Don't shoot me! If you see anything that looks like a threat, shoot first. Our survival is the most important thing. Do you understand?"

Eric nodded and crouched in anticipation.

"Is your safety catch off?"

"Yes," Eric almost whispered.

"I'm going to open this door now and if I identify any cover I will point and you need to run to it as fast as possible. I'll lay down covering fire while you move and, once you are there, cover me. One last thing, don't shoot me! Did you get that?"

Eric nodded.

"Did you get that, I said?"

"Yes I got it," Eric replied, his anger from his encounter with Will seeming to resurface.

Pepper could see Frank smiling broadly, almost laughing on the steps below them. He realised that he sounded more like a father talking to his young son but Eric wasn't as experienced at this kind of action and all their lives could depend on his movements.

He grabbed the door handle and yanked open the door, catching the people on the roof off-guard. Pepper motioned to Eric to run to a small brick structure while he opened fire on the roofs occupants. Continuing to fire, he managed to blurt out to Eric, "Quick, get behind that wall."

Eric sprinted for the cover as rounds seemed to ricochet off every hard surface.

With Eric gone, Frank filled the lower position in the doorway, firing two round bursts at their prey.

Pepper and Frank had already dropped three of the roof guards before they had a chance to react. Suddenly the rebels had the superior numbers and the three of them quickly disposed of the remaining two sentries.

Cautiously Pepper shouted, "Eric, can you see any other people on the roof?"

"No I think we got them all," came a hesitant reply.

"Okay, we're coming out, do not shoot us!"

"I understand."

As Pepper and Frank emerged out into the open, Eric continued to scan the roof for potential threats, glancing back at them every so often.

Nobody else was there. A large letter H was painted on the roof but there was no sign of an aircraft.

It was clear that these troops had been guarding something but, with nothing of value present now, whatever they'd been guarding had left before the rebels had arrived.

They checked the bodies and relieved them of any weapons as a precaution. These five soldiers were dead and no longer posed a threat but neither Frank nor Pepper was about to give up the habits that had kept them alive to this point.

"It appears that Brand has somehow slipped through

our net," Frank shouted to Pepper across the open rooftop.

"But we do have his right-hand man trussed up downstairs and we've also managed to take out the last of the resistance targets," Pepper replied.

"Let's hope the resistance council were right that when we cut the head off the snake, the remaining Company troops stand down."

"And now comes the fun bit of rebuilding the system and trying to feed the starving masses while we do so."

"I'm glad you are such an optimist Pepper," Frank said sarcastically. "Now let's get off this roof before we are blown off and then we can learn to make peace instead of war."

EPILOGUE

10 January 2206

It had been three years since Zap and Flo had discovered that they were siblings. Even though they were constantly busy, they tried to meet up at least once a week for breakfast.

In the last 12 months, the twins had instigated a programme to identify other telepaths and to corral them into a centre for education and training. It had reaped some promising results.

The centre had become the safe haven for the scared individuals with strange abilities. Most of them were young and the help they received to develop their skills without being treated as freaks had borne fruit.

Zap was key to the infrastructure of the Sanctuary now and his technical skills had been used extensively. Flo was becoming an influential young woman. The skills she had developed in the last few years and her blossoming friendship with Frank had made her a key resource in the new government.

Frank had become one of the main leaders in this new regime. He was ideally suited to deal with the influx of immigrants into the Sanctuary. With his knowledge of the outside world and his previous management of a resistance stronghold, he was able to deal not just with the influx but also with the distribution of resources to other parts of the kingdom.

In working towards the goal of weaning people off the gel packs, his previous experience in building an infrastructure with the farm that had supported his stronghold was invaluable in organising the supply and distribution of resources and assets, as well as the workforces supporting them.

Initially he had rejected the mantle of leader but it was obvious to the other council members that he was the best choice.

Although the twins only talked in person once a week, they talked in their heads all the time.

Over the last few weeks, it had become increasingly obvious to them that something was coming. Their conversations had felt strange. It was as though someone was mentally blocking them.

They had decided to tell Pepper first and he had informed the other members of the council that something strange was happening. They trusted his instincts and instructed him to take whatever actions he deemed necessary to identify and combat the threat.

SANCTUARY SERIES BOOK TWO PREVIEW

14 February 2206 – Assault on the Sanctuary

Barry was out of his comfort zone. He had served the Kompaniya for seven years now but this was the first time he had left his homeland.

Ever since the Kompaniya had received its new leader, Barry and his comrades had been preparing for this mission. Their previous jobs contained nowhere near this much risk. They had always had the upper hand. They had always had superior firepower when they faced the masses.

Of course, they had been at risk of a minor chance of injury on their previous missions. Most missions, though, had consisted of facing down lightly armed civilians and sometimes the enemy were even unarmed. Either way, the results were more massacres than battles.

When Barry got off of the boat in this strange land, he had felt wary, almost scared. Having mind readers for companions didn't help. They were supposed to be there to mask his thoughts of destruction but they also made him feel that everything he did was being second-guessed.

The security people at the docks had their own telepaths. He imagined them searching his mind and knowing what he intended. He tried not to focus on being a bomb technician whose sole reason for visiting this Sanctuary was to kill and dismember people.

Barry didn't have a conscience about killing. He remembered his first kill like it was yesterday. At the age of sixteen, he had shot a rebel in the distance. The boy had been running away from their raid and Barry took him down at a distance of eight hundred metres. The rest of the squad had shouted and screamed and called him "Hot Shot". That nickname had stuck with him for several years, even after he became a bomb technician.

After the vehicle crash had damaged his shoulder, he could still kill someone at a short distance but his days of taking out a distant target were over. Their society had little use for damaged soldiers but he was fortunate that his bosses respected him for his previous shooting successes. His companions in the truck had not been as lucky, as all but one had died in the crash.

Malik, the driver, had lost his leg and had supposedly been given a medical discharge to spend time with his family. Yet Malik had never contacted Barry or any other members of the squad, fuelling suspicions that injured Kompaniya soldiers ended up in the liquidation plants.

If injured soldiers could be discarded like everybody else, this could ruin discipline in the military. The illusion of injured soldiers being cared for was part of the story that the Kompaniya perpetuated, as they could do by keeping someone like Barry on helped to support this narrative.

On this mission, Barry's task was pretty simple. He had four devices to place around the capital of this Sanctuary. Two of his bombs would create damage to the physical infrastructure – one was for the power plant and the other for the water plant. The remaining devices were targeted at the political infrastructure. It was hoped that killing or maiming as many of the leaders as possible at once would cause maximum disruption.

It had been a challenge to smuggle the devices into the Sanctuary without detection. This Sanctuary was littered with spies just like his own. When life was worthless and resources were scarce, loyalties could easily be bought. People would inform on their own family members for even a small reward.

The smallest of suspicions could inspire people to raise an alarm, alerting either the authorities or criminals. The returns from black marketers or local hoods tended to be more beneficial than anybody in any type of government. Smuggling of anything was thus difficult no matter what the size of the cargo.

Conventional wisdom would dictate that transporting explosives not already assembled would be safer. Barry had decided that shipping components separately increased the chances of a crucial component being intercepted, which would leave him with no bombs at all. He chose to ship each bomb separately but each with all of its components.

Of the ten bombs that they had started with, only four had made it. Barry had calculated that a minimum of three bombs would be required for the mission and felt lucky to have four.

Shortly after exiting the boat, Barry had been reunited with the bombs and in only a short time they were ready to go.

Since then, the two bombs at the utility plants had been installed by other team members with no issues. As expected, the security for the council buildings was a lot tighter.

Anya and Gabe were here to stop anyone from scanning his mind and to act as lookouts. He had already placed one of the bombs in the council buildings. With only one left, he was ecstatic, he was achieving the impossible. Just this last device and he might actually succeed.

Barry had always included an escape strategy as part of his planning but no matter what the odds, he had no choice but to try to complete the assignment. Deploying on this mission guaranteed that his family would receive extra rations and supplies. Failing to deploy would leave his family to the same fate as any other criminals or traitors to the realm. They would end up in the liquidation plants.

Barry had hoped for perhaps two of the four bombs to be placed before he was caught but this was going better than expected. He had only one bomb left and there was a chance that he could set the timer and escape, clear and free.

As he walked towards the large set of stairs, something seemed off. They had been briefed that security would be intense upstairs but there shouldn't be this much downstairs in the open area. More security people were around here than expected, checking bags. You even had to pass through a security barrier before you could reach the stairs.

When he looked to Anya and Gabe, their faces appeared strained. These were not two people who were always smiling but they generally seemed happy with their lot.

Maybe the telepaths normally felt superior because

of their powers. At the moment, thought, they didn't look superior.

Gabe looked to be in pain. Both were holding their hands to the sides of their head. This drew the attention of men in grey overalls, who began heading towards the mind readers.

Suddenly Barry had his own problems. A young man and woman had interlinked one hand with each other. They were pointing their free hands towards him.

More armed men in grey overalls were moving but this time towards Barry. They reminded him of the security guards in his own Sanctuary but these people had different triangle emblems on their shoulders.

Barry was unsure what to do. Should he abort the mission? He noticed that grey-clad men now stood at every door, stopping anyone from leaving. He had a decision to make. There was a good chance that he was going to get shot by one of the many armed men. If he was taken alive, they would no doubt torture him.

Everyone gave in to torture eventually and if he was considered a traitor, his family would likely suffer. Barry wasn't a coward but he was a survivor and he had many thoughts running through his mind, all at once.

His hand was on the timer in his pocket. It had a button that automatically set the timer to go off after twenty seconds, as a fail-safe for bombers who thought they were likely to be captured.

Barry decided that he had no choice. Placing the parcel on the floor, he pressed the timer as he walked away with the rest of the crowd.

"Oy you, pick up that parcel!" someone called out to him.

Deciding that his priority was to get as far away from

the bomb as possible, Barry continued to walk away, without turning around.

"Stop, stop," he heard. Barry didn't slow his pace. He hoped that he would be far enough away to be safe. Perhaps the blast would be enough of a distraction to allow him to escape.

"Stop, stop or I'll shoot," he heard. Perhaps the voice was talking to Gabe or Anya? He knew in his heart that it wasn't.

Suddenly there was a loud bang and Barry felt a searing pain in his left shoulder. The impact made his body spin around. As he began to crumple to the ground, he could see someone holding a pistol in both hands and pointing it at him. The man had a startled expression on his face and it was obvious that he was the shooter.

Before Barry had time to hit the ground, there was a blinding flash. The ear-shattering bang was the last sound that he heard before he was engulfed by the explosion.

Attack The Best Form of Defence (Sanctuary Series Book Two) is now available, wherever you purchased this copy of The Hunger Rebellion.

ACKNOWLEDGMENTS

For every minute a writer spends writing a book, there are others providing more time in support.

I'd like to thank my amazing siblings (Trish, Pete & Teresa) for always providing positive support.

I'd also like to acknowledge the fantastic efforts of my editor Tanya for turning a rough draft into a better book for the reader.

Kudos to my cover designer Sara for turning a vision into a reality.

ABOUT THE AUTHOR

Ged is a child of the sixties and has always been passionate about reading, learning and all forms of knowledge.

He served for over twenty years as a British Army Royal Engineer, relocating to New Zealand after completing his final tour of Iraq in 2004.

Since entering civilian life he has embraced new challenges including: trading foreign exchange currencies and other financial derivatives on international markets, building Amazon businesses and later leading a team rebuilding Canterbury after a major earthquake.

His wealth of experience contributed to him becoming the author of six non-fiction books.

The Hunger Rebellion is book one of his Sanctuary Series, his first published fiction, a dystopian world that he has been nurturing in his mind for many years.

Ged finds inspiration living in the stunning countryside of the South Island of New Zealand, where he enjoys breathtaking views of the Southern Alps.